A Captive Heart

By Sherry Foley

Winter Goose Publishing
2701 Del Paso Road, 130-92
Sacramento, CA 95835

www.wintergoosepublishing.com
Contact Information: info@wintergoosepublishing.com

A Captive Heart

First Edition, November 2012

Hardback ISBN: 978-0-9881845-1-0
Paperback ISBN: 978-0-9881845-2-7

Cover Art by Winter Goose Publishing
Typeset by Michelle Lovi

Published in the United States of America

Sherry Foley is the author of
the fiction suspense novel

Switched in Death

Available at all major retailers

For Liz
In memory of Chaz's German Shepherd, Rosie

Chapter 1

Nicole Hewett unlocked the back door of her home and stepped into fear. Masculine arms pinned her in a crushing grip. Shock tore through her system. She gasped as a large hand clamped over her mouth making it impossible to scream. Gut-twisting panic welled up in her throat.

The drawings her kindergarten students colored for her on the last day of school fell from her fingers and fluttered to the floor. She bit the inside of her cheek trying again to scream. The taste of blood made her stomach lurch. She pried at her assailant's hands and lost her footing as she slid on the mangled papers beneath her sandals. Now frantic, she fought hard to break from his grasp.

He jerked her up against him hard. Nicole's muffled sounds were useless with his fierce hold. There was no way she could even bite him.

Please. Dear God, no.

Her heart vibrated in her ears, as she thrashed at the solid mass wedged between her and the door. Her foot slammed alongside his shin, but his vise grip didn't loosen. He was too strong. Tears of desperation stung her eyes.

Nicole wrenched her head to the side and tried to scream again. Nothing worked. The arm around her neck tightened, choking her.

"Stop fighting me," he rasped in her ear.

The voice wasn't familiar.

What does he want?

If she could trick him into thinking she would cooperate, it might be possible to catch him off guard. She closed her eyes and willed her body to relax. It took all of her concentration to regulate her breathing. Dropping her hands to her sides, she fought with her instincts and tried to nod against his chest.

The assailant's hold slackened as he shifted his weight.

She made her move. Nicole rammed her elbow into his gut with all the force she could put behind it.

He doubled slightly, letting out a grunt. When she turned and tried to push him back, a sharp pinprick shot into her right arm and her eyes widened in horror.

Dear God.

With his hold firm, he kept his hand pressed over her mouth. "Just give in, sweetheart. Let go. That's it."

She shook her head.

"Just relax. Don't fight it, Brandy. Come on."

Brandy? No. No. Please. What's happening?

Heat trailed up her arm like a fire spiraling out of control. Nicole struggled furiously, giving her last bit of strength. He was like a fortress. She managed to claw one of his arms but he held her firmly alongside the length of him.

Tears spilled from her eyes.

Against her will, her fingers lost their grip.

No ... no. She fought to stay conscious. Thoughts of her parents finding out what happened pained her.

She strained to keep her eyes open. *Focus.* Her head drooped slightly. She tried to lift her chin but her body was so heavy. She stared down at the images her students had drawn for her. They lay crumpled at her feet. Their colors blurred and her eyes fluttered in their heaviness. *No ... I have to ...*

Warmth from the light faded as shadows claimed her.

Ian Mulherin tipped the wooden chair back and stretched his long legs out on the porch railing of his log cabin. He scanned the row of fragrant pine trees lining the woods in front of him. His ears strained to detect anything out of the norm. Carefree robins trilled their songs of summer, unconcerned. He rolled his neck in hopes of releasing the mounting tension.

He was tired of waiting for the damned phone to ring. There couldn't be any screw ups. Ian had already done his fair share of those, he supposed, if his relationship with his father was anything to gauge. He rotated his shoulders and a crack on his right side loosened his neck. Maybe the last years of his mother's life would've been better if he'd just knuckled under to the old man.

Maybe his partner on the force would still be alive.

The cell phone on his hip vibrated. This was it. The call everything hinged on. He looked at the number and took a deep breath. "Yeah?"

"What's the status of that little matter I asked you to run down for me?" the voice on the other end demanded.

Ian's grip tightened on the phone. *Show time.* "It's a done deal."

"You're sure there won't be anything to trace back?"

"Acid is a beautiful thing," Ian promised, thinking of the woman in question.

"Good enough." The caller hung up.

Ian snapped his phone shut. His pulse escalated a notch. He'd pulled off the next phase of his plan. He could feel it. Ian's smile sobered as he glanced down at the angry claw marks running up his right hand. He flexed his fingers and shook his head. Over his years as an FBI agent, he had taken men twice that woman's size down with more ease. Brandy Mullins had fought him like a hellion.

He rubbed the cell phone along his jaw line, the day's growth making a scratchy sound. Why did his boss, Roark, want her killed? What did the woman have on him? Things had started happening within the FBI and it could be traced back to Roark. If the man was on the take, how many others within the organization did it involve?

Questions deserved answers. He smiled. It would be a challenge to find those answers, good thing he loved a challenge.

Ian dropped his feet from the railing and stood. His muscles rippled along the length of his frame as he stretched. Another week and he'd be off medical leave and could work out again.

Dusk descended, causing shadows to knit their web of darkness. The winding dirt road which led to his ten acres would make it easy to hear if anyone approached by car. A faint sound of an airplane's roaring engine passed over and trailed off. He waited and listened. Nothing out of the norm triggered his senses. Once satisfied no one lurked around his property, he went into the cabin and twisted the lock, attempting to bolt out the world behind him.

Ian walked into the oak-beamed kitchen he had built with his own hands. Virginia would always be his home. He loved the land. It had been a dream to build a cabin on this land once he'd paid it off. Just having that goal in the back of his mind enabled him to endure his work with the FBI. Four years ago, his dream became a reality and he'd built the cabin from the ground up.

Coffee was next on his agenda. Night came all too soon. The demons of the dead would be coming to offer him their nightly company. It was hard not to be cold in a job where you had to shoot the bad guys or be shot. He rubbed his thumb along his right side out of habit, distracted in thought.

How long has it been since I had a good night's sleep? He shrugged. *Too long to remember.* With his cup in one hand, he pulled his shirttail out with the other, and made his way down the hall to the bedroom.

Ian stopped at the threshold and stared at the unconscious woman handcuffed to his bed. Jaw clenched, his fingers tightened around the handle of the mug. He needed answers her pretty little head held. That was all.

Still, he was distracted by the way her golden hair spilled across his pillow. She looked damn good. In her sleep, the woman appeared almost angelic. He shook his head, trying to free himself of his thoughts. She was arm candy and he was choosier with his women. This little number had landed herself in trouble because she'd shared a pillow with some scumbag.

He frowned. The sedative should have worn off by now. Restless, he moved further into the room and stood by the bed. Ian leaned down to pick up her slender wrist and feel for a pulse. Steady. He dropped her hand and rubbed his palm along the leg of his jeans. The memory of her velvety soft skin still lingered. Stepping back, he withdrew to the window, opting to analyze the shadows outside. Ian took a swig of coffee and reviewed what he knew about her. Brandy Mullins, twenty-four, various odd jobs, one arrest for hooking, parents lived in Connecticut. One sister. That didn't give him much. He looked back at the woman who warmed his bed. There were ways of finding out more. He took another drink of his coffee and decided to count them.

Maybe the night wasn't going to be so lonely after all.

Nicole was falling and she couldn't catch herself. Her arms wouldn't help break her fall. She moaned as her eyes blinked open. The room was dim, unfamiliar. She ached all over and her parched throat burned.

She was lying on her back, on a bed. Frowning, she tried to sit up, but something stopped her. Realization slapped her like horrific thunder.

Handcuffs!

She yanked both hands against the cuffs chained to the metal spindles of the white wrought-iron bed.

A shape to the left of her moved. She opened her mouth and screamed. Chest heaving, she sucked air back into her exhausted lungs and looked wildly around.

The figure of a man lurked just inside the shadows.

"Who ... who are you?"

"Your new best friend," the man replied and shrugged his broad shoulders. "You're tucked away in a remote cabin, so scream all you like. No one will hear."

She strained to make out his features. Nicole recognized his voice as the one who had attacked her. Would she know him by sight?

He stood perfectly still.

"What do you want?" She observed her surroundings looking for something as a possible weapon.

"Answers."

"To what?"

He moved closer. A streak of moonlight snaked through the blinds, laying shadows across his face. He leaned over her, his coffee breath fanning her cheeks. "Just whose bed have you been sleeping in, Goldilocks?"

"What?" she croaked, trying to move away from him as she fought the handcuffs. "Please. I don't know what you're talking about."

He sat on the mattress beside her, his weight shifting the bed, dipping her towards him. She froze. He reached out and ran the back of his roughened fingers along the side of her face. Her bottom lip trembled.

"Cut the innocent act with me, Brandy."

Brandy?

Nicole wracked her brain trying to figure out what he meant. *He has the wrong person. This is all a mistake of some kind.* "I-I don't know what you mean. My name isn't—"

"Stop playing games," he demanded. "I'm going to get the answers I need, one way ... or another."

"You've got the wrong person; my name is Nicole. Nicole Hewett," she argued.

Her attacker stood, the sudden movement causing her to flinch. She braced herself, fearing he would strike her.

To her shock, a light flickered on overhead. Nicole squinted as her eyes adjusted to the change. When the kidnapper came into focus he was standing by a lamp, dressed in a gray ribbed shirt and snug black jeans. Dark hair fell to his collar in waves. He had a face she would have remembered. Ruthless. A hint of danger rimmed his eyes. Angled cheekbones trailed down to tightly drawn lips. Cold blue eyes caused him to look haunted.

She shivered.

Nicole realized two things in that instant. She'd never seen him before, and now that she had, he wouldn't let her live.

Tears blurred him out.

She heard what sounded like a drawer opening. Eyes stinging, she tried to blink the tears away to see what he was doing.

He turned to face her from the foot of the bed. She watched him fix those icy blue eyes on her as he held up a manila folder.

"*This* is proof you're lying."

She stared at him. Numb.

"You wanna change your story now, Brandy?"

Her head shaking, she pleaded, "I'm not who you think I am."

"These tell a different story," he said, flicking up photos for her to see.

Nicole gasped at her image in the pictures. Black and white photos. There was one of her getting out of her Toyota. Another of her entering the gym. Others of her taking her morning run, unaware eyes watched. Chills trailed down her spine. The only thing she could do was shake her head in horror and disbelief.

"You've been investigated, Brandy. Do you still deny this is you?"

"Those are of me, but that isn't my name. There's been some mistake." Her brain raced to figure out something that would make him believe her. "That's me in the photo, but my name is Nicole."

Ian stared down at the woman lying on his bed. Her brown eyes were flecked with fear. Real fear. She was either a hell of an actress or something was very wrong here.

"Your age?" he demanded, putting his foot up on the bed frame and leaning in to watch every movement she made.

"What?"

"Just answer the damn question."

"Twenty-four."

"Address?"

"You should know that, it's where you kidnapped me from!"

He gritted his teeth, but refused to take the bait. "Siblings?"

"I … one. A sister."

"What make of a car do you own?"

"Toyota."

"Color?"

"Red."

"What'd you have for breakfast?"

"I don't eat breakfast."

"Full name?"

"Nicole Lynn Hewett."

Ian stopped. He watched her carefully the whole time he interrogated her. If she so much as blinked, he knew it. She had met his every question without hesitating and looked straight at him. He lifted his eyes to stare at the seams where the logs of the cabin met until the lines fused together.

He had escaped death before thanks to an inherent ability to accurately read people. Realization that this woman just might be telling the truth snaked through him. A sick feeling blazed in his stomach. Here he thought he was going to trap his boss, catch him in his double life by pretending to take Brandy out for him.

Instead, he'd walked into quicksand.

If his gut was right, there was only one other answer. A setup. Orders handed down from the largest gun on the rack. *But why? Surely no one is onto me. Or are they?*

Letting out a breath of frustration, he rubbed his fingertips down his ribs. He unhooked his cell phone from its clip and strode away from the bed.

He punched the number of the one man he hoped was still trustworthy in this sick world. Trey should be at headquarters and could pull up information on the name Nicole Hewett. After several seconds Trey's voicemail clicked on. "This is you-know-who. I'm not you-know-where. So, leave a message at the you-know-what." The beep echoed in his ears.

"Where the hell are you?" he yelled into the phone. His thumb jabbed the button to end the call as he slammed the cell phone down on the dresser beside him.

He turned to stare silently at the woman for several moments. Her eyes, rounded with worry, were fixed on him. She obviously was terrified.

Something pulled at him. Something he could have sworn was too cynical to be reached. He forced his body to relax and tried not to look as grim as he felt. If his instincts were right, she was as much of a victim in all of this as he was.

"I just might believe you," Ian offered.

Skeptical, Nicole blinked. She looked from the cell phone he had all but crushed back to his face. His sudden change in attitude put her on guard. "You mean you'll let me go?"

"No."

"But you said you might—"

"We should begin again. Let me introduce myself. The name's Ian Mulherin. I'm with the FBI, investigating a murder for hire … yours."

It took her a few minutes to replay his words in her brain. "You mean, Brandy."

He shrugged his shoulders.

"I take it you have a badge for me to see," she demanded.

He regarded her for a moment and then reached into his back pocket. With a flip of his wrist, a badge appeared along with his picture.

Satisfied he was the man in the photo, she looked up at him. *Same sour expression.* "I see the scowl is a trademark of yours."

His only answer was a thin-lipped frown. He came closer as he fished a key out of his pocket, and unlocked the left side of the cuffs. Her hand fell to the bed and she instinctively moved it to rub her other wrist. "Thank you."

"I'm afraid I can't undo the other."

"But … I thought you believed me," she spoke in a soothing tone, much like she used on her students when they were frustrated with a subject. If she could calm him down with reason maybe she could convince him.

"I said I might."

"But I—"

"No."

"Can't you just—"

"No."

She glared at him. "Some agent you are. Why couldn't you have simply knocked on my door and asked me your questions?"

"I wasn't hired to find out answers from you, only to kill you."

Nicole stared at Ian's mouth, she couldn't believe he'd just uttered those words. A ringing vibrated in her ears. "You mean Brandy."

"Whatever."

"I don't understand any of this. You're working for the FBI and you were hired to kill me?"

"I'm the one asking questions here," he growled. "The name Peter Roark ring your bell?"

All she could do was shake her head. She'd never heard the name before.

He studied her intently. She refused to look away. "I don't know anyone by that name."

"Your safest bet is still with me," he said, cupping her chin in his hand. The agent was too close. She could see the flecks of green in his blue eyes. "And just how do you figure that?"

"Simple. It's like this, sweetheart, I didn't kill you. And the man who hired me thinks I did."

Ian moved away and stalked over to the window. With his hand braced against the wall he peered through the blinds. Apparently, he didn't detect anything moving in the moonlight because he moved to lean against the wall.

"So, you're working undercover?" Nicole asked, trying to sort through and make some sense of things.

He turned those hard, cold blue eyes on her and stared. "Just accept that I'm your guardian angel and we'll get along fine."

"Are we still in Virginia?"

"In the hills thereof."

Nicole could only stare at him. *How could this happen? Someone has gotten me mixed up with this Brandy Mullins. But how to prove it?*

The cell phone on the dresser vibrated before the ring sounded and interrupted them.

Ian must have known the caller by the set ring because he moved quickly.

Ian answered. "It's about damn time."

"Nobody leaves a message like you, pal," joked the voice on the other end. "What's up besides your blood pressure?"

Ian glanced over at Nicole handcuffed to the bed. He walked into the hallway and headed to the living room. "How's Roark?"

"Same demanding boss we've always had. Why?"

"He called me a couple a days ago for a special assignment."

"Congrats. You're off medical leave? This means you've decided to come back then?"

Ian paused for a moment. He hadn't decided anything. After being shot and on medical leave, he'd wrestled with the idea of opening a private investigation office. "Maybe. I took care of my assignment earlier tonight."

"Why do I get the feeling you've yet to tell the story?"

Ian hesitated. *What if Trey was in on this?* He'd be able to tell better from Trey's facial expressions by telling him in person. "I'll fill you in when you get here."

"Okay ... sounds serious."

"It is."

"So, I assume you want me there soon?"

"Yesterday."

A chuckle crackled through the connection. "I see a little R & R hasn't mellowed you any."

"Not hardly. Just get your sorry ass up here to the cabin."

"I've got to wrap up some things here. I can be there first thing tomorrow."

"I need anything you can dig up on a Nicole Hewett. Check all variations of spellings, too."

"Gotcha. Anything else?"

"Make sure you come alone. I will be watching."

"Ian, are you in some kinda trouble?"

"No more than usual."

Trey chuckled. "For that I risk life and limb, huh?"

"Trey, watch your back on this. Your head could be on a block."

"Thanks for reminding me I need a haircut. I want to be a good-looking corpse for all the women I leave behind."

Ian snorted and snapped the phone shut. Trey, ever the ladies' man, would have that last wish. Ian sobered and ran his thumb along his side. His next move would be to wait and see what happened with Trey. Would he come alone? Ian would be ready either way.

His mind wandered back to the woman handcuffed to his bed.

What should I do with her now?

Chapter 2

Time was slipping away. *No telling how long he'll stay on the phone.* Nicole stole a glance at the white pine nightstand.

With a jerk she rolled onto her side and strained against the handcuff holding her hostage. The top of the stand was bare. She grasped the knob. *Oh, let there be something inside I can use to get this cuff off.*

After a quick glance at the door, she gently drew in her bottom lip to chew on it, and eased the drawer open. She slid her hand inside, groping for something, anything.

The drawer was empty. *No. What kind of a man has an empty drawer in his bedroom?* Her eyes ran a quick survey around the room.

Think, Nicole. Think.

She reached down and patted the pockets on her jeans with her free hand to see if she had anything to use.

Empty.

A scan of the immediate area within reach didn't give her much hope either. She looked at the wall above the bed, hoping for a picture hanging on a nail, something she could use to pick the lock. The white antique-iron bed up against the wall provided nothing. The only other item in the room was an oak, pattern-back chair with a wicker bottom that sat angled in the corner.

With a wistful glance across the room, Nicole saw freedom just beyond her reach. Through the window, darkness fell, ready to blanket out the world. *There must be a way to escape.*

Her immediate chances of being reported missing weren't very good. Most of her neighbors were retired. Summer break started tomorrow and her parents were in Peru doing missionary work. Nicole's heart squeezed at the thought of her mother finding out her daughter was missing. She and her sister had just spoken recently. Neither kept tabs on the other. Her ex-boyfriend was probably still too busy sleeping with her ex-best friend. Nicole's heart raced against her thoughts.

She shifted her attention to the wooden knob she still had her fingers on. *Yes.*

As she unscrewed the handle, a washer fell with a quiet *ching* in the bottom of the wooden drawer. A small screw protruded from the knob. It took all her concentration to maneuver the screw into the keyhole of the cuff.

Frustrated and in a hurry, beads of perspiration dotted her forehead as she gritted her teeth.

Come on.

She fumbled with the screw, trying to line it up. The knob slipped from her fingers, hit her foot and rolled under the bed.

"No," she gasped as it disappeared from her sight.

She stretched to bend and retrieve it. The handcuff halted her motion, painfully twisting her wrist.

Fatigue and worry fused like a noose around her neck. Eyes stinging, she gulped for air. *Maybe if I—*

The bedroom door flung open behind her. Startled, she jumped and turned to face her captor. His large frame filled out the doorway. Ian stood there with a bowl in each hand.

Fear held her frozen, unable to look away. His cool blue eyes seized hers, while his gaze transferred to the open drawer and cut back to her. "The room has been stripped clean. You're wasting your time."

Nicole swallowed her disappointment and sank down on the side of the bed. The handcuff scraped down the iron spindle. She never liked to be out of control, and being held captive was a claustrophobic as it got.

"I brought dinner."

He walked over and placed both bowls on the nightstand, then pushed it around in front of her and stepped back.

A whiff of spiciness spiraled around her. In that moment she realized she'd skipped lunch to help a student in the library. She backed up against the headboard and rubbed her cuffed wrist. There was no way she was touching any food he supplied. It was probably drugged. Her stomach growled, reminding her of just how long ago breakfast was.

"Tell you what, you pick which ever bowl you want and I'll eat from the other. That ought to convince you I'm not trying to drug you."

He had read her thoughts. She looked from him to the bowls. Her mind whirled, wondering if she could hit him hard enough with one of the bowls to knock him out and frisk him for the key to the handcuff. "You forgot to add the word *again*."

"Perhaps you'd prefer to dine alone."

"I'd prefer to be somewhere else."

"That makes two of us, sweetheart. If you need something, holler."

His footsteps echoed against a hard surface as he retreated down the hall. She relaxed a fraction. Steam rose from the stoneware bowls heaped with chili. Chunks of tomatoes and onion brimming to the top made her mouth water. It looked as good as it smelled.

She sighed in defeat as she moved restlessly on the bed and stared at the oak beams across the ceiling. None of this made sense. The man had taken pictures of her. The idea of being watched, photographed unaware, made goose bumps raise on her flesh. There was a mix up somewhere. There had to be. Somehow the FBI had the wrong person. Maybe this Brandy and she looked similar. That had to be it. The other alternative made her stomach churn. Her mind started to recount everyone she had ever known. Someone couldn't really want her dead, could they?

Ian slumped down in his worn leather chair in the living room and took his gun out of its holster. He reached over to the end table beside him and flipped open a leather box. The cloth he used to clean the gun remained right where he had left it. This cabin had been his getaway for over a year now. No one but Trey and Dan knew about it.

He sighed and his hand stilled on the gun. Dan's murder put him out of the picture, so that narrowed things a bit. He threw the cloth down and holstered his gun.

His partner's death was a wound as raw as it had been that first day. His muscles bunched and his jaw hardened. The two of them had watched each other's back for the better part of ten years, and been best friends for longer.

Now, because of him, Dan was dead.

He dug his fingers under the hobnails in the leather chair while the memories closed in again. With one shove against the chair arms, he stood.

Always distance yourself from emotion. Focus. That had been one of many survival lessons he'd learned. He paced like a panther down a path he knew too well. The braided rug in front of the limestone fireplace already showed signs of a road well-traveled.

It was his fault Dan took the hit. Ian swore as he remembered that day. He had been helpless while he watched the life slip away from his partner. The guilt threatened to choke him as he thought about how he had shut his friend's eyes for the last time.

He gripped either side of his head and bent over as if sucker punched. "Why couldn't it have been me instead, dammit!"

His hands fell to his sides, clenching in tight balls. *It should've been me.* Remorse raging inside, he raised his eyes to the mantel in front of him. It was barren, just like his life.

A familiar scratching noise at the door pulled him back from the dark clouds that draped over his mind. He strode over to the door and yanked it open. "About time you showed your hairy butt back here."

A hundred-pound dog jumped up to rest his paws on Ian's shoulders. "Okay, Dickens. Heel."

The German Sheppard parked his hindquarters on the hardwood floor and thumped his tail wildly.

"Where you been, huh?" Ian rubbed Dickens behind the ears. The dog fell over on his back to have his belly given the attention his ears enjoyed. His paws were wet from being in the nearby creek that ran through the property. Giving Dickens a rub down, Ian turned to shut and bolt the door. "We've got company so I don't want you to do any—"

He heard the dog take off, his nails tapping on the hardwood floors. Ian turned in time to see the dog's massive body bound along the hallway and around the corner out of sight. Ian feared once Nicole was spotted, Dickens would become territorial and growl at her. He braced himself for screams as he charged down the hallway after the dog.

When Ian made it to the doorway, Nicole's startled brown eyes looked up at him.

"Dickens. Heel!" he demanded.

The beast wouldn't be thwarted from his mission. Ian lunged for the dog's leather collar. Dickens jumped up on the bed and began wiping his tongue up the side of the Nicole's face.

"Dickens. I said heel." Ian stared at his dog, bewildered. Dickens never took up with strangers. Yet, there was his skilled police dog, trained to kill, licking the woman to death.

"Oh …" She was trying to hold the dog back a bit with her hand. "You're beautiful."

Ian grabbed Dickens' collar and hauled him off the bed. "Heel, dammit."

The dog sat on the floor beside the bed and looked hopeful. Ian returned his attention to Nicole. "Did he hurt you?"

"I'm fine."

Not taking her word for it, he ran his hands down her arm and turned her hand over. Her skin felt smooth, soft. He cupped her chin to inspect her face. Her eyes lowered and she pulled away.

The thought ran through his head, he wanted to make her look at him, see him. He cleared his throat and stepped back. *Heel Ian. Down, yourself, boy.*

"I'm sorry. He seems to have forgotten he's been trained to take commands."

He blew out breath, relieved to know she wasn't scared out of her mind. The dog looked from him to Nicole sitting in the bed, and back to his master. He didn't look like he had any intention of minding.

"Dickens. Bed," he ordered again.

The dog hung his head, sauntered out the door, and down the hall.

Ian looked back at Nicole. "You sure you're all right?"

She nodded.

"I'll shut your door and keep Dickens out."

"No ... please ... leave it open."

He regarded her with a puzzled look. Her eyes were dilated with fear. "But Dickens will—"

"I ... I'm claustrophobic."

"Okay. Door open it is then."

"Thank you." She gave him a slight smile.

His breath hitched, glad she hadn't given him the full wattage. "I can't guarantee Dickens won't be back in here to slobber on you some more."

"I'd rather take my chances with an over-excited oaf than feel the walls closing in on me."

He glanced at her untouched food. "You didn't eat."

She shook her head.

"Want me to warm it up?" he asked, starting to walk over to the bowl. He couldn't let her go hungry.

"No."

"Can I bring you something else? A salad? Sandwich?"

"No."

"Let me know if you change your mind." He gave her one last glance and headed back into the living room.

Dickens was sprawled in front of the fireplace gnawing on a bone when Ian walked into the room.

Ian lowered back down in his chair and reached for his latest issue of *Magnum Gun*, hoping it would distract him. It bugged him that she wouldn't eat. Annoyed, he flipped the page. He read the first line twice. It was no use. He snapped the pages together and dropped the magazine in his lap. Dickens looked over at him and whimpered. "You're blaming me, aren't you?"

He gave a defeated sighed, hauled himself out of his chair and retraced his steps down the hallway.

He stopped at the threshold of the bedroom door and paused. She had her back to the door. Maybe things were better left alone. He turned to leave.

"What do you intend on doing with me?"

He paused and turned to face her. "Try to keep us both alive."

"Your dog, he's a trained police dog?"

"That appears to be a matter of opinion."

"Were you a cop?"

"Used to be. Then decided I wanted to swing from a higher rung. I became an agent about ten years ago."

"What made you—"

"I can't tell you any more than I already have until I know for sure you're on the up and up."

"Are you one of the good guys or bad guys?" she asked.

The question threw him. He leaned back against the door jam. If asked a couple of months ago his answer would have been easy. Now he wasn't so sure. "I'm a good guy who's had to do some bad things."

"And now?"

"Now … I don't know what I am," he said quietly and sighed. "I work for someone I'm convinced has turned into one of the bad guys."

"I'm sorry."

"It happens. Hazard of the job."

"What will you do next?"

"Try to figure out how to go about proving it."

"I guess you have to decide if you want to be on the winning side, or the losing."

"Oh, I fully plan to be the one left standing," he assured her. "Try to get some sleep. Tomorrow's a new day."

He parted with that comment and hurried back into the living room. Nicole was getting to him. It ate at him that he had opened up to her so much. What the hell was that all about? He must be getting soft. His mouth formed a grim line. He didn't like it one damn bit.

A couple of beers would right things. He marched into the kitchen and yanked open the refrigerator door. Dickens followed him in and sat on the floor.

"What?" Ian asked, twisting off the tab to the beer. "Your buddy, Trey, will be here tomorrow with some answers on your newfound friend."

Dickens sat up, barked, and thumped his tail.

"Huh, we'll find out if she's as innocent as those chocolate-brown eyes suggest. Satisfied?" Dickens looked to be indeed satisfied and went over to his food bowl to chow down.

Tomorrow would prove a lot. Ian figured he'd have the truth about her one way or another, but still he wondered which way it would go.

Chapter 3

Somewhere, a distant noise registered in Nicole's brain, dragging her from a restless night's sleep. Her eyes fluttered open and squinted against the sunlight streaking into the room. It wasn't until she caught sight of the chair in the corner of the room that she remembered where she was. *So much for yesterday being only a bad dream.*

A new day, Ian said. She could think of a million better ways to start it than a hostage shackled to a bed. She wondered how far out this cabin was from town or the nearest neighbor. Her legs stretched until they brushed against a warm body.

Startled, she gasped and jerked herself to a sitting position. Two pointed ears perked up over alert black eyes. Her free hand flew to her chest. "Dickens. You scared me."

Dickens belly-crawled up the bed to tuck his wet nose under her hand.

"I see how it is," she said, running her hand over his soft coat. He really was a beautiful dog. She always loved them but her parents never let her or her sister have one. "You're expecting a morning rub down."

Dickens whimpered and rolled over onto his back.

She scraped her handcuff up the iron spindle on the headboard to sit up better. She combed her fingers through the underside of her hair, pausing to work through the tangles. "I don't suppose you know how to fetch a hacksaw to help me get out of this thing?"

Dickens went on rolling from side to side until she ruffled his belly fur.

"It's okay, pal. I'm worried enough for the both of us."

She continued to give Dickens his rub down while she absently stared off in thought. Her captor hadn't killed her when he could have. Nor had he harmed her in any way. Still, she didn't trust him any more than he did her. His partner would show up with the correct information and Ian would have to believe her then and let her go.

Wouldn't he?

Her hand stilled against Dickens' collar. She looked down at the strip of black leather and realized what she was seeing. A collar with a metal buckle. "Hold still, boy."

With her left hand, she worked awkwardly trying to maneuver the clasp. Maybe she could use the buckle's little metal-tongue piece as a pick.

"Yes." She would be back in control of the situation.

The collar fell from around the dog's neck. She grabbed it and scooted up to the head of the bed. Using the metal prong, she tried to guide it into the keyhole.

It was too big to fit.

"Damn." Nicole's shoulders sagged. This was just a setback. She wasn't giving up. She'd have to figure out a way to knock Ian in the head with something and get the key.

Dickens sat up at attention. His ears twitched like he was picking up a sound. He barked and bounded off the bed. She heard the sound, too.

A car.

Ian plugged in the percolator at the same time Dickens barked and shot through to the front of the cabin. Ian wiped his hands on the dishtowel, threw it over his shoulder, and pushed open the door to the living room. The dog was going nuts at the front door. "Dickens. Pipe down."

Ian put his hand on his holster while walking to the front window. He scanned the area. There was just enough dust flying across the road to be from one car. His new partner and old friend's black Trailblazer pulled up next to the house. Trey emerged from the vehicle carrying a brown paper bag and manila folder. Ian yanked open the front door and pushed the screen door wide with a creak.

"Don't shoot. I come bearing breakfast." Trey raised the bag to chest level.

"I oughta shoot you for what's probably in that bag," Ian growled as he stepped aside. "Knowing you, it's some kinda multi-grain crap and yogurt."

"And a treat for Dickens." His partner stepped inside and smacked the bag square against Ian's stomach. "I also brought the information you asked for."

"Did you get a rundown on both women?" Ian asked, motioning him through to the kitchen."

"I didn't find anything on a Brandy Mullins. I ran checks on all variations of names. No such person exists."

Ian ran his fingers along the night's growth on his chin thoughtfully. Things weren't looking good for him. If there was no Brandy, he was being set up. They were on to him. "You checked the name against the alias list?"

"Of course. Nothing."

Ian processed the information as he walked into the kitchen. If they were onto him, they were using Nicole to take him down. What was the angle, or Nicole's involvement in all of this? He opened the cabinet and passed a mug to Trey. He selected his favorite pottery mug with the large handle. Ian turned to see Trey inspecting the inside of his cup.

"What?"

"Just checking to see what I was seasoning my coffee with."

"Asshole. It's clean." Ian poured himself the first cup and didn't offer to serve any. "I'm surprised you didn't bring your own frou-frou latte."

"Already polished it off on the way here." Trey winked and helped himself to the coffee.

"What did you find on the name Nicole Hewett?"

"She's a straight arrow. School teacher and is—"

"Currently handcuffed to my bed," Ian said, watching Trey closely to gauge his reaction.

"No shit?" A smile spread across the other man's face.

Satisfied, Ian relaxed a fraction after his partner's easy response. "No shit. Honest Injun."

"Kinky."

Ian rolled his eyes, shrugged, and tossed the offensive paper bag Trey brought over on the kitchen table. "Just needed her to answer a few questions and thought it the best way."

"Your bedside manner really needs work, Ian."

"Help yourself. She fought me like a hell cat when I nabbed her."

"Purrfect."

Trey led the way and Ian followed with Dickens bringing up the rear. Ian had spent half the night nursing two pots of coffee, trying to figure out how she fit into this mess. He was interested in hearing the rest of what Trey had dug up on her.

"Well, well, cabin fever never looked so good," announced a voice that drew Nicole's attention to the doorway.

She regarded the new man with curiosity. This had to be Ian's partner, Trey. He looked more like a male model than an FBI agent. While not as tall and broad as Ian, he had boyish charm written across his face. Grey-green eyes twinkled at her, eyes which probably brought the women in droves.

"I think between the two of us we can manage her, don't you, partner?" He smiled and put his hand out for the key.

Ian watched her from the doorway. "Let's just hear what else you've found out and see how closely it matches her story."

"Okay. Nicole Hewett. Twenty-four. Kindergarten teacher. Today is the first day of summer break for her," he said. "She whistles clean all through her file."

She continued to glare at Ian, refusing to even blink. He pulled a key from his pocket and worked it between his fingers. She raised her chin in defiance. "It would appear you owe me an apology."

Her eyes never left his as he came toward her. He reached for the handcuff. The cuff popped open. She felt the singe of his touch as his fingers brushed against her. Surprised, she rubbed at her hand, working the blood flow into it once she was free. She dismissed the odd sensations as vented anger.

"Nicole, my name is Agent Trey Bollinger. Agent Mulherin and I need to ask you a few questions."

"As I told Mr. Agent here last night, he nabbed the wrong woman. I don't know anything."

"It's unfortunate you were pulled into this. Our humble apologies." Trey bowed slightly, producing a killer smile.

Oh, yeah. A ladies' man, all right. For some reason she couldn't explain, she liked Trey despite that fact.

"Nicole, you may know something and not even realize it," Trey said.

"He's right." Ian spoke up, his intense gaze trained on her. "We need to question you about your comings and goings over recent weeks."

Nicole's eyes narrowed on him. "And here I thought you'd captured it all on film."

Their gazes locked.

"Those pictures were handed to me in a file. I didn't take them."

Trey cleared his throat. "Breakfast is on me." He turned to lead the way to the kitchen.

She scooted off the bed, tried to smooth out her shirt, and brushed at her rumpled jeans. Spying her shoes over by the chair, she slipped into them and turned towards the door.

Ian stood leaning against the doorframe with arms folded across his chest. He straightened and made a sweeping motion indicating passage. She waltzed right past him without a glance. "I would like to use the restroom. That is if you don't mind?"

Ian grumbled something she didn't quite catch and gestured to the right.

She darted into the room and shut the door. Snapping the lock in place, she was drawn to a small frosted window. She could make out the shadows of trees, but nothing else. The window was too small to crawl out of.

Hopefully I can just answer their questions and go home.

Nicole stepped out into the hallway and headed towards the smell of coffee. Just what she needed, a strong shot of caffeine. The hallway opened to a large living room with high timbered ceilings. Braided rugs were scattered on the hardwood floor giving the space a cozy feel. A brown leather sofa and chair faced a limestone fireplace with an impressive pine mantle. A gun rack was mounted on the north wall, and on the opposing wall hung a beautiful old quilt in a colorful circled pattern.

Intrigued by the room's charm, she followed the voices around a corner and into a kitchen. The two men sat in ladder-backed pine chairs at a matching table with spindle legs. Pine cabinets lined the wall with wooden leaves for handles. Whoever had built this cabin had done a beautifully detailed job. The men stopped talking as she walked in. Her eyes focused on the coffee pot.

Ian must have seen her drool because he got up, poured her a cup, and brought it over to the table.

"Bless you," she said gratefully and sat down to worship the brew. She waved off the cream and sugar offered to her. Black, rich, and real was the way she preferred it.

"I have yogurt, seven grain bagels, cream cheese, and for our connoisseur of food, donut gems." Trey laughed and tossed the chocolate donuts at Ian.

"You're all heart, partner." Ian caught them and pulled out a chair opposite Nicole's.

She took one of the bagels and slathered it with cream cheese. The first bite tasted moist and delightful.

"We'd like to ask you a few questions, Miss Hewett," Ian said.

Ignoring Ian, she nodded at Trey. "What would you like to know, Agent Bollinger?"

Trey smiled a kind smile that made his eyes soften. "Trey, please."

"Okay, Trey then. What would you like to ask me?" She was really enjoying her breakfast.

"Ian, what's a lovely girl like this supposed to be involved in?"

She looked at Trey and he winked. *Oh yeah, a ladies' man. Definitely.*

It's a shame his partner couldn't learn something from him in the charm department. She chanced a glance at Ian and caught her breath. His expression was thunderous.

Ian was not amused. It pissed him off that there was business to be done and Trey was flirting. Nicole didn't look like she minded his attention either. She sat there watching Trey and licking cream cheese off her fingers with that dainty little tongue of hers. Something stirred in his groin. He cleared his throat. She must've finally remembered he was in the room because she turned her attention to him.

He glared at both of them. "Okay, do you think you two are ready to begin here?"

"Sorry, big shot. The floor's yours. You said someone gave you the photos of Nicole with the name Brandy Mullins on it. Who?"

Ian studied the other man's face with a head-on look. There was no turning back now. "Roark."

"What?" Trey looked genuinely surprised, then shocked. "Ian, the way you say that, you sound as if you think Roark knew about the mix up of names."

Ian waited a heartbeat before answering. "I do."

"But that would mean …" Trey's voice trailed off into a whistle.

"Yeah."

"Maybe he's just passing the photos on to you from someone higher up."

"Nice try." Ian gripped his pen between his thumb and forefingers, giving it a twirl. "About six months ago Dan and I suspected Roark of some underhanded deals."

"Do you have any proof?" Trey asked, leaning forward.

"Suspicions more than anything. A lost file on the Monroe case. A file that was last in Roark's hands. The case was dismissed because of it. No file. No case."

"What about electronic backup files?"

"Right. There should have been those. It's protocol. When we checked into it, there wasn't a trace the file ever existed." Ian said.

"Wasn't Monroe one of the Mosconi Mafia men in the news for drug trafficking?" Nicole asked.

"Bingo." Ian got up and poured himself another cup of coffee. He waved the coffee pot, Trey passed, and Nicole nodded. He refilled her cup. "I also have reason to believe Roark helped Joe Talence Fisher get off. Another Mosconi man."

Trey whistled again. "You're going to need something concrete, man."

Ian sat back down and took a swig of his coffee before answering. He was this far into it; there was no backing out now. He regarded Trey a moment before continuing. "Back when I first went on medical leave, I implied to Roark that I was tired of this shit. I told him playing by the books only made you a candidate for a corpse. And the hell of it was, if you made it out alive, you couldn't afford to retire anywhere warm."

"What was his response?" Trey asked.

"Nothing, right away. Last month he called me in and asked me how I was enjoying my medical leave. I told him it was a helluva lot better than being used as target practice." Ian stopped. This was where the lines blurred. "He asked me to fake a report on the last case I'd handled before being off, omitting Cordoza's name from any involvement."

He watched comprehension drain the color from Trey's face. Nicole had leaned forward while he was talking, taking it all in, now she slumped back in her chair and closed her eyes. Ian looked away. He wasn't proud of what he'd done.

"Tell me you didn't," Trey said quietly.

"I can't." Ian wiped the back of his hand across his mouth. Self-disgust welled up from his stomach.

"Shit, Ian." Trey pushed away from the table and stood. He paced around the kitchen, and ran his hand through his hair. On his second trip around, he rubbed the back of his neck and stopped in front of Ian. "Okay ... so tell me the rest."

"The act of compliance got my foot in the door," Ian told him quietly.

He didn't expect his partner to understand.

Trey swung around and threw a hand up in the air. "Well, that's just great."

"I needed to prove to him that I wanted a cut and was worthy of his trust. I just needed to buy some time."

Trey turned straight on and looked at him thoughtfully. "Wait. Cordoza is up against charges again."

Ian raised his brow at Trey, crossed his arm and leaned back in his chair. "And where, oh where, could that anonymous tip have come from, do you suppose?"

Trey's eyes narrowed on him. "It damn well have better been you."

"I made sure the bastard wasn't going to walk free."

"Ian, you're playing with fire." Trey pounded his fist on the table.

"Don't you think I know that?" he tossed back at the other man. "Two days ago Roark called me in to show me the file of photos on one Brandy Mullins. He told me she needed to be taken out of the picture. No trace-backs. Quoted me a fee and asked if I was in. I knew it was my chance."

Ian looked at Nicole who was regarding both of them with fascination. He picked up the folder his partner had set on the table and thumbed through it.

"And you told Roark to count you in?" Trey asked.

"Yeah."

"And then you devised this plan to kidnap her instead?"

"You're a sharp one today. You're three to nothing."

"And you're insane if you think you can pull this off and not get yourself killed."

"But why me? I don't know any Roark," Nicole interrupted.

"We need to get back to questioning you, Nicole. To find out," Trey said.

"What else can I answer?"

"Let's start with what you do for a living. It says here in your file that you're a kindergarten teacher at Mark Twain elementary. Is that your current position?" Ian asked.

"Yes, I am."

"Do you know why anyone might want to harm you?" Ian asked watching her closely, his eyes narrowed on her face.

"No."

"Have you had any disputes with anyone recently?" Trey asked.

"No."

"Look, Miss Hewett, we need your total cooperation here," Ian snapped at her.

Nicole dropped her bagel back down on the plate, grabbed up her napkin, and wiped her mouth. "I don't believe I'll say another thing until I have a lawyer present hot shot."

"You just don't get it, do you?" Ian raised his voice at her. "Someone wants you dead!"

She stared at his mouth as though the words coming out were from another language. It all was very hard to process. "Why? I-I don't understand."

"Right now we don't either. Perhaps in questioning you, we can find a link." Trey said in soothing tones and shot Ian a look. "Let's start at the beginning and see what we come up with."

Nicole pushed her plate away. Eating was now an unappealing thought.

"You do have a right to a lawyer, Nicole, but we want to lie low with this," Trey explained. "At the moment, you're in danger and we're trying to keep you safe."

Nicole's mouth went dry. *This couldn't be happening. Could it?*

"How long have you been a teacher?" Ian asked.

She inhaled a deep breath and released it. "I've just completed my second year."

Ian got up, walked over to a drawer, and took out a legal pad and pen. He plopped it onto the table as he sat back down. "Two years. Summer job?"

"No."

"No?"

"No. That's what I said, no," she snapped.

His pen stroke ceased and he looked up at her. "You own the house you live in?"

"Yes."

"You're twenty-four, teach, but take summers off, and you own your own home?"

"The house was left to me by my grandmother. I live modestly."

"I see." Ian went back to scribbling. "Do you live alone?"

"Yes."

"Boyfriend's name?"

Nicole reached for her coffee. Great. She was going to have to explain her love life, or the lack thereof. Images of Mark and Angela on her bed flooded to the front of her mind. The old pain started to creep back in. On a whim she'd decided to bop home that day on her lunch hour and surprise Mark. Only it was she who'd gotten the shock of her life. She pinched the bridge of her nose, her fingers still warm from holding the coffee mug. "I don't really see that it's any of your business."

"Listen, Miss Hewett, we have a job to do here and that begins with trying to find out who would like to see your pretty neck snapped in two," Ian said.

Nicole slammed her hand down on the table, sloshing her coffee out of her cup. "You can just—"

"Time out," Trey called, forming a *T* with his hands. "To your corners, both of you."

Nicole blinked. She'd forgotten the other man was even in the room. Folding her arms across her chest, she glared at Ian. *The man is impossible. By the look on his face, he doesn't think any more of me than I do of him.* "Fine."

"What we have here is a problem," Trey said. "We need to get to the bottom of it."

Ian shifted in his chair and jotted more notes onto his paper.

"Nicole," Trey said, "we need to know if you have a boyfriend who might be involved in anything that would endanger you."

"No," she replied lifting her chin. The last thing she wanted to do was talk about him. "I'm not seeing anyone currently."

"The name of your last boyfriend was what?" Ian cut back in, not looking at her, but still writing.

She gritted her teeth. *It's been, what, almost a year since I found Mark and my best friend having sex like wild monkeys?* "I'd say ... ten, maybe eleven months."

Ian looked up and arched an eyebrow at her. A very attractive eyebrow, she thought. *Whoa. He's a first class jerk, remember. You've already dated plenty of that.*

"And what was the lucky guy's name?"

She didn't much care for his sarcastic emphasis on the word lucky and answered sweetly, "Mark Reynolds. He's a doctor at St. Peter's Medical."

The dratted pen scratched over the legal pad again. The questions went on for another two hours. Ian fired questions at her, his pen recording, and Trey refereeing. With each answer, Nicole grew more and more disgusted with how mundane her life sounded in this little interview. She taught all day, went home to lead a quiet life, with cross-stitching her only hobby. Her shoulders ached and her stomach protested the bagel she'd ingested.

When Trey's cell phone went off, Nicole had a chance to come up for air.

"Bollinger," the detective answered, then held up his hand for silence. He continued to listen, stood up, and retreated to the front porch, shutting the door behind him.

Ian turned his attention back to her.

"So, do you see now that this has all been some sort of mix up?" she asked. "I'm not sure how this happened, but—"

"Things don't just happen, Miss Hewett. I don't believe in random chance."

"I can assure you that I want to find out what's going on here, too, and clear my name."

"I haven't found the connection yet, but somehow ... there is a reason for your involvement."

He doesn't get it. "I've just recounted my entire life and there isn't a connection, apparent or otherwise."

"I hope you're telling us everything."

"And just why would I lie?"

"You tell me."

"I have been telling you the truth. You're just not listening."

The wooden screen door creaked open, drawing their attention. They both stopped talking to glance toward the door. Trey appeared in the entryway, his expression grim. His hand rested on his holster.

Tension unfolded across the room, snuffing out the oxygen.

Ian's chair scraped the floor as he slowly rose to his feet. His hand traveled down to cover his gun. His expression stern. The only movement Nicole detected was the bunched muscles along Ian's jaw line.

Dickens' whine was the only noise in the room.

Nicole swallowed nervously. Speechless, she tried to figure out what was going on. Some drastic change had taken hold of Trey after his phone call on the porch. *What could have happened?*

"I take it that was Roark on the phone," Ian said quietly.

"No. It wasn't." Trey responded unsmiling. His pose was stiff, rigid, and unyielding.

Nicole looked from one man to the other. She felt she should say something, but couldn't think what it would be.

Ian took a deep breath. "Then what's this all about, Trey?"

"I was told to hunt you down and haul you in."

Chapter 4

Ian remained still. He kept his face impassive. The expression on Trey's face mirrored the grimness of the situation. A standoff. His heart racing along with his mind, he tried to process what was happening. A lot hinged on his reactions. He had to play this out right.

Trey stared him down.

"If it wasn't Roark, care to venture a guess as to who else it could be?" Ian asked quietly. "I'm not wanting to play games. If you've got something to say, say it."

Ian recognized the inner conflict going on in Trey. A man fighting himself. Wrestling instinct against orders.

"Well?" Ian demanded to know.

"That was Brad Garret. The lab has the report in on Dan's death. It states the bullet that killed him … was from your gun."

Trey's voice faded, as did the room around Ian. Ian's vision blurred with the hammering of his heart in his ears. *This isn't happening.* He sank back into his chair, curled his fists and pressed them against his eyes. The tightness in his chest exploded. He then pounded his clenched fists on the table. "It's a lie!"

"Ian, then how do you explain the evidence the lab is holding?"

Ian beat the table again, sloshing coffee everywhere this time. He jumped to his feet, and threw the chair backwards. "I didn't kill Dan, dammit. This is a set up. Can't you see that?"

He heard Nicole gasp.

Trey stared at him long and hard without blinking. He shook his head as if he was trying to clear it. "Garret said the bullet was a match to your gun."

"Forget the lab. Forget Roark right now. This is me, Trey. Me! You know what's right here. Could I really have offed Dan? What does your gut tell you?"

Trey regarded him for several moments. In the end, he blew out a long, slow breath. His hand fell to his side. "That I'm between a best friend and a Roark," Trey said, running his hand through his hair and attempting a weak smile.

Ian relaxed a fraction.

"We need to go over and over this, Ian, until we find out what the hell we're missing."

"Yeah." Ian bent and picked up the fallen chair, but stood there for a moment trying to right himself.

"I'm sorry, Nicole," Trey offered. "We must've scared you a moment ago there. We'll try to act more like grown men from here on out."

Ian watched her nod as she exhaled. She looked pale. He'd give anything if she hadn't been drug into his nightmare. Too many had already paid a price.

The two men returned to their places at the table and sat in silence for several awkward minutes. The tension in the room faded to a lower level.

"Shall we get back to the business at hand?" Ian asked.

"You were testing me with my coming here, weren't you?" Trey accused. "You wanted to see if I was in cahoots with Roark."

Ian hesitated and then looked his friend straight in the eye. "Yes. And you're going to tell me you wouldn't have done the same?"

After a few moments of careful consideration, Trey blew out a breath. "No. I don't know what came over me. It's still raw, you know?"

"Yeah." *I do. You'll never know how well I know. Dan was my best friend and I held him while he died.*

"I know you couldn't have pulled the trigger on Dan."

"Forget it," Ian replied and shrugged. "We're trained to take orders."

"This raises the bar on your theory concerning Roark even more; that he's on the take. He has to be involved in this new development somehow."

Ian's lips formed a grim line. "But how to prove it?"

"Garret said Roark gave instructions that you were to be brought in and it kept quiet. He wants to talk to you first. It's what he's telling everyone."

"I'll just bet. Trying to look like the ever faithful boss."

"We'd better take it from the morning Dan was killed," Trey suggested, pulling the legal pad in front of him and flipping the page over. "Maybe we'll run into a tie-in with Nicole."

Ian released a deep sigh and rolled his neck from side to side. He hated going over it again. Over the last month, that morning played daily on a wide screen behind his eyes. The reruns haunted him at night.

"It happened just before dawn on that Friday morning. Dan and I were on an all-night stake out. Down on the north side of Kearney Street."

Ian stared over his partner's shoulder. "An informant tipped us off that a guy named Metcalfe would be peddling cocaine."

"I remember the case. Metcalfe was already wanted for murder."

"Yeah. That's where we came in." Ian ran a hand through his wavy hair. "We'd gotten an anonymous tip. The two of us hid outside an old abandoned warehouse for hours. Finally, a black sedan pulled up. It was still dark out. We could barely make out the three men going in."

Ian paused for a moment. His eyes shifted from the spot he'd been staring at to focus on Trey. The memories of that night still seemed at times like he was there, walking through the motions all over again.

"We called for backup. The men inside started to disband. Things began to happen; we couldn't wait and decided to proceed. Dan had my back. He always did."

Ian twisted his napkin in a tight swirl and then tore it in two. Clearing his throat, he hoped the shakes in his voice would stop. He was conscious of Nicole watching. He could feel her eyes on him.

"I called out a warning, kicked the door open, and we pushed in. They fired first. The room was a haze of smoke. Dan and I both fired. Metcalf went down first. More shots rained around the room. At least one got away."

He closed his eyes. He heard the shots. Over and over in his mind he could see the scene unfold. Smell the gunpowder. Each time another part of him died. "Things get confusing after that. They were going in different directions."

One man he'd shot in the shoulder. Another fired at him from the left. He'd ducked behind a bunch of boxes and fired back. "I yelled to Dan one was getting away … he never answered, he …"

His throat closed. The back of his eyes burned. He knew the tears wouldn't come, though. They never did.

The silence in the room was deafening.

Nicole cleared her throat and got up to walk over to the coffee pot.

"I can't bring Dan back," Ian said, "but I can bring Roark down. I acted like I was going to off this Brandy, but planned to kidnap her instead and find out what she knew about Roark. I hoped to get some answers that way."

Trey addressed Nicole, "Do you know a Peter Roark?"

"No, not until Ian mentioned him last night."

"I wonder if it's possible you know him by another name," Trey said jotting something down on his paper. "I'll see what I can do about getting you a picture."

"That's a good idea. We also need to find out why he made a bogus file with Nicole's info," Ian said.

"I agree. This wasn't an accident."

"Trey, thanks for being with me on this, man."

Trey's phone buzzed before it rang. After checking the screen he held up his hand. "This is Roark. Quiet. 'Lo."

Ian watched the expressions play over Trey's face. He was nodding and listening.

"Got it, sir. I'm on it. I'll be in touch." He flipped the phone shut. His eyes went from Nicole to Ian.

"Well, Trey?" Ian asked, leaning his elbow on the table. "What's up?"

His partner considered him for a long moment before answering. "Roark wants you tracked down and brought in."

"Well, we knew that was coming." Ian said, nodding.

"Yes. But what we didn't know was how he was going to spin it."

Ian narrowed his eyes and inhaled, bracing himself. "And that would be?"

"He's putting the word out that the lab has proof a bullet from your gun killed Dan," Trey recounted the phone call, "and it gets better. There's supposedly evidence that you've snapped because Dan was making it with your girlfriend behind your back. The girlfriend is missing. One Nicole Hewett."

"Damn."

"Yeah." Trey nodded.

"And if I'd really killed her, he could pin it on me that I killed my lover."

"What?" Nicole jumped in. "Well, I could just show up very much alive then and discredit this Roark."

"It's not that easy. Ian will still be wanted for Dan's death. And you're tied in somehow. That means you aren't safe either."

Ian watched the color drain from her face. "I'm sorry you've been dragged into this, Nicole."

"So, I was picked to be the girlfriend. That's why I'm involved?"

Ian looked at her thoughtfully and shook his head. "No. I don't buy it. Too easy."

"No, I don't either. There has to be more than a random name pulled out of a hat." Trey agreed. "I mean, you two have never met before this have you?"

"No." They both chimed.

Ian chuckled to himself. *That's the first time we've agreed on anything.*

"We'll figure out why you were targeted," Trey told her.

She nodded slightly again and looked away. Something kicked in Ian's gut. There was a vulnerability about her and at the same time, a quiet strength. He felt the strong urge to protect her. He discounted it; he was trained to protect, that was all it was. He turned his attention back to Trey. "A picture of Roark for her to look at is a good idea."

"I'll get on it."

"I just don't see how I could be connected in all this" Nicole said.

"I think this is where I came in," Trey said twisting his pen and clipping it to the legal pad. He grabbed up his coffee cup and carried it to the sink. "Ian, how many people know about this cabin of yours?"

"Nicole. You. Dan did."

The last name hung in the air for a moment.

"I'd better head back and see what I can do on my end," Trey said. "If either of you come up with the missing link, give me a call."

Nicole smiled faintly and nodded at Trey. Ian moved to the door to walk him out.

Both men went out on the front porch, the screen door clanging behind them. The late morning air was thick with heat. It amused Ian to notice his partner doing the same panning of the area that he was.

"Thanks for everything, Trey."

"Don't mention it. It'll be interesting to see who'll be left standing to answer the door when I come next time," Trey joked, fishing out his keys to click the lock open.

"Very funny."

The humor died as they exchanged glances at one another.

With a slap on the back, Trey said, "Watch yourself. Let me know how I can help."

"Sure. Yeah."

Resolve settled over Ian while he watched his friend drive off. He wouldn't be in contact with him again. Ties needed to be severed or he'd be the cause of another partner's death. Roark would calculate every move Trey made from here on out. One slip and Trey could end up six feet under. There was no way in hell he was risking another friend's life.

He leaned forward and rested his hands on the banister of the porch. The dust kicked up as he watched the Trailblazer drive away. He flexed the muscles along his jaw line as he thought of the trail he'd need to blaze. The first order of business was to deal with the little missy inside.

Chapter 5

Nicole calmed herself by clearing away the table. Keeping busy might help to process the morning's information. She needed that picture of Roark. She hoped Trey would return soon with one. Maybe they could get the horrible mess cleared up quickly. She didn't like the idea of being stuck with Ian or at his mercy. Still, if whoever was behind this outlandish action thought she was dead, she couldn't very well show up alive. They would kill her for sure then. Fear threatened to close in on her. She stood at the sink and stared out the window at a robin fluttering freely from tree limb to limb. *Oh, to be so free. Please let this all be over soon.*

The screen door creaked behind her. Holding her chin high, she wiped her hands on the dishtowel and turned in the direction of the noise. Ian stood looking at her, eyes narrowed. She cleared her throat. "Ah … there's a little coffee left."

"My eyeballs are floating already. I've had enough."

"How soon do you think Trey will have a picture for me to look at?"

He shrugged and sat down at the table, flipping through the pages of the legal pad. "We have to go over this again."

"What difference will that make?"

"It has to."

"I don't see how I'll know anything differently than what I've already told you."

"That's just it. We have to go over your life and keep going over it until we do see it."

"I think if we just wait until Trey comes back with a picture, I might recognize this Roark person."

"He's not coming back."

"What?" *What did I miss when they were out on the front porch?*

"Trey is out of this."

"What do you mean?"

"I'm not risking his life with my problems. I've already lost one partner. It's me they're after, for what they think I know, or may find out."

"You think you're going to be a one-man show, is that it?" *He's the most maddening man I've ever met.* "You're ... you're insane."

"Ohhhh, is that the best you can do, Miss Schoolmarm?"

She gritted her teeth. "You can't pull this off alone."

"I've got some contacts that can come in on this."

"You need Trey's help."

"Listen, woman, I've kept myself alive until I met you, I can damn well keep it up."

She stared at him while he sat calmly. "You're serious about this aren't you?"

"Never more so."

"I can't tell you how safe I feel right now," she returned dryly, snapping the dishcloth and placing it over the handle of the stove to dry.

"Nicole, listen, I'll make sure you're safe," he said, coming to stand behind her.

"This is bigger than you," she said, flailing her arms in the air and pacing about the room.

"Ideally, I would have you placed in protective custody, but I'm not sure just who all Roark has under his thumb at this point," Ian told her as he went back and lowered himself in his chair and picked up his pen.

With the tension and voices in the room raised, Dickens picked himself up and padded over to sit by his master's chair.

"It's all right, boy," Ian leaned over to rub the dog's neck and head in reassurance. "Check this out, Nicole."

He pointed to Dickens and told him to stay. The dog sat at attention and watched his owner go over to the refrigerator. Ian came back and placed a hot dog in the German Shepherd's mouth.

"You and I, Nicole," he continued as he sat back down and turned his attention to Dickens, "are going to figure out why Roark wanted you out of the picture. There is a tie-in somewhere."

Nicole stood fascinated as Dickens sat on his haunches and looked at Ian attentively. The hot dog was still sticking out of Dickens' mouth.

Ian turned to look at her. "When we find that answer, we'll have yet another piece to this hellish puzzle."

The dog was drooling now, but other than that, Nicole hadn't detected movement. *Incredible.*

"Until such a time, you will do as I say. If not, you'll find yourself handcuffed to the bed again."

Arrogant brows over hard blue glaciers stared back at her. He didn't even look away from her when he snapped his fingers. Dickens swallowed the hot dog in one gulp.

"And this is the only faithful friend I need," Ian said smugly, rubbing the dog down as praise. "There's nothing like man's best friend."

Nicole was still stuck back at him boasting that she would do as he said. *As if.* "Really? Well, here's a little trick for you."

She smiled sweetly at Dickens and crooked her index finger. The dog cocked his beautiful head to one side and rose to a standing position. Nicole tossed a glare Ian's way and marched down the hall with Dickens bringing up the rear. *The man really is insane.*

The cabin vibrated when she slammed the door.

"I'm gonna wring her pretty neck yet," Ian growled in disgust to an empty room.

His eyes narrowed. He knew she wasn't the type to sulk. She probably thought he hadn't noticed Dickens' collar was missing. He could just see her trying to pick the lock on her handcuff. Chuckling to himself, he admired her for her resourcefulness. She certainly was a feisty one. He liked it when her temper caused her eyes to flash from chocolate-brown to black. He bet her eyes did that in bed, too. His mind ran back to her trying to pick her handcuff.

Ian didn't even let another minute slip by before he was out of his chair, easing the screen door open. An arrogant smile tugged at one corner of his mouth as he stepped off the porch and dropped behind a fire bush. She would try to make a run for it out the bedroom window.

He'd show her. The heat was at a high with the sun beaming down. *She must think I started to work for the agency just yesterday.* He waited, bent on one knee and ready for action.

Nicole massaged her fingertips into Dickens' fur coat. "He makes me so mad, Dickens."

The dog laid down on the bed and rolled over on his back. She rubbed his stomach. "He just thinks he knows it all." The dog's tail thumped on the bed.

"He thinks he has me right where he wants me," Nicole huffed out through her teeth. Her eyes started to sting. She sniffed. Dickens leaned up and licked her face. "It's okay, boy, I always cry when I get angry."

Dickens sat up and cocked his head to look at her.

"I know. It's a terrible nuisance." She laughed, sniffed again, and hugged his neck. "I'm going to prove to Mr. Moody Broody that he can't push me around."

Dickens barked.

"I guess you like him, so he can't be all that bad," Nicole told the dog. "Still, he's in for a few surprises."

Several minutes passed while the sun blazed down on the back of his head. Beads of perspiration dotted Ian's forehead. He swiped the heel of his hand across his forehead. He shifted positions to allow blood flow back to the leg he had tucked under him. *What the hell is she doing in there, anyway?*

He'd had enough. Staying low, he approached the edge of the window and leaned in. Twigs snapped beneath his feet. He peeked through the glass and stilled in surprise. Nicole's back was turned from the window, her legs curled under her on the bed, arms flung around Dickens' neck. A shard of unexpected tenderness slammed into him. This wasn't the image of the woman whose eyes flashed daggers and argued with him at every turn. His breath hitched when she moved to wipe the back of her hand across her face. She was crying.

"Damn."

He tried to pass off his feelings for aggravation. After all, since he hadn't caught her trying to escape, it robbed him of an excuse to wring her neck.

Ian turned to retrace his steps. He shut the door quietly behind him and faced the hallway. *Great. Just great. What the hell am I supposed to do now?*

He rubbed his fingertips down his side and looked around at a loss. Weeping women were not something they included in training at the force. They could be lethal.

With deliberate noisy steps, he tromped down the hallway in hope she'd had time to pull herself together.

He raised his hand to tap on the door and paused. Hearing nothing, he rapped on the door.

No response.

Then it came to him. "If you're through sulking in there we need to get back to the business at hand."

After a couple of minutes the door was wrenched open and he saw one furious woman glaring at him. He bit back a smile. *Ah, Miss Feisty Fire is back. This I can deal with.*

"I do not sulk," she crossed her arms across her breasts and stared him down.

"Whatever." Ian shrugged, trying his damnedest not to notice her chest heaving. "Come on and let's get going."

"Going? Where?"

"We're going to play dress up." He enjoyed the incredulous look that washed over her face. Keeping her off guard agreed with him. His hand encircled her wrist and he tugged her down the hall into the spare bedroom.

"W-what are we doing?"

He went over to the closet, swung the doors open and rifled through a packing box to the left on the floor. "We're going to disguise our appearance. Ladies first."

After tossing her a bottle of dark brown hair wash and a tube of cream, he chose some other things for himself.

She caught the first, but dropped the second. He brought over a small box and sat it on the bed. Flipping open the lid, he pulled out fake facial hair of every color.

He rummaged through the rest of the contents and brought out a black mustache with grey flecks in it. The sideburns to match were stuck to it.

"Why are we doing this?" she asked.

He looked over at her still rooted to the spot, holding her supplies.

"We're going to change our appearance," he explained.

"Where are we going after we do that?"

"In search of answers. We can't just sit here. First, we'll stop in somewhere and buy you some clothes."

"Can't we just go by my house after dark?"

"No. It'll be safer if we go to a store in disguise than returning to the scene of the crime. Someone could be watching your house."

A worried look furrowed her brows. "But, I've got to have my prescription. I can't go without it."

Ian walked over to where she stood, cupped her chin and turned her face up to his. His eyes sought hers. "What medicine?"

"For my migraines. I have to have a high-powered prescription."

Great. Just great. He regarded her thoughtfully. Her dark brown eyes rounded with fear and desperation. She was telling the truth. *Damn.*

"Okay, plan B, we head to your house."

"I'm sorry."

He let go of her chin and stepped back. The thought of taking her in his arms, soothing away worry, and holding her close teased him. *She's right. I am insane. That would so not be a good idea.* "We'll deal with it."

He went over, grabbed the duffle bag, and crammed some of his clothes in it. It was risky returning to her house. It was even a worse idea to try to get her prescription refilled when she was supposed to be dead.

Ian went through to the bathroom and grabbed a towel. He turned on the faucet and leaned over to soak his head. Toweling off his hair, he chewed off the cap to the color and began brushing the applicator through his hair lightly, paying close attention to the temples.

It was then that he noticed movement in the mirror. Nicole bent over and rummaged through another box. Her tight, form-fitting jeans emphasized her sweet curves even more.

Stay focused, pal. You need to clear this mess up and deposit her back into her safe little world teaching kids. She's too good for you.

He turned his attention back to his hair. *Damn.* If he left the solution on his hair too long, he was going to be snow white. With his head back under the faucet, he cranked the water to a cooler temperature.

Nicole was trying on different glasses when he returned.

"I don't see how this stuff is going to make us look any different because—"

She stopped, looked up at him and stared. He guessed she was surprised at his appearance after following the directions and putting heat with the blow dryer on his hair.

"You do look different," she finished. She studied him closer now, walking around him.

"Well, could I pass for someone other than me?" he asked.

"Yeah … you do look like someone other than yourself. You're kinda debonair looking now."

"As opposed to?" he baited her.

"A plain, ordinary, run-of-the-mill agent," she tossed at him, and shrugged.

He narrowed his eyes and she looked away. She was flustered. Blushing even. Did women still do that? He'd seen her watching him with those dark brown eyes when she thought he wasn't looking. A slight smile was all he would allow himself. She was lying. He knew it and she knew it. *Well, hell, two could play that way.*

"Did you find anything in those boxes that might … spruce your looks up a bit?"

She rewarded with the rise he'd been going for. Those brown eyes swept back at him and danced with fire.

"I think I found some things suitable. I'm not sure what I'm looking for, though."

He sauntered over and took the bag from her. Their hands grazed and his eyes met hers. She quickly looked down into the bag. Run of the mill looking agent his ass. She wanted him.

The thought of it pleased him. Sure. But, it wasn't something he would act on. She was too sweet for him. He preferred women who knew the score and only wanted to dance a few dances. Nothing permanent. This girl smelled of permanence. Nope, she wasn't his type at all.

"What's our next step in this crazy dance?" he heard her ask.

Chapter 6

Why is he staring at me like that? Nicole wondered what she'd said to warrant such a startled look on Ian's face.

"What did you just say?"

She repeated it for him. "I asked what the next dance step was in this little dress up game of yours."

"Ah ... you ... need to wash your hair in that darkening stuff. It's for blonde to brunette. It'll wash out after a while." he said, turning away from her.

He kicked off his tennis shoes before dropping a pair of leather boat shoes onto the floor. He leaned over and shoved a thick insert in one but not the other.

"What is that for?" She didn't have a clue what he was doing to his shoe.

"It'll give me the appearance of a limp."

His expertise with disguises intrigued her. Her thoughts were jarred when he pulled his T-shirt over his head. Well-honed muscles rippled from broad shoulder to narrow waistband. Her mouth went dry. Perfect pecs adorned by chest hair trailing downward. He leaned over to grab a plaid shirt off the bed. Once he tugged it on, she blinked from her stupor and cleared her throat.

It was then that she noticed his face. She studied him closer. His wet hair was drying and the colors were more noticeable. He had done something to give it a salt and pepper look.

Buttoning his shirt, he turned to look at her. "What?"

"I was just noticing your hair now that it's drier."

"I have sideburns and a mustache to go with it."

He disappeared into the bathroom.

She went over and picked up the bottle of color rinse for her hair to examine it. The thought of coloring her hair didn't appeal to her.

"Well? What do you think?"

She turned to look up into an older face. With the application of the sideburns and mustache to match his hair, he appeared several years older. More distinguished. *He'll age well. Figures.* He was already devastatingly attractive. In a dangerous sort of way.

Dangerous. She would do well to remember that. There was no way she needed man trouble again after what she'd been through with her ex-boyfriend. She should learn from that, move on down the road, and keep her heart with her.

"Um ... yeah, you look different." Her eyes fell back to the shampoo bottle in her hand. Pretending the utmost concentration, she trailed her finger along the directions. For some reason the information wasn't registering in her brain. She needed some space.

With her head down, she walked into a bathroom off to the right of the bedroom. She faced a white pedestal sink with an oval mirror positioned above it. Pulling the door forward to look behind it for towels, she stopped when she spotted the large porcelain, claw-foot tub. She swallowed. A tub made for fantasies.

"Can I help you out with anything?"

Her mouth formed a thin line.

"Have you located everything you need? Towels?" Ian called, his voice getting closer.

"Ah ... towels. I need a ... towel."

"Behind the door on the corner shelf."

"Right. Thanks."

She hadn't even noticed the floor-to-ceiling cabinet with old fashioned handles. *Who could see past the glorious tub?*

Forcing her attention on the cabinet, she pulled open a door and retrieved a fluffy beige towel. She moved to stand in front of the oval mirror over the sink. Before sticking her head under the water, she twisted the knobs to get the temperature right.

The cool water rushed over her head and felt refreshing. She reached for the shampoo on the side of the sink, the back of her hand knocking the bottle to the floor with a clatter. "Oh, crap."

She squeezed the water out of the length of her hair hanging down so it wouldn't drip everywhere.

"Here. I got it."

She froze. A snap of the cap sounded to her right. Before she had time to react, Ian's large hands were in her hair. He used his fingertips to rub her scalp. Her eyes fell closed and she tried to make herself relax. It was a losing battle. The heat from his body leaning over her distracted her determination.

"We need to work this in good for optimal coloring. The bottle said three to five minutes," he told her.

Great. I could combust. She tried to think of something else. Anything but him being so close.

He kept up the massage for several minutes then pushed her head gently beneath the warm water.

"I can take it from here. Thanks," she muttered.

"Suit yourself."

She was relieved when he moved back and took his all too capable hands with him. Cool air circulating between them helped her senses to return. Almost. Once her hands rid her hair of the excess water, she grabbed the towel, and wrapped it around her head. Straightening, her eyes met his in the mirror. She tried to act nonchalant. The bathroom had shrunk in size and the air had left the room. There certainly wasn't any extra in her lungs.

"Here, you'll need this tanning lotion," he told her.

"I do?"

"Yes. Have you used any before?"

She shook her head and kept her eyes on the tube she took from him. This was turning out to be quite an adventure. It was a self-tanning lotion for medium to dark skin.

"Rub it over your body evenly and then wash your hands well when you're done," he explained. "Unless … you need some help with that, too?"

Her cheeks warmed as she all but memorized the instructions on the tube. "I got it."

"Pity."

She gave him a scathing look and then turned away.

"Well, if you're sure, I'm going to pack a few things so we can take off."

"I'm quite sure."

"Suit yourself. Be sure to pack that goop because you'll need to keep reapplying over the next few days for it to really make a difference."

When he left, she exhaled, almost falling on the floor with relief. The bathroom suddenly seemed much larger. *Whew.* He had flirted a bit, but he was a man. She hadn't returned any signals. End of story. She glared at the antique tub. It had been the cause of her riotous thoughts.

She gladly shut the bathroom door and locked it. Squeezing out the recommended pea-sized dab she rubbed the cream into her face, careful not to get it into her eyes. She continued the process with her arms and legs and thought about her grandmother talking about a farmer's tan. She tried to make sure she smoothed it over herself evenly in circular motions so there wouldn't be any streaks. Once finished, she returned to the sink to wash her hands well. The last thing she needed was orangey-brown palms. The pine-scented soap in the dispenser was fitting for the cabin's atmosphere.

Nicole pulled the towel from her head and ran her fingers through her hair. With it wet, it didn't seem too much different in color, maybe a bit darker. It was then she noticed Ian must have set out a blow dryer on the back of the toilet for her. She plugged it in and tousled her hair against the warmth.

After a few minutes, a woman with strawberry-blonde hair stared back at her. Nicole was left stunned at how it really changed her appearance. She imagined after a few hours her skin would darken as well. She wasn't sure she cared for the look at all.

"We need to get moving. Are you ready?" he called out to her.

"Oh, yeah, I'm ready." *To kill you.* She yanked the plug for the blow dryer out of the wall and wrapped the cord around it.

She found him in the living room zipping a duffle bag. He looked up when she came in, narrowing his eyes in assessment of her newfound appearance.

"Hmm."

He dropped the bag and walked around her before coming to stop in front of her. His expression thoughtful, his eyes roved over her. "Different. That was what we were going for."

"I look like a freak. My hair isn't darker blonde or brown. It has red in it."

"Not a freak, just different from Miss Prim and Proper," he said with a maddening twinkle in his eyes. "Now you've got red to match the fire I've seen glimpses of since we met. You look kinda wild and sexy."

"I oughta—"

"Get in the car. Right. Let's go. The sooner we get on the road and get this solved, the sooner we can part company."

That stopped her. The sooner the better was right. A part of her wondered how much teasing had gone into his words "wild and sexy."

He whistled for Dickens. The dog bounded from the kitchen to sit at his master's feet.

"You're going, too, pal." He retrieved the dog's leash from a hanger on the wall, replaced the collar on Dickens' neck from where Nicole had taken it off, and opened the door.

She stepped out onto the front porch, the boards creaking beneath her feet, and peered into the evening's dimming light. Two large pine rockers adorned the platform with a porch swing swaying invitingly to the right. Shrubs outlined the porch, the landscaping had a mixture of red roses, and hostas mingled throughout. Tall pine trees loomed around the frame of the yard. She was about to inquire on the roses, as she was surprised by their presence, when he cupped her elbow and led her down the steps.

They circled around the porch to the left of the house. Gravel crunched beneath their feet on a path that led toward a barn-like structure nestled between two large, old oak trees. Ian tugged on the handles of the wide doors. They opened with a groan and he pushed the doors back against the sides of the barn.

Nicole peered in and saw a seventy-something refurbished dark blue Mustang. She wasn't sure what she'd been expecting to see, but this type of car wasn't on her realm of possibilities.

"I thought all agents drove sedate, unmarked cars." She commented as she lined up behind him to drop her bag in the trunk.

"We do. My neighbor drove over and swapped out cars with me yesterday. He and I go way back and he can be trusted. Mine's parked in his barn until this all blows over," Ian explained taking her bags from her. "They'll be looking for me to be driving something low key. Let 'em look."

He gave off a masculine, cocky laugh. It startled her how the sound of it raised prickles to her skin. Heat spread through her. Unprepared for the sensation, she rubbed at her arms. Dickens sniffed at the tire of the Mustang. Wearing an impatient look on his face, Ian opened the door and nodded for her to get into the car. She slid in onto smooth, cream-colored leather seats. He shut the door, went around to the driver's side, and let Dickens in the back.

The engine hummed to life as Ian backed them out. She couldn't help but think how this was all so bizarre. Here she was being whisked off by a man she'd known less than twenty-four hours. Kidnapped by, no less. She was involved in some mystery and preparing to sneak like a thief into her own house. She was afraid to ask what else could happen.

All of it was a bit too much to take into her system.

She turned to look at the man beside her. Ian really was devastatingly handsome. His haughty eyebrows went well with the arrogant personality.

Ian put the car in park and got out to shut and padlock the barn doors. He scanned the area as he walked back to the car and got in.

"If you want water, there are bottles behind your seat."

"Thank you. I'm fine."

Dickens took that moment to sit up in the back seat and stick his nose between them. She leaned around and scruffed his neck.

The trees flew by as Ian gunned the Mustang down a winding gravel road and out onto the highway. They drove for another thirty minutes before things started to look familiar to her. She was surprised to find they were coming out on the north side of Anderson. With it getting darker each mile, she really hadn't known where they'd end up until Ian pulled onto Madison Street near Hadley's Hardware store. She checked the clock on the dash. It had just reached ten.

It was odd to pass familiar places she'd just driven by yesterday and feel so detached from them. Like she'd been gone for days. So much had happened in the last twenty-four hours. They took another fifteen minutes to navigate through town before turning onto her street.

"Do you think my house is being watched?"

"I would say no because they think I killed you. Still, we'll want to keep a low profile and use precautions."

She wasn't sure she wanted to ask what those were.

Her neighborhood was an older one but well kept. Her house was nestled around retired people who had nothing better to do with their time than plant flowers and work in their yards.

"With this being more of a seniors' neighborhood, it will be quiet. A point for our side." Ian was saying, "When I staked out your place I only remember seeing the raisin generation about."

"Right. That sums it up, really. It was my grandmother's house. The whole neighborhood falls asleep in their chairs before the time the news comes on."

"Good. I'll park the car on this side street, and we'll walk back a few houses." Ian eased the Mustang along the curb and killed the lights. He pushed the button to lower the dog's window. "Dickens, stay, but keep your ears alert."

"You're going to park by a street lamp?"

"To the side of it. Close, but not direct. The trick is, if you want to hide something, you do it in plain sight."

"Really?" She was getting quite the education in sneaking around in disguise. Shaking her head, she hoped she'd never need to reference any of it again.

"Yeah, people will expect someone with something to hide to slink around in the dark bushes and hide in the shadows."

"Oh." She'd never really thought about it, but he was right. She coiled her hair behind her ear and tried to brace herself against what was to come.

He opened the door and ducked down to look at her. "Just get out, we'll go for a walk. We'll hold hands and act like star-struck lovers."

"That'll take some acting."

"It's dark, so that'll cover your lack of acting ability."

She was about to snap back at him but he shut the door behind him. In the time it took him to walk around the car she was able to count to ten and take a deep breath before he opened her door. She stepped out and flashed him a sharp look. His lazy grin showed in the glow of the light through the trees from the street lamp. *He is maddening.*

He caught her hand in his and they walked side by side down the walk. The rest of her body seemed to fade away, all she could feel was her hand warm in his. She watched him look up and down the street. He looked casual but she could tell he was on alert. There didn't seem to be anyone out and about this late. Always a good sign. She hoped their luck held out.

A car passed as they strolled along acting nonchalant. Fresh-cut grass permeated the air. A sprinkler system sprayed across a lawn making rhythmic noises as the force of the water shot around.

"I can't believe I'm sneaking into my own house."

"Once in, we don't want to call attention to ourselves so don't flip on any lights. We make it quick. In. Out."

She noticed her next-door neighbor, Mrs. Malcahaney, had her house all dark. "My neighbor there on the left has gone to bed already and the other, Mrs. Dorsh, is probably still in the hospital."

"Works for us."

Ian tugged on her hand and led the way behind a row of boxwood shrubs. They went deeper into the shadows and sprinted between her house and the neighbor's who was in the hospital. Her heart raced her footsteps. They made it behind the elm tree where he held his finger up to his lips for silence. He must not have detected anything because he crouched down and darted to the back steps. She didn't have a choice but to follow suit because of his death grip on her hand.

"I don't have my key," she whispered.

"No prob, I'll just pick it and …"

She peered up at him to see why he'd stopped talking. His hand was on the knob. He reached behind him and from somewhere produced a gun.

"What's going on?" she whispered worriedly. She gazed into the darkness, but didn't see anything.

"I locked this door when I left."

"But how—"

"Stay here and stay down," he instructed, barely whispering.

He pressed the keys to the Mustang into the palm of her hand and she gripped them. Heart pounding a thunderous drumbeat, she crouched beside the stoop to the left of the door. Her shrub rose dug into her leg. Ian pushed through the door, gun ready for whatever he might find.

She strained to hear. Her lips formed a grim line. *What could I possibly hear over the wild beating of my heart?*

After an agonizing few minutes, Ian poked his head through the door. He tucked his gun behind him.

"It's all clear. You'd better come in and … Nicole …" His voice held a hesitant tone that made her nervous. She pushed past him and stepped into the house. Her mouth dropped open.

Moonlight filtered through the blinds to cast wicked shadows across a utility room in chaos. Cabinets flung open wide. The laundry hamper upside down. A hand whipped around her waist and another hand clamped over her mouth. For a frozen moment they just stood there.

"You can't make a sound," he breathed in her ear.

She nodded. He was right. She had to fight the panic. He waited a minute, then slackened his hold and released her.

"You gonna be okay?" He ran his hands up and down her arms.

She nodded but didn't trust herself to speak because she wasn't sure she'd ever be all right again. Like a sleepwalker, traipsing through a bad dream unable to come to, she wandered into her kitchen. Her mouth fell open to say something, but words didn't form. She shook her head in awe as what she saw wasn't sinking into her brain. Drawers were yanked out, some dumped on the floor. Cupboards gaped open, now empty cavities. The floor was littered with dishtowels and the items she recognized from her phone drawer. Even the contents of the trashcan were strewn about the room.

She moved in slow motion toward the door that led into the dining room and pushed through it to find the same scenario.

Trashed.

She placed one hand over her forehead and the other fisted at her stomach. "I'm ... involved. Oh, dear God ... I'm somehow involved. What could they have been after?"

He was beside her then. His hand cupped her shoulder and turned her toward him.

"What on earth could they have been looking for to do all this?" she murmured.

"Nicole. Focus. We need to get your medicine, some clothes, and get out. Do you hear me?"

She nodded. He was right. They had to get her things and get out. He leaned her over and asked her to breath. She tried to do as asked but it wasn't as easy as it sounded. The whole time he rubbed a hand along her back. She exhaled and took a deep breath and nodded again. "Yes. Okay. Yes, you're right."

She turned and staggered down the hall and turned toward her bedroom. "I'm going to be okay. I can do this."

"Damn right you can."

He brushed past her down the hallway and disappeared into her room. She followed slowly, her bottom lip caught between her teeth, she fought to stay focused. Tears threatened to take over, but she pushed them back.

Now was not the time. She'd fall apart later. After they were gone from what was once her haven.

Dazed, she walked into her room at the same time she heard Ian whip back her shower curtain in the bathroom. Her bedroom was a disaster. Everything felt dirty. Someone's filthy hands had roved over her personal things tossing them aside as if they were nothing.

She stumbled over something on the floor and kicked it out of the way. Her mattress was off to the side of her box springs. They'd left nothing untouched.

Ian appeared in the doorway of her bathroom. "All clear. I'm going to check the rest of the house."

She nodded absently as he left. In the dimly lit room, she felt for her closet door handle. On the top shelf was a carry-on bag she'd bought to take on her trip to Mexico a few weeks ago with her friend Kelly. She ran her hand along the shelf. It was gone. She sighed and peered around the room until her eyes fell on a bag in the corner.

Her dresser drawers were flung wide open and tilted down. Whoever had gone through her things had rifled through her underwear. *Oh God. Think about it later. Not now. You have to get out. Think about it later.* She grabbed some under garments and went over to her T-shirt drawer. There were only two left in the bottom. The rest she had to pick up across the room.

For the life of her, she couldn't think what they'd be after. Her nice stereo was still there. She flipped the leather jewelry box open that adorned the top of her dresser. Her rings were still there. The large sapphire pendant that had belonged to her grandmother rested in its spot. She retrieved it from the box and put it deep in her pocket.

What could they have been after then if all this stuff is still here?

A movement in the next room brought her back to the present. Ian was roaming about inspecting things, no doubt. Maybe he'd have some insight after his thorough search of the place.

She hurried over to the drawer where she kept her shorts. She just pulled out a hand full of whatever had been scrambled on top. After stuffing those in the bag, she worked her way over the right side of her bed.

Her medicine bottle was still in the nightstand, but even that drawer was in disarray. Thankful to have the prescription in her possession, she hugged it to her chest before dropping it inside her bag. She went into the bathroom, took her makeup bag, and quickly selected some other toiletries. After tossing them into her carry on, she zipped it up.

Assessing the bedroom with one last glance, her house no longer felt familiar. The shadows were eerie. She walked carefully into the hallway so as not to stumble over clutter.

"Ian?"

"In here."

She followed the sound of his voice. It led her to the living room where he stood in the dim light provided from the streetlamps through the window. He was looking between the blinds, his gun drawn.

"Do you see anyone?"

"No. We're good."

The living room told the same story as the others. Sofa cushions tossed, drawers opened and chairs turned over. In dismay, she noted her grandmother's Victorian lamp overturned and the base broken. She tried to swallow the bitterness that burned her throat. That had been a fiftieth anniversary gift from her grandfather to her grandmother. She shook her head. *This mess would take forever to weed through.*

Her antique, cherry, roll-top desk in the corner looked as if it had exploded and her hall closet like a couple of dogs had dug it out.

"What do you think they were looking for? I don't have anything much of value," Nicole whispered. "My stereo, TV, and computer are all still here."

"I believe I may know. Follow me," he said. She watched Ian walk over to her dining room table and stop.

"What did you find?"

She went to stand beside him. He gestured to her camera bag lying on its side on the table.

"It's what I didn't find. Your camera bag is empty. It would appear they stole your camera."

Nicole frowned. "No, they didn't. I don't have it here."

He turned to look at her and then stepped closer. "What?"

"My camera. I don't have it here. It's at my friend Kelly's house."

He grabbed her elbow. "Did you get your medicine?"

"Yes."

"Let's go then. You can explain in the car on the way."

He urged her through the house and guided her toward the back door and out into the night.

Chapter 7

Ian steered the car away from the curb as he checked the rear-view mirror to ensure they weren't being followed. The neighborhood appeared to be sleeping and none the wiser. No new porch lights detected. He took a few calming breaths and tried to think of a way to approach Nicole with his new line of questions so as not to excite her. She was already upset enough with her house tossed and dissected.

Ian flipped his signal and turned right. Still, no one appeared to be tailing them. He glanced over at Nicole and noted her serious expression. He imagined it would take a while to digest the condition they had found her house in. Whoever ransacked the place had done a thorough job. Probably one of Roark's men looking for whatever damning evidence he thought Nicole had on him. *Yep, there's a connection there all right. But what?*

"Tell me about this Kelly, your camera, and when you used it last."

"It was three weekends ago. In Mexico, at Trish's wedding."

"Mexico? You didn't say anything to Trey and I about Mexico when we questioned you this morning."

"I told you about going to the wedding of a lifelong friend."

"You conveniently left out the part about Mexico," he snapped before getting himself under check.

"Well, excuse me. I've had a little bit of stress in my life in the last twenty-four hours," she flung back at him.

"Okay. Okay." He rolled his neck and gripped the steering wheel tighter. "Just tell me about Mexico. What part?"

"Guadalajara. Kelly and I flew out on that Friday. Trish and Jack—"

"Jack who?"

"Benson."

"Okay. Continue."

"I took hordes of pictures. I minored in photography in college. Jack and Trish couldn't afford a fancy photographer and a trip to Mexico for their honeymoon," she explained. "So, I offered to take their wedding pictures."

"And this Kelly? Where does she come in and why does she have your camera?"

"She was going to develop the pictures and size them for the frames and wedding album."

"You couldn't develop them at your place?"

"Kelly and I met in college in photog class. She has a larger house than I do, with equipment set up in a small back bathroom that dubs for a darkroom."

"I see."

"Well, I wish I did."

The facts were beginning to add up. His fingers tightened on the steering wheel. If his hunches were right, those wedding pictures could be the next piece of the puzzle.

"Where does Kelly live?"

She gave him the address. It was about a forty-minute drive west.

"We can't go there tonight. It'll be well after eleven before we arrive," Nicole said.

"We need answers. Now."

"But she's an airline stewardess. She may have gotten in late on a flight. We can't just—"

"We can. And we will."

"But—"

"Nicole, the people who tossed your place were looking for something. Your missing camera and film are the only clues we have to go on right now."

She turned toward him in her seat, opened her mouth to say something, but must have thought better of it. She twisted back to face the road and stared.

"Look, if we have to wake your friend, I'm sorry, but this is really important. She'll get over it when she realizes we're trying to save your life."

He winced at the harshness in his tone. She flinched and looked out her passenger window away from him. He took the slight slump of her shoulders as her resign.

They drove on in silence for a few miles.

Ian wracked his brain. *It has to be the pictures. It has to be.* "So, you took pictures of your friends getting married. Did you know everyone who attended the wedding?"

"It was just the four of us and another man, Jack's best friend ... um, Eric ... I can't remember his last name at the moment. Kelly would know. He hit on her."

"Okay. We'll get his last name and I'll have him checked out. Go on. Do you remember taking pictures of anything or anyone else while you were there?"

"Well, of the scenery of course. A mission church. The landscape. Pizza delivery mopeds we laughed about ... I don't know. What does anyone take pictures of when they're on vacation?"

"It'll be interesting to see what you have."

"I can't imagine what would be so troublesome."

Ian sat thoughtful while he tried to figure out that angle as he drove. He wondered if her father being a missionary in another country had anything to do with it. The pieces weren't adding up.

He made it about twenty minutes down the road before he asked, "Are you cool enough?"

"Hmm."

What the hell was that supposed to mean? He adjusted the air anyway.

"Mind if I turn on some music?" he asked her.

"No."

"Fine."

The awkward silence was replaced with the local station coming over the air. They drove within a few blocks of the address she'd given him to Kelly's house.

"Left or right from here?"

"Left."

He cranked the steering wheel to the left and guided the car down the street. "Now?"

"Right this time."

He complied with the directions and found Ashford Court. "Which house is it?"

"The one with the shrubs and large mailbox over there."

He hugged the car to the curb and killed the motor. The ranch-style house sat back, sprawled behind elm trees. All the windows were dark. He eyed the windows in the two-car garage. They'd be able to see her car if it was parked in there. "Let's see if she's home. If she is, we really need to speak to her, Nicole."

"Okay. I know. You're right."

They climbed out and shut their doors, leaving Dickens lying on the backseat.

Ian headed up the driveway to the garage doors, cupped his hands and peered inside.

"No car."

"She must be on a layover flight or doing a red eye. We'll have to come back tomorrow."

"Yeah. Let's go," he said, and turned to head back to the car.

Ian noticed she had looked up at him, probably shocked by how agreeable he seemed. He hadn't said how soon they would come back.

Taking her elbow, he guided her to the Mustang and held the car door open for her. Ian surveyed the street for a better place to park as he walked around the car to slide in. He decided to drive down the street and come up the next block to park. After finding a spot he liked, he pulled over and turned off the engine.

"What are we doing?" Nicole asked.

"I'm going back to retrieve that camera and either the film or the developed pictures," he said.

"You're going to break into Kelly's house?"

"Yep. With or without you."

"I won't be a part of that. I feel bad breaking into her house."

"Okay. Lock the doors." He pushed his door open, then ducked his head down and looked at her. "It would be quicker if you'd show me where the makeshift darkroom is, and safer if you'd stay with me."

She sighed and reached for the door handle. "I know, I know, it's necessary."

"Now you're learning." He closed the door and smiled to himself. She was aggravatingly adorable. He shouldn't have so much fun baiting her, but he did.

They met in front of the car and he took her hand. She tensed.

"Okay, Nicole, same as before. Strolling lovers out to admire the stars."

He turned his attention to the row of houses and tried to forget how incredibly soft her hand was in his. The subdivision was one cookie-cutter house after another. Groomed yards, driveways littered with cars, and basketball hoops on the sides. A white cat crouched on a porch rail, unconcerned. No dogs detected. Quiet, just the way he liked it.

"What are you doing?" Nicole asked, breaking his reverie.

"Getting a feel for the neighborhood."

"How does it feel?"

"Asleep."

"Let's hope it stays that way," she said. "I don't like doing this."

"Neither do I, but I like it even less that someone is trying to kill you and frame me for the murder." He assumed he'd made his point with her because her hand clenched inside of his. "Does Kelly live alone?"

"Yes."

"Pets?"

"A fish tank."

"Wonderful. Piece of cake."

The next house was Kelly's. Ian swung his gaze up and down the street before tugging on Nicole's arm and leading her between the two houses. They paused behind an arched trellis covered in vines. Ian listened for any sound that would indicate they'd been spotted.

All remained quiet.

Nicole couldn't believe they were breaking and entering into her best friend's house. She curled her bottom lip in to chew on it. Always one to do the right thing, she'd never snuck out of the house like her friends did in high school. Her nerves were wired tight. She grasped her throat half expecting someone to jump out at her and demand to know what they were doing.

What would we say?

Ian let go of her hand and pulled his wallet from his pocket. He flipped it open, took something out that gleamed in the moonlight and headed for the back door. "See anything?"

"No. Nor do I hear anything," she whispered back.

"You stay ten paces behind me. Understand? And keep a look out."

"Yes, master." Her voice dripped with sarcasm to the point she doubted even he would miss it.

He knelt down and examined the lock. Fascinated, she forgot to watch out for any neighbors moving about. He slipped something that made a scraping noise into the lock. Next, he tried the door and then ran the metal tool back into the key hole again.

The second time he tried the door, it opened. She let out a breath, not knowing if she felt more relieved or anxious. She hoped Kelly would forgive her for this.

They stepped quietly into the dark kitchen. The room was unlit except for the surface light on the stove, which created a golden glow.

"Where's her darkroom?"

"Through here." She took the lead and felt her way across the room. The toe of her sandal rammed into a kitchenette chair and made a scooting noise on the linoleum, shattering the quiet.

"Don't take up being a cat burglar," Ian said from behind her, catching her arm.

"Very funny."

She groped her way across the living room and into the hallway that led back to the bedrooms. Past the master bedroom, a hallway closet, the next door on the right was the bathroom. "In through there."

"Don't turn on the light. Slip in and I'll be right behind you. Is there a window in the room?"

"No."

She opened the door and stepped inside. Ian came in behind her and shut the door with a soft snap.

"There's a switch over there. It's a darkroom light."

She could hear his hand swipe along the wall, a click, and then the room illuminated with a red cast.

It was rectangle shaped with a long vanity that lined one full wall and a large mirror behind it. There were developing trays between two double sinks. A laundry cord strung across the basins from wall to wall displaying recently developed pictures of kids in black and white poses.

"I don't see my camera," she said, rifling through the shelves behind her. Kelly's camera bag and paraphernalia sat on the top shelf. The second shelf held photo albums with more examples of Kelly's work.

"What's this here?"

Ian stood to the left of her and opened a door that appeared to have once been a linen closet. They both peered inside. More photo albums and cameras decorated the shelves.

"There's my camera."

"It's not a digital?"

Nicole brushed ahead of him and reached for her Nikon to inspect it. "My dad bought me this camera for my high school graduation. I'm partial to it."

"Hopefully the roll of film is still in it."

She checked the window. The loader was empty. "No, it's not."

"Maybe she's developed it."

Nicole nodded and flipped through the albums, none of which were wedding pictures. On the next shelf was a box the size of a scrapbook. She pulled it out and stepped back to examine it in the dim light. Taking off the lid her eyes fell to the words "Our Wedding."

"This may be it."

She took the book out of the box and quickly opened it. The happy couple posed by the ocean, staring up at her. "Bingo."

Ian grasped the right side of the book as she moved over. Page by page, they pored over each photo. Nothing was out of the ordinary, as far as she could tell. They showed Jack and Trish standing at the altar, being announced man and wife, and then pictures of them cutting the cake. She noticed Ian paused at each photo and inspected each one closely.

"Do you see anything?"

Ian didn't answer until he'd made his second trip through each picture. She remained silent so he could concentrate, but it was killing her. Her breath caught in her chest.

"Nothing."

Her shoulders slumped and eyes sank shut as she drew her lips inward. *Nothing.*

She opened her eyes and blinked, not even sure what she thought they'd find. Some kind of key that would unlock the mystery to this horrible nightmare she was trapped in. She went to put the album back into the box. Her hand brushed something in the bottom. An envelope. She ran a fingernail under the paper and turned it over. Her name was written across the front of it.

"Ian."

She set the album down on the vanity. Opening the flap, she shook out a handful of pictures. The first was of the beautiful bougainvillea in Mexico that she had admired and snapped the shot, the ocean in the background. The next was one of the sunset.

"These are my pictures."

Ian studied them over her shoulder as she shuffled through them one by one. There were about twenty photos in all.

"Go back."

Nicole stopped and looked up at him. "What? What did you see? She shuffled back to the one she thought he meant.

"One more."

She turned the pictures back one by one. The ocean. Someone parasailing against the red morning sky. Men standing off to the side on the beach ...

"Stop."

Ian grabbed the photo to scrutinize it under the light.

She opened a drawer, picked up a magnifying glass and handed it to him.

"What is it?" she asked, trying to peer around his shoulder.

He just stared at the photo with a funny expression on his face. She looked from him to the photo and back again, puzzled. "What is it? What do you see?"

"You're a helluva good photographer."

"What do you mean?"

"You've just taken a picture of one of our top agents," he said, turning to face her. "And he looks damned good for someone who's been dead for five years."

Chapter 8

This is it. Ian held his ticket to pass go and nail Roark's ass to a jail wall in the process. His fingers tightened on the edges of the picture as his pulse ricocheted. He'd found Nicole's connection in this hellish mess.

"You're saying this man is supposed to be dead?" Nicole looked up from the picture, confused. "I don't understand."

"I think I'm beginning to. See this man here?" he said, indicating the taller of the three men. "His name is Agent Derek Borland."

"Yeah. Okay."

"Borland worked undercover about five years back trying to locate a leak coming from the Pentagon."

"What happened?"

"He came close to discovering the source, but someone killed him before he could point a finger," Ian told her. "There was an explosion, and we never recovered his body. He was presumed dead. Until you snapped this photo, that is."

"This is how I'm involved," Nicole whispered.

"Exactly. Someone must've spotted you taking pictures and tracked you down."

"But, I wouldn't have known who this man was."

"Doesn't matter. You're a loose end," Ian explained as he put the photos back in the folder. "You have to consider how many people view wedding photos."

"A lot."

"Exactly."

"What do we do next?"

"We get out of here." He un-tucked his shirt, pushed the folder into his shorts, and pulled his shirt down over it. He straightened the darkroom back like they'd found it.

Ian reached in front of her and snapped off the darkroom light. "Let's give our eyes a minute to adjust before we make our way through the house."

With darkness blanketing the room, he was conscious of Nicole's warmth next to him. *Time to get out.*

"Let's go."

Ian reached around her and groped for the doorknob. She leaned into him as he opened the door. Her soft silky hair brushed against his chin. *Oh, yeah, definitely time to go.*

Careful not to bump into anything, Ian retraced their steps. He paused near the back door and moved the curtains ever so slightly to peer into the night. The streets still appeared to be quiet.

"Looks good," he whispered.

He opened the door and stepped out and into the warm summer evening air. The only movement he detected was the slight swaying of leaves. He motioned for Nicole to follow. Once she came out and into the yard, he palmed the pick from his pocket. He locked the door behind them.

He caught Nicole's hand in his. "Same drill as before."

They darted over to the bushes beside the house. Ian froze, listening. Down the sidewalk on the left, a man's legs were visible beneath the low growth of tree limbs. The glow of a cigarette bobbed in the air. The man was leaning over doing something on the ground. A sputtering noise followed by a *whoosh* as water sprayed in all directions over the lawn. After a few minutes, the man put out his cigarette and trotted up the steps to his house and shut the door.

"Let's go." He tugged on Nicole's hand, pulling her towards the sidewalk. "Just stroll like we have all the time in the world. Lovers, remember?"

He set the pace, as they sauntered back to where the Mustang sat. Not ready to let go of Nicole's hand, he retrieved his keys from his pocket and walked her around to the passenger side of the car. He smiled and wondered what she'd do if he completed their little lovers act and pushed her up against the car and kissed her hard. Instead, he shook his head, trying to regain sanity, and opened the door for her. Dickens sat up and rolled his tongue out in a yawn.

"Sorry to wake you, pal."

He shut her door and mentally kicked himself as he made his way over to the driver's side and climbed in. The woman was getting to him. He needed to rein in his hormones and think with his brain.

Ian stole a glance at Nicole. He wished he could protect her from the anxiety written on her face. Without a thought, he reached out and put his hand on her knee.

"Are you all right?"

"I'm involved. All this for something I didn't even know was … something."

"We'll get to the bottom of it." He tried to assure her by giving her knee a squeeze and then realizing what he was doing, removed his hand. "Remember, knowledge is power."

He checked his mirrors. Not many cars were out this late. It would be easy to tell if a car was tailing them.

"What do we have the power to do, Ian?"

"The first thing I need to do is prove that the picture and negatives haven't been altered. Borland had to have inside help to pull faking his death off."

"Roark?"

"Exactly. Roark. And this means he's been on the take for longer than Dan and I suspected. A good five years."

"A lot of damage could have been done in that time."

"Exactly. The fallout from this could be huge," Ian said, his mind humming with the possibilities. No wonder Roark had gone to elaborate methods to set him up.

"How are you going to have the picture's authenticity checked?"

"I have a connection who could help," Ian said, an old friend's name coming to mind. He really couldn't use anyone at the agency. It would be too risky.

"How will you know who you can trust and who you can't?"

His eyes never left the road. "I won't."

Silence fell between them. The night swallowed them up as he drove and tried to work out a strategy in his mind. His friend, Brian Helms, now lived about two hours away. They'd go to him.

After a while, he said, "We're going to need sleep first, then get a fresh start on things tomorrow."

"I'm too keyed up to sleep."

"You'll have settled down by the time we get to where we're going."

"Aren't we headed back to the cabin?" Nicole asked.

"No. After finding this picture, I've decided we're heading north. There were three men in that picture. I only know one. We need to find out who the other two are. I've got a buddy I think can help us."

Nicole stared out the car window. The shadows were as dark as her mood. Her trip to Mexico had been brief and focused on the wedding. Who would've thought all of this would come from just snapping photos of beautiful scenery? All she'd wanted was a good photo of the hills dotted with those small houses and red thatched roofs. They had made a lovely backdrop for the gorgeous red bougainvillea growing everywhere. She'd planned to enlarge the best photo and put it in a frame over her couch. Something to remember her trip by.

Now all she could do was wish she could forget it.

Ian flipped stations on the radio until smooth jazz filled the Mustang's confines. The balanced rhythms helped calmed her frayed nerves a bit. She took a deep breath as she glanced over at him. He was lost in thought she could tell. She prayed he would come up with a way for them to get out of their situation.

The city lights of Charleston twinkled in the distance. She raised her hand to her mouth to suppress a yawn. The day had been long, and the night was rolling into tomorrow. She yawned a second time.

"It won't be long now. I'll pull over at the first motel that will take animals."

"I didn't realize I was so tired."

"It's late and it's been a long day."

"I'll say. Breaking and entering wears you out."

Crossing into the city limits, they slowed. "Just follow my lead. We're married and traveling east along Virginia Beach way, and up to Boston to visit relatives."

"But ... that means we'll be in the same room."

"I'm not worried you'll jump my bones, unless you don't think you can keep yourself under control."

"Oh, I think I can manage." She rolled her eyes.

"I know it'll be hard for you." He laughed and then said in a serious tone, "It will be better if we stay together."

Although she hated to admit it, she knew he was right.

After passing five hotels, they found one that had a "Pets Allowed" sign hanging. She pushed her feet against the floorboard and stretched out her legs. Her whole body was stiff as a post.

"Stay here with the door locked," Ian told her as he eased the car into a parking space near the lobby entrance.

She merely nodded and watched him walk over to the double doors and push his way through. Dickens whimpered in the seat behind her and nuzzled her left ear.

"Let me guess, you hear the call of nature, Dickens?" She pulled up on her door handle and hopped out. She opened the door for the German Shepherd to bound from the back seat. He gave his body a good shake and then sat down.

"Good boy." She reached in the car, felt along the floor until she found his leash. With a snap, the leash hooked into place and she led him over to a grove of trees alongside the parking lot.

Through the front window, Nicole could see Ian talking to the desk clerk. He would check them in as a married couple. She tried not to worry about the sleeping arrangements. It wasn't like he could request double beds. She could do this. She was a grown woman. The trouble was, he was a grown man, and a very attractive one at that. There would surely be a chair to sleep in, or, if not, she'd take the floor. She pressed her lips together. It wouldn't be easy bedding down in the same room with him.

Lost in thought, she didn't notice that someone had walked up behind her. A heavy hand clapped her shoulder and she gasped at the sharp squeeze. The hand spun her around where she stood face to face with Ian's thunderous expression.

Chapter 9

"What were you thinking?" Ian demanded, his heart echoing in his ears.

Her hand flew to her chest. "You scared me half to death."

"I should strangle the other half and finish the job," he growled.

"I'm sorry. Dickens needed to go, and I just didn't think of—"

"You just didn't think. Period." He should handcuff her to him.

He let his hand fall away and then raised it to pinch the bridge of his nose. She didn't have a clue how badly shaken he'd been when he got back to the car and found her gone. She couldn't. Hell, he didn't even understand it, much less expect her to. Sure, she was his responsibility to protect, but this was something else. Something he didn't want to think about. Fear.

"Okay. It's okay. Just don't let there be a next time," he warned her. Before he did something else stupid like touch her again, he turned back to the Mustang and opened the trunk. "Let's take our bags up to our room, Anne, dear."

"Yes, sir," she muttered, "And you are …?"

"Your adoring husband, Mike."

"Pity. You look more like a Fred to me."

He fisted the handles of the duffle bags and yanked them both out of the trunk instead of doing what he wanted to do. Kiss her. Hard. Kiss that smirk right off her beautiful upturned face. The thought of tasting those luscious lips of hers made his blood hum. Other parts of him, too, he realized.

It's going to be a long night. He sighed, slammed the trunk harder than necessary, and stormed off toward the lobby. Nicole trailed behind with Dickens in tow. If he let her, she'd make a damned slave of him just like the dog. He was going to have to get his hormones under check. This was just another assignment. Plain and simple.

Ian held the lobby door for her and Dickens. He caught a whiff of her fragrance as she passed by. Some kind of floral scent. He refused to breathe too deeply until she was farther ahead of him. The pause allowed him a moment to look over her head and nod at the hotel clerk that checked him in. The man wasn't looking at him but instead tracking Nicole's sweet little backside all the way to the elevator.

"My wife and I won't be needing a wakeup call in the morning," he tossed at the clerk, then gave him a cocky wink when the pervert finally dragged his eyes off Nicole. Realizing he'd been caught, the guy turned to look at his computer. *Asshole.*

They stepped onto the elevator, and the moment the door closed, he found Nicole's elbow in his gut.

"Just what was that all about?" she demanded, folding her arms across her chest.

He doubled forward sucking in a sharp breath. *Her elbows should be registered.* "Just trying to act the part of a happily married couple. I've no real experience. Cut me some slack."

He punched the button for the second floor. The elevator started to ascend. "We're in room two-thirteen."

The elevator slowed to a stop and with a *ding* the doors glided open. He noted the signs indicating which way to turn for their room and took a left. Half way down the hall he located their room. Ian shifted his cargo and slid the room key into the slot.

Nicole stepped into the room first while Ian held the door with his foot. He went in and dropped the bags. The serene earth-toned colors of the room did little to quell the rise of panic raging inside her. She stared at the lone bed in the room. Ian must have sensed by her rigid pose, she was having trouble with all of this.

"Relax, Goldilocks. I couldn't very well ask for two beds, now could I? You'll sleep in it by yourself." He closed the door behind him, slid the chain over, and bolted the door.

His eyes held amusement when he turned to look at her. She brushed past him and headed over to perch on the side of the bed to kick off her shoes. Both the lateness of the hour and the days mounting stress hit her like a tidal wave. She couldn't remember a time when she'd been this tired before.

"You get first dibs on the bathroom," Ian announced, and paced over to the window to look out.

Nicole didn't wait to be asked twice. She grabbed up her duffle bag and headed into the bathroom. Her eyes watered with a suppressed yawn. The shower encased in glass was inviting, but she was too tired. She pulled her T-shirt over her head and stepped out of her jeans. Thinking she might have to wear them again before this was over, she folded each article of clothing neatly to place them in a drawer when she went back out. After rummaging through her bag, she selected the pink camie and white cotton shorts she'd brought to sleep in, and grimaced. *I wished I'd thought to bring something more covering.*

After dressing, she stood and assessed herself in the mirror. Everything was covered up modestly enough. *So, why do I feel so exposed?*

She raked her brush through her hair. Ian could be heard moving around in the bedroom and talking to Dickens. It was stupid to hide in the bathroom. She sucked in her bottom lip, opened the door, and went to stand in front of the other vanity outside. Unzipping her cosmetic bag, she rooted through it until she found her toothbrush. "Your turn."

Despite her resolve to keep her eyes averted, she looked up when he walked behind her, completely missing her brush with the toothpaste. The blue gel slid down her shirt.

Her eyes watched in the mirror as his gaze traveled the length of her and back up, a lazy smile spreading across his face. Her body tingled with awareness. He patted her on the head and said, "Cute."

And just like that, he sauntered into the bathroom and shut the door behind him.

She set her jaw and narrowed her eyes. Staring back at herself in the mirror she turned the water on full blast from the sink outside the bathroom door. *Cute?* The man was infuriating. The very idea, patting her on the head. She smooshed two days' worth of the minty gel out and hit her bristles this time. She brushed her teeth with a fury as she tried to work out her aggravation. By the time she'd patted her mouth dry with a towel, she was determined to go to bed and sleep the day off.

Dickens lay at the foot of her bed on a make-shift pallet Ian had prepared for himself. The sight brought a smile to her face. The large dog took up over half of Ian's bed.

"You're such a treasure, Dickens." She leaned down to rub his neck in circular motions. "Just a delight. Stretch out and sleep well my friend."

She threw back the scattered leaf-print bedspread and climbed between the cool sheets. The bed was comfortable enough, although the way she felt, being able to pause and sleep on a rock would do, too. She tried to look on the bright side. At least she wasn't handcuffed to a bed tonight.

A sudden and familiar noise jolted her from her thoughts. Her mouth went dry. It was the sound a bar of soap made when it slipped through your fingers and hit the shower floor.

She swallowed hard.

Forbidden images of Ian's lathered bare chest, and other body parts, floated to the front of her mind. His body covered in creamy lather. Her hands over his slick wet shoulders. Touching him. Kissing a trail down to … she reached out to snap off the bedside lamp and scooted down in the bed. He could just super sleuth his way to his dog-filled pallet in the dark. It would serve him right if he stubbed his cocky toe.

"Cute," he says.

She leaned up and turned to thump her pillow. Once. Twice. Semi-satisfied, she laid back down again and closed her eyes. *I'm very tired. I'm going right to sleep I'm so tired.*

Minutes later, her eyes sprang open as she heard the water shut off and the shower door glide back. He was probably reaching for a towel. Images of him towel drying off every inch of his body tormented her.

She let her eyes fall shut as she expelled a long sigh.

After a moment, the bathroom door clicked. She squeezed her eyes shut and tried to pretend she was asleep. Curiosity got the better of her and she peeked through squinted eyelashes trying to detect his motions. At first, he stood against the silhouetted backdrop of the bathroom light. He must've been allowing his eyes time to adjust to the darkness of the room. He eased the bathroom door forward to just a slight crack, letting the light seep into the room. His shadow passed through the line of light on the wall and she heard him moving about the room. He was checking out the window again. She realized she was holding her breath and tried to let it sneak out slowly so as not to give herself away.

"Good night, Nicole."

"How'd you know I wasn't asleep yet?" she whispered.

"Because your breathing hasn't gone into a rhythm yet."

Well that's just great.

"Tomorrow's a new day. Things will look better."

"I hope you're right."

He was evidently repositioning Dickens on the blankets to make room for himself. Tomorrow was a new day and she hoped it held the answers they needed.

After a few minutes, she noticed his breathing had become rhythmic. *How did he do that so quick? Great. It was going to be a long night of listening to him breathe.*

A yawn crept up on her as she curled on her right side and slipped a hand under the pillow. After several minutes, warmth spread over her like a soft quilt. The air conditioner shifted on. Her eyes rocked closed as the hum of sleep beckoned.

Lavender. The only thing not covered in the scented bubbles was her head poking out of the warm creamy water. Her hands glided through the mounds of suds. She stretched languorously in the claw-foot tub, loving the silky caress of the foam against her skin. She opened her eyes drowsily when she heard a faint noise. Ian stood over her with that sexy devilish grin of his. It was the only thing he wore. Her eyes took their time to wander down his glorious well-toned, tan body. Such perfection. And all hers. By the looks of things, his body was more than ready for their union. She laughed and swept the bubbles closer to her chin.

"What do you want?" she teased giving a coy look out of the corner of her eye lashes.

"I just thought you might be in need of my services."

"Hmm. What's your expertise?" she bated.

"A little of this. And a whole lotta that."

"You're hired. When can you start?" she purred.

Ian knelt beside the tub and sifted his strong fingers through her hair. He worked shampoo gently into her scalp and massaged her temples. She moaned from the sheer pleasure of it. Life didn't get any better than this.

Or did it?

The water rose to her chin. Her eyes fluttered open as he slipped into the water beside her, his left arm curling under her body, his legs entwining with hers. His hard-muscled, very male thigh cradled her hip.

They were off to a delicious start.

He looked down at her with a wicked glint and produced a bar of soap between his long tanned fingers. His smile said it all. With slow deliberation, he caressed the soap over her neck in circular motions.

"This may take a while," he told her. "You're a very dirty girl."

She laughed and outlined his bottom lip with the tip of her index finger. "And you're one naughty boy."

"I'm prepared to show you just how good I can be."

"Mmm." She moaned as he snaked the soap across her shoulders. He lightly grazed her already erect nipples. She moaned again and arched her back. More throaty whimpers escaped from her.

She wanted to feel the length of him. Her hand started at his biceps and trailed down his torso. Her fingertip traced swirls in his dampened chest hair and crept lower. The soap continued its downward spiral, the heat spreading throughout her entire body. She was on fire. He was fanning the flames by blowing in her ear and nipping at her lobe. She didn't think she could wait much longer.

Her finger trailed from his chest along his very male body and slid over his rippled stomach muscles.

"Take it easy, sweetheart. There's no rush. We've got all night. Let's take it slow and easy the first time. We can switch to fast and hard after that."

"Oh, I do love the way you think."

"You've not heard anything yet. I can be very creative when given the right incentive."

She pressed into him. All the bubbles escaped from between them. They were skin to skin. She ran the tip of her tongue along his neck and kissed the area right behind his ear.

"That works." He laughed that throaty laugh that gave her chills, even when she was going up in flames.

She smiled and raised her eyes to search his. "Make love to me."

He licked the side of her face.

"Huh? What?" She sputtered and bolted up from the bed.

"Nicole."

"Wh-what?" Hands gripped her shoulders and she opened her eyes. She was disoriented. She realized she wasn't even wet. And in fact, had clothes on. "What?"

"I asked if you were all right."

She struggled to make sense of things. She was dry. There was no claw-foot tub. The room was dark. She was in a hotel bed. "I—um …"

Dickens licked her face again.

"Dickens, I told you to get back."

Realization began to push its way to the forefront of her mind. It had all been just a dream.

He was sitting on the bed beside her. He was far too close.

Ian stood up and reached for the lamp on the nightstand.

"No." Nicole shot out a hand to stop him and winced at how harsh her voice sounded. "I … sorry."

She couldn't allow him to see the twin flames in her cheeks. She was on fire. Her whole body felt like it was blushing. Embarrassment coursed through her veins; she wanted to wither up and die.

"Okay, I'll leave it off."

"Thank you." *How am I ever going to explain my way out of this?*

"Are you having one of your migraines?"

She sat and stared at his neck. The bathroom light seeping through the cracked door was the only illumination in the room. She hoped the shadows would help to hide her embarrassment. "No. I … no."

"I tried to wake you."

"Ah … did I, um, happen to say anything?"

Chapter 10

"You were moaning," Ian said, "and I thought you might be having a bad dream or a migraine."

Oh, yeah, it had been bad dream all right. Her eyes closed as she tried to keep from fanning her face. She just knew her body was experiencing its first hot flash. The flush was creeping up her neck and heading straight for her cheeks.

"I-I'm sorry I woke you," she whispered over the lump in her throat. She tried to swallow.

"Don't worry about it."

He sat back down on the side of the bed. Close enough for her to touch him. It was at that moment she realized his chest was bare.

She was fully awake now.

Her eyes followed the line of his chest hair down to the band on his jeans. She swallowed hard. They weren't zipped. He must have just thrown them on in a hurry. A strangled noise escaped from her lips.

The bed shifted as Ian stood and walked away. Nicole let out the breath caught in her throat. The air in the room started to circulate again. She needed to get a grip. The dream had felt so real. Her body was tingling all over. Her skin flushed.

Ian came back and pressed a glass of water into her hands. She took a sip and tried not to choke.

He then held out a wet cloth and picked up her hand.

"What ... is this for?"

"I don't know. My mother always brought me a cold wash cloth when I wasn't well."

"Thanks."

She rested back against the pillows and spun it around and laid it across her forehead. Yeah, it did feel refreshing. Now if she could just cool the rest of herself down.

Ian moved to the foot of the bed and sat back on his pallet. She heard him shift out of his jeans, one leg at a time.

She inwardly groaned. He was killing her here.

"Nicole?"

She cleared her throat. "Y-yes?"

"If you need me for anything, wake me up, okay?"

"Okay," she whispered hoarsely and pulled the washcloth down over her face.

Ian lay on the floor staring at shadows streaked across the ceiling. He was in over his head and way past the gray areas here. You never became involved with someone you were protecting. It clouds your judgment and puts you both at risk. The results could be deadly.

He knew the rules.

He felt too much alive, that was the problem. When he'd awakened and heard Nicole's soft little throaty noises, his body came to life. After she started moaning, he couldn't even get his jeans fastened over his erection.

He wiped a hand over his face. They needed to find answers and get out of this situation fast. He was losing it.

How he longed for a brisk run or swim to work off his present state. Neither was an option at the moment.

Tomorrow was another day. First on the agenda was to locate Brian Helms and have him run tests on the photos. Roark was in on this. Ian could feel it. That would mean Roark had been on the take for at least five years, maybe more. There was no telling what else would be unearthed when they began digging into the past.

Or who else was involved.

Roark couldn't be a one man show. He wondered how many other agents were involved. He and Dan may have only uncovered the tip of the iceberg. He couldn't place the other two men in the photo but he was determined to find out who they were.

Ian rolled up on one side and repositioned himself more comfortably. It burned him that he'd laid a trap for Roark only to get caught in his own snare. He still didn't understand how Roark figured out that he was on to him. *What went wrong?*

He strained to hear Nicole's breathing. Her breaths were becoming rhythmic. She was asleep.

Sounds of people walking in the corridor mingled with laughter distracted him. He rolled back over and stared into the darkness. Things outside the door quieted down as the voices faded. He shifted his legs and grazed Dickens. He wished he could rest his mind. There was still the matter of the trump card. Nicole. Roark just thought he had killed the girl for the money. And now there was the matter of the pictures of Borland. Roark would lie down tonight with a false sense of security, while Ian, on the other hand, had a clear conscience for a soft pillow.

A slight smile tugged at the corners of his mouth as his eyes drifted closed.

Nicole's brain registered the sound of a drawer being eased open. She barely peeked through her eyelashes in time to see Ian pull his wallet out and tuck it in the back pocket of his khaki shorts. She averted her eyes when he turned.

"Good morning," Ian said, coming to stand at the foot of the bed.

"Morning." She raised up on an elbow and stretched her legs.

"I thought I'd take Dickens out and bring back coffee. We have the pot in our room but they didn't supply any coffee."

"Bless you."

He paused and scrutinized her a moment longer. She glanced away. She wondered how bad her bed head looked.

"Are you doing okay?"

She shrugged and nodded. *Please don't let me blush.*

He went through to the bathroom. Her elbow collapsed and she landed back on the bed to stare at the ceiling. What a night. That dream had seemed so real. Maybe they could get the answers they needed today and then this would all be over.

A few minutes passed and Ian came out of the bathroom, his fake facial hair in place. He whistled and Dickens stood up and headed for the door. "I need you to pull the chain across the door after I leave. Don't answer it for anyone."

He walked over to the door and took Dickens' leash off the handle where it had been draped the night before. Escorting the dog out, he closed the door quietly behind them.

Alone at last. She tossed back the sheet and stood up to stretch. A soft tap at the door broke into her thoughts. She tiptoed over to the door to peek through the peephole. All she could see was an eye staring back at her. Glaring was more like it.

"I don't hear the chain moving across the door yet," Ian called out.

"Aye, aye, sir." She grabbed the chain guard and trailed it along the groove. If only she could erase the memory of that dream as easily.

She chose her clothes for the day and took them through to the bathroom. She turned the shower on to allow time for the water to get hot and locked the door. Ian was good looking. There was no denying it. They were in a dangerous situation. Sometimes that gave people a rush of adrenaline and she was just reacting.

Stepping into the shower, she let the warm water sluice over her body. She reached for the shampoo and laughed to herself. She thought of the old commercial where the woman was going to wash that man right out of her hair. A good lather was what she needed about now.

This connection of Ian's they were going to see would hopefully be able to prove the picture hadn't been tampered with. They could blow it up and get detailed evidence to prove the agent was still alive.

And she could go home. End of story. She needed to get out before she completely lost her heart. After her last relationship had ended badly, she didn't want to be that vulnerable ever again.

She reached for the bar of soap and lathered up. Ian had said today would be a new day. In it they would find the answers they needed. She smiled and let the water wash the suds off of her.

The smile faded from her face as she held up the soap she'd been using. She swallowed. The same soap that had ran all over Ian's body, too. She turned the knob to cold.

Nicole had just gotten dressed when there was a tap at the door. She peered through the peephole to confirm that Ian was the cause.

"What's the pass word?"

She saw him raise a Styrofoam cup of coffee.

"That's it!" She pushed the chain to the side and swung the door open. "My hero."

Fifteen minutes later they took off in the Mustang, leaving Dickens behind in the room. Just having missed morning rush hour, they made their way down the highway in good time. The morning sun blazed along their chosen path.

"We're headed to see a man about a picture," Ian told her as he switched lanes to make his exit.

"How do you know you can trust him?"

Chapter 11

"Brian has always maintained he owes me," Ian told her. "He keeps score. I don't. But, I could use him about now."

"Just like that, you think he'll be loyal?"

"About three years back I tracked down the man who killed his brother and hauled him in."

"Oh." Nicole didn't know what else to say. She couldn't imagine Ian's life and the things he had to have seen and done. She shuddered. Drug busts, shootouts, and killing must be all in a day's work for him.

"Okay?"

She turned to look at him. It was then she realized he'd been talking and she hadn't heard a thing he said. "What?"

"I was telling you not to use my cell phone. They can trace it. I've taken the battery out and it's in the glove box for now."

"Okay."

"We're almost to Brian's photo lab. He's a little rough around the edges," Ian warned her as he signaled to pass a Ford truck driving too slow in front of them. "He quit the HRT to stay home with his small daughter after his wife died."

"How sad."

"It was a hard time for a lot of people. Brian's a good man though."

"What's the HRT?"

"Hostage Rescue Team. They're paramilitary-tactical for FBI counter-terrorism."

"Wow." She was sure she didn't want to know any more than that.

They turned off Market Street into the downtown area of Arcola and slowed to take in the shop names.

It was a red brick store with a white awning set back into an indention between a pet store and little Italian café. Passing the Italian café was hard given the wonderful aroma permeating the air. Ian opened the door to Brian's place and a bell jingled as they entered the store. Nicole spotted a big, burly, middle-aged man standing behind the counter. A jagged scar ran along his left jaw line and ended where tattoos picked up and trailed down his neck. *This must be Brian.*

She was glad he was on their side.

"Good morning. You folks need your picture taken?"

"No," Ian replied, then set the manila folder on the counter and tapped it with his index finger. "I need a little of your backroom expertise in checking to see if a picture is authentic or not."

The man's eyes surveyed Ian first and then ran over Nicole. He seemed to be assessing both of them and the situation very carefully.

"I don't know who you've been talking to, mister, but I don't offer any service of that nature and—"

"Ian Mulherin."

The man stopped in mid-sentence, his eyes narrowing as he scrutinized Ian closer. He put his hand on the folder. "Good enough. Let's take a look here and see what we have."

"How's Cindy Lou Who?"

The man's head jerked up. He grabbed hold of the corner of the counter and stormed around it to stand in front of them. He glared at Ian for a moment. Recognition dawned over his face.

A smile spread and transformed his looks. "I'll be damned. Mulherin, how in the hell are you?"

The two men grabbed each other by the shoulders and exchanged slaps and smiles.

"You look the same, Brian."

"You've aged twenty years, man."

Ian shrugged. "It's a piece," he said, stroking his fake beard.

"You dressing up like your father these days, are you?"

Ian chuckled, but she noticed the look on his face at the reference to looking like his dad. It hadn't set well.

"Cindy's great, Ian. You wouldn't believe how she's grown."

To prove it the big, burly man whipped out his wallet and flashed several pictures of a cute little toothless blonde in pigtails.

"She's a doll, Brian."

Brian's face stilled. "Thank you. She's looking more and more like her mother every day."

"Well, that's a good thing. If she looked like you ... well ...." He laughed and slapped Brian on the shoulder.

"You know, she's almost five and already on a collision course for puberty. Training to be HRT didn't prepare me for this, man." He replaced his wallet in his back pocket and cleared his throat. "I was sorry to hear about Dan."

If she hadn't been looking right at Ian she would have missed the flash of pain that streaked across his face. Her heart turned over for him.

"Thanks." Ian nodded, and looked away.

"What brings you here?"

"I'm a dog on the run."

Brian's face sobered, he let his hand drop from the counter as he straightened. "What do you need?"

"Answers. First, I'd like to introduce you to someone I'm supposed to have killed a couple of nights ago." Ian turned to her. "This is Nicole. Nicole, Brian."

"And might I say, you make a fine looking corpse," Brian said, taking her hand in his and winking.

She was surprised to find that it wasn't a crushing grip. "Hello. Thank you."

"Let's take a look at what you've brought," Brian said, turning back to pick the folder up. He bent the tab on the folder and slid the pictures out.

Ian leaned over to point at the picture of the men. "This one. I need this blown up to where I can see their nose hairs. Then I need tests run to prove the pictures' authenticity."

"I'll get right on it. There are several tests I can run on this, Ian."

"I need it iron clad, Brian. I know who one of them is, but not the other two. I'm hoping a blow up of the picture could help with that."

The two men went on talking specifics and she decided to wander the shop. Brides' portraits decorated the south wall along with family photos. He was artistic. On the opposing wall were mostly pictures of cherubic-looking children. She thought of her snapshot at home on her fridge of Emily. She had many pictures of her niece that she treasured.

Maybe one day she would have her own child to take for portraits. A little dark haired boy with the same grin as—

She froze.

What was I thinking?

She turned to look at Ian's profile and closed her mouth. Heat spread from her core until her skin tingled. Vivid images of her dream danced across her mind. She put her fingers over her lips.

"Did you say something, Nicole?"

Her eyes flew open and she stiffened. She didn't even turn to look at Ian when she answered. "Um … no, I was just admiring the pictures. They're really good."

"Thank you, Nicole. I've owned the business for five years now and love doing what I do."

"It certainly shows," she said, turning to smile weakly at Brian, all the while she was careful not to meet Ian's eyes.

"Well, thank you for your help on this, Brian."

"Not a problem. I've got your hotel number. I'll be in touch, say, in a couple of days."

"The sooner the better," Ian told him.

"Ian, you watch your ass," Brian called to him as they walked out. "Hers too."

Chapter 12

"Brian was certainly an interesting character," Nicole said as she shut the car door. She immediately reached for her water bottle in the drink holder. They hadn't left any windows cracked and it was steamy inside the car. The day was turning into a scorcher.

"Brian's a good man. Of course, I've heard Trey say 'he was a killer HRT-man,'" Ian said.

Nicole winced at the bad pun but then chuckled despite her initial disapproval. "If there is anyone who could speak on character it would be Trey."

They laughed together on that one as Ian steered them back onto the highway.

Nicole shook her head, her thoughts slipping away with the passing of the billboards that littered the highway out her window. There was no way she could fathom killing another person. Just as there was no way she could begin to understand Ian's life. Wanting to be in the thick of all that danger. Thriving on it. She'd had enough in the last forty-eight hours to last her the rest of her life.

"What are we going to do while Brian tests the pictures?"

"I'd like to find a payphone and make some calls," Ian replied. "Then I suggest we run by the hotel and let Dickens out and afterwards we can scout a place for lunch."

"A payphone?"

"Yeah, it's my safest bet but they are a rarity. It's a pain not to be able to use my cell. I need to get some information from some other contacts."

They drove around for a good fifteen minutes before spotting a payphone on the side of an older gas station. Ian inserted the nozzle into his gas tank, climbed back in, and reached across her to unlock his glove box. He retrieved a small book and pushed the door shut.

"Ah, the little black book," Nicole said, eyeing the spiral bound note-book.

Ian looked at her sideways and shrugged. The pump clicked off and he swung the door open to take care of things.

Nicole's eyes fell to the book resting on the console. Her fingers curled in her lap.

"I'll go in and pay. You want anything?"

She jumped. Ian had poked his head in the window. "Um … no. Thanks anyway."

Nicole watched as Ian walked into the convenience store to pay, her eyes returned to the book. She knew she shouldn't look. Pulling down the visor, she ran her fingers through her hair in the vanity mirror, and then snapped it back in place. Ian was standing in the back of a lengthy line waiting to pay. Curiosity got the better of her. It wouldn't hurt anything to just take a peek. She plucked up the book and flipped it open in her lap.

"Probably a fair share of Barbie names," she muttered to herself.

Thumbing to the first page, she scanned the names listed. It was just a bunch of jibberish with phone numbers beside it. She turned the page and ran her French-tipped nail down the columns and across, finding more strange names. It was the same way with the next three pages.

"Didn't you know that curiosity killed the cat?" Ian inquired of her as he slid into the driver's seat and slammed the door.

Startled, she jumped. "This probably could get me killed if I knew what I was reading."

Ian rolled his eyes at her as he drove them over to the payphone.

"With friends like these, you don't need enemies," she said, leafing through the rest of the pages before handing it back to him. "Ice pick. Jumpdog. Ratterman. One-eyed."

Ian looked sideways at her and smiled. "It's all in code. Things I associate these people with, but nothing to say who they really are."

"Hmm."

"It wouldn't be good for me to write Brian Helms, ex-HRT, now would it?"

"Which is his code name?"

"Jackknife."

"I don't wanna know." She held up a hand and slumped down in her seat to prove her point.

"Class dismissed, teacher." He gave that throaty chuckle that did things to her. Things she didn't want to think about. It was too reminiscent of her dream. She sat back up and snapped her seat belt back against her.

"Who was Pretty Boy?" she asked, thinking that was a safer subject.

"Oh, you've already met him," Ian informed her. "Trey, of course. That number is his home phone. Play Boy is his cell number."

Nicole grinned big on that one. So appropriate. "Go and make your calls to your cronies."

Nicole watched him fish change out of his pocket and place his first call. It didn't put her at ease that she was in danger from the man that was her protector. He was too sexy for his own good, let alone hers. When this was all over, if they lived to see the end, she would go back to her safe life and he would go back to whatever danger lie ahead.

She drew in her bottom lip and wished she didn't feel so pulled apart by the thought.

He stuck his head back in the car. "You got any change?"

Changed. That's what she was since meeting him.

After retrieving coins from the bottom of her purse, she handed them over to him. "An investment in my future, I hope."

He took the money and closed her hand. "You can count on it."

"I've already gotten a lot more than I banked on."

"Ah, I aim to please." He winked at her and was gone.

Let that be a lesson to you. He'll flirt with you and hit the road. She'd already done that with her previous boyfriend and was wiser this time around. Needing a distraction, she flipped on the radio and stared out over the hood.

She wasn't sure how long she'd waited while he made one call after another but she had tidied her purse and gone through her wallet. She stepped out of the car to throw her trash in a nearby can and got back in when she saw him heading toward the car.

"What did you find out?" she asked as he took his place behind the wheel.

"I've got several contacts that owe me, working to see what other agents were on the case with Borland," Ian told her while he fastened his seat belt into place. "I want info on who else might've been involved and could be on the take."

"I hope these ice packs and knife men can track down the answers you need."

"That would be ice *pick*," Ian said. "And believe me, these guys are good."

"They live up to their names, huh?"

"You got it, babe."

They cruised ahead to the hotel and took Dickens for a long walk. The edge was backing off the late afternoon heat. Clouds were rolling in and a slight breeze worked its way across their path. A comfortable silence fell between them and they strolled along just enjoying the fresh air.

"So, you wanted to be a teacher when you grew up?"

Nicole shook her head as she smoothed her errant hair back up and redid her ponytail. "No. I wanted to be a boy."

Ian stopped and trailed his eyes down her body slowly and then let his eyes wander back to her face. "Now that would've been a real waste."

She flushed and curled the last band around her hair. *I must look terrible.* "Well, I thought my dad would take me on his missionary trips if I'd been a boy instead of a girl."

"Your father was a missionary the whole time you were growing up?"

"No, he went to Africa when I was fourteen. His trips grew longer and longer," she explained, walking beside him. Dickens strained against his leash as a cat pranced around a trash can behind the hotel. "After my sister and I left home he took Mom with him."

"You missed him?"

"Terribly, although I understood. He's always been good at what he does. And he's helped so many. We've always been very close."

"Must be nice. I can't relate."

Nicole looked sideways at Ian and chewed on her bottom lip. "You and your dad weren't close?"

"It's all right. My father and I aren't cut from the same cloth."

"What's he like?" she asked. She thought she might try a different angle.

"Hard. Unbending. An Army man in special intelligence. He was away a lot, too."

"That had to be hard with him gone." She stopped walking and turned to face him.

He paused in his step and glanced at her and shrugged. "It's okay. I got used to it."

By the set of his jaw, she realized he wanted the subject closed. They finished their walk in silence. Crickets chirped while frogs chimed in and sang their songs of summer. Dickens seemed content to sniff the ground.

It was killing her to know more about his growing up. "So, tell me about your mom. Siblings?"

"I'm an only child." he tugged on Dickens' leash. "I lost my mother to breast cancer two years ago."

Nicole's heart went out to him, hearing the pain in his voice. "Oh, Ian, how terrible. I'm so sorry."

"I got through it." He lifted his shoulders and let them fall. "And I've been left with some wonderful memories. She was a terrific mother. We should start back now."

They headed across the parking lot to the side door of the hotel. The dusk to dawn lights popped on as they reached their entrance. Ian led their way back to their room.

"You go ahead and shower first, Nicole. I'm going to make some notes," Ian offered.

Later she lay in bed with her back to the light, praying she wouldn't dream of him again tonight. *Ian must still be working something out in his mind.* She was very aware of him sitting there with his freshly showered hair, shirt off, jotting notes on his notepad. Every once in a while his chair would creak. He was so engrossed in what he was doing, he'd probably forgotten she was even in the room.

"Are you having trouble sleeping?" His voice sounded from across the room.

"What?"

"You're twitchy."

"Excuse me?" She rolled over on her back and glared at him.

"The lamp being on probably isn't helping you. Sorry." He reached up, snapped the light off, and pushed his chair away from the desk.

She shrugged and rolled up on her side. He shuffled his way through the room. She heard the bathroom light click on and the light narrowed on the wall. Ian must be pulling the door up to allow just enough light to come through to see.

"Are you afraid to go to sleep after the dream you had last night?"

If you only knew. "I guess I am a bit restless."

"Do you need me to tell you a bedtime story?" he offered.

"Oh, that would send me right off the edge." She laughed. "I'm sure with all the cops and robbers firing at one another I wouldn't sleep a wink for weeks."

She heard him padding toward her, he'd kicked off his shoes, and then the bed sagged with his weight.

Her breath caught in her throat.

"There once was a beautiful princess named Nicolette."

She couldn't help it, she smiled.

"She was as sweet as she was beautiful and because of that, she had many, many admirers."

Nicole didn't realize she'd been holding her breath while she waited on his next words. "And? And?"

"You don't think I can do this, do you?"

She didn't even try to hide her laughter this time. "Nope. You're already beginning to flounder and you just started."

"Huh, says you. Now be still. A suitor came to town riding on a sleek black horse and—"

"White."

"What?"

"White. The horses are always white in these kinda stories."

"Well, in this one the horse is black. I like to shake things up a bit."

She chuckled. "So I've noticed."

"Be quiet. I'm telling the story here."

She curled her lips inward and pressed them together. Her eyes focused on his shadow moving along the wall. The strength of his profile was comforting to her.

"So, this suitor comes to town on a black horse, armed and dangerous."

"Oh, Ian."

"Be quiet."

She turned her face into her pillow to stifle the laughter.

"His name was Sir Bad."

Her toes curled as she fought the bubbling pressure in her throat. He really was just trying to make her feel better she knew.

"He asked Princess Nicolette for her lovely hand in marriage. She batted her beautiful eyes at him but snubbed him. So, he grabbed her and threw her over his shoulder and rode off."

"Oh, no." She faked a gasp in mock seriousness and covered her mouth with her hand.

"Oh, yes. And all the king's horses and all the king's men searched across the land for her. No trace of her could be found. A king's ransom went out to anyone who would be brave enough to rescue and bring back the beautiful princess."

She rolled over to face him. "Now, in rides Mr. Good on a white horse, right?"

"No." He tapped her nose with his index finger.

She knew she shouldn't ask, but couldn't help herself. "Who then?"

"Sir Noble on his gray steed."

"Ah, but of course."

"He rescued the lovely princess from the snares of Sir Bad and brought her before her father. Instead of the ransom money, Sir Noble asked for the dearly beloved princess' hand in marriage."

"But what if she really wanted Sir Bad?" The words rushed out of her mouth before she could stop them.

The air conditioner kicked on in the room. Somewhere an elevator *dinged* and distant voices were heard from people milling about the halls.

"She would soon realize she was better off with Sir Noble and would live happily ever after. The end."

She laughed and faked a yawn and patted her mouth.

His weight shifted off the bed as he stood up. He moved across the room and she watched his frame lower to the floor. He went to the task of sorting out his make-shift bed and lying down.

"Good night, Nicolette."

"Good night, Sir Bad."

Ian never said anything more. She heard him change positions on his pallet and then all was silent. Nicole lay there for a long time staring at the ceiling. If she wasn't awake before she sure was now.

Ian was the first to stir the next morning. He stretched and sat up. The digital clock showed it was just a little past seven. It would appear the princess had finally conked out and was still collecting her beauty sleep. And what a beauty she was. Her long tanned legs were uncovered with the sheet tangled around her midriff. His fingers tightened on the sheet. An urge to run those fingers along her silky limbs nagged at him. He ran his hands through his hair instead. He needed to get answers today and get her back to her life fast before she became a fixture in his. She was too good for him. He'd screw up the relationship just like he had with everyone else in his life. She belonged to someone noble all right and it sure as hell wasn't him.

The very thought of her with someone else clawed at him. He pulled his jeans out of the drawer, grabbed a shirt and headed to the bathroom. A nice brisk shower would clear his head, followed by a strong cup of coffee.

When he emerged from the bathroom a good twenty minutes later, he found Nicole dressed in shorts and a tank top. She started to give a slight wave but covered a yawn instead.

"Morning." He nodded, trying to keep it all conversational.

"Mm."

She wasn't a bad morning person but he knew what she needed. "Coffee?"

"Please."

"Gotcha." He laughed as he reached for the coffee pot and filter. The maid had left them coffee this time when she had picked up the room. "After we've split the pot, we'll head over to see Brian. Fasten your seat belt. Things are bound to get interesting."

Chapter 13

Ian drove them back to the same payphone they'd used the day before. He put a call through to each of his contacts to find out if they had any leads yet for him. He scribbled down the new information and headed to the car.

"Have you seen a library sign anywhere around here?" he asked.

"I think I saw one over by that car wash we commented on, why?" Nicole replied, scanning the billboard signs along the row of businesses.

"I want to look at some back issues of certain newspapers," he explained. "One of my contacts gave me a list of agent names that were on the case with Borland. I'd like to research them. If we're lucky it might give us a lead to who the other two men are."

He turned right at the stoplight and traversed back down toward where they had seen the carwash. The morning sun beat through the windshield. He reached for his sunglasses to fight the glare. The day was going to be another scorcher. Watching for the blue library sign, he turned another corner.

"What are we hoping to find at the library?" Nicole asked him, unlatching her seat belt and leaning over to retrieve her purse.

"Articles in the news around the time of Borland's death. I'm trying to find out who the witnesses were," Ian said, "and what else was going on in the world at that same time."

They entered the north door and stepped into a lobby where a white haired woman at the information desk greeted them. She directed them to where the computers were and helped them get set up.

He typed the name of the Chicago paper they needed to research. For the next hour they poured over the archives of the newspaper looking for any kind of lead.

"Bingo," Ian announced as he jotted down the information in his legal pad. "See this man here?"

Nicole leaned over from her computer to look at his screen. "He's the same man in the photo, isn't he?"

"Yes, meet dead man number two. Kevin Adams."

Ian settled back in his chair and stared over the top of the computer while he tapped the point of his pen on the pad. This would complicate things for them even more.

"Ian, it says here this Adams is with the Mafia."

"Yeah, he's one of Alberto's men."

"So, now we have the Mafia after us, too?"

Ian looked at her worried eyes and wanted to lie. The facts were staring them both in the face. "We're going to get to the bottom this."

"Yeah, the bottom of a lake with cement blocks tied to our ankles." She shuddered.

He put a reassuring hand on her shoulder. She had panic written across her face. He wished he could shield her from all of this. From his world. "Nicole, we need to focus here. We're going to figure this out and turn it over to the proper authorities."

Her hand covered his. "Okay. Okay, I'm trying to think positively."

"That's my girl," he said, and gave her shoulder a squeeze.

"That just leaves us with man number three," Nicole said. "Who do you suppose he is?"

He looked over at her thoughtfully and shrugged his shoulders. Nothing about the mystery man stood out to him. "Perhaps he was a bodyguard. I don't know, but I plan on finding out."

They searched through the archives for another hour hoping to find more leads. Other people came and went around them unnoticed. Not finding anything new, Ian stood up and stretched. "You hungry?"

"Starved."

Ian checked his watch. He couldn't believe it was almost noon. He must've been engrossed in the research because his stomach hadn't even gone off. "How did it get to be so late in the morning?"

"We were too busy digging up dead men?" she replied dryly as she stood up and pushed her chair in.

"Don't smart mouth me," he scolded her as he flipped his legal pad closed and grabbed his pens up. "With it being this late, we should run back by the hotel and walk Dickens and then grab a bite."

"Sounds good to me," Nicole said, hooking her purse onto her shoulder and pushing Ian's chair into the desk.

They took a side door out that was closer to the parking lot. The heat enveloped them, erasing any reprieve they'd gotten from the coolness inside the library. He started the car and cranked the air on full blast.

While weaving through traffic they went over the information they'd learned again. He made a mental note of a few more calls to make and drove back to the hotel.

The moment they unlocked their hotel door, Dickens trotted over to them with his leash in his mouth and laid it at their feet.

"You ready to go out, boy?" Ian laughed and fastened the leash to the dog's collar. "Come on."

"Why don't we just pick something up and find a park somewhere to eat while he runs?" Nicole suggested.

Ian looked up from his crouched position to where Nicole stood. She had her brows knitted together like she did when she was all serious. It was cute. Surprised at the thought, he cleared his throat. "That's a good idea, and better than eating in the Mustang, we need to keep a low profile."

They drove into the flow of noon traffic that dumped them into the cluttered line up of food chains.

"They seem to have everything. See anything that sounds good to you?" Ian asked while pulling behind a silver Honda Accord in the slower lane. This offered them a chance to take it at an easier pace and scan the signs. His stomach growled.

"Hm. Do you like Chinese?" she asked.

"Love it."

She pointed to a row of stores on the left with the sign overhead, "Wok and Roll," and laughed.

"My kinda place," he said, laughing as well while flipping his turn signal on.

They pulled over in front of the restaurant, but had to go around to the side to find a place to park.

"It's a sign they do a good business." Ian killed the motor.

Opening the door of the Chinese restaurant for Nicole, he caught the smell of something tangy that made him crave sweet and sour chicken.

The place was a good size, but packed. An array of people dressed from shorts to business suits on lunch break took up every table.

"Good thing we'd decided to take our food somewhere else," Nicole turned and said to him.

"Yeah."

They got in line behind a mother and her little girl who couldn't seem to make up her mind what to order.

"You know what you want?" he asked her.

"Yeah, but you take your time," Nicole said, and then wandered across the room to inspect the ten-gallon tank of salt-water fish.

When it was his turn at the counter, the young Asian woman greeted him with a smile. "What may I order from our kitchen for you?"

"I'd like the sweet and sour chicken."

"And for the lady?" the woman inquired.

"I'll make it easy, I'll have the same," Nicole replied, coming to stand beside him. "Make it two to go please."

The woman in the black kimono with the red and yellow dragon embroidered on it smiled sweetly and nodded again. "I have easy job. Be ready for you in a moment."

She disappeared into the kitchen with the order slip.

"It all looks good," Ian said, glancing over some of the dishes on the other tables.

"After smelling cabbage cooking for the egg rolls, I'm really getting hungry," Nicole said.

A tall Asian man entered from a side door carrying a clipboard. He spotted them, smiled, and nodded. "I help you?"

Ian rested his hands on the counter and nodded back. "We've already placed our order. Thanks. Maybe you could tell us where we might find a park nearby, though?"

"There was a park down the road. It shut down when they open new water park. They no have ground equipment any more. They have some of their picnic tables left."

"Perfect. We've got a dog to let run."

"Oh. Good park for that. Yeah. A mile down the road you will see a red sign for Mara resort. Turn left there. Follow and see park on left."

"Thank you," Ian said.

The lady came back with their food boxed up and in a sack. She pointed to the shelves on the left where diners collected their own paper plates and sauces. While Ian and Nicole chose their utensils and condiments, they failed to notice the man behind them slip out of line and hurry out the front door.

Chapter 14

"There. Anderson Park," Nicole announced, pointing out the weathered sign partially hidden by bushes of yellow daylilies.

Ian flipped the signal for their last turn to take them into the park. Massive oak trees stretched across the road leading to the picnic tables. The two remaining tables were both shaded from the sweltering sun. Sparse weeds poked up from what once was a baseball field. Dickens bounded out of the car to seek the nearest tree. Ian followed Nicole to a nearby table trying not to be mesmerized by the way her hips swayed.

Nicole turned to say something to Ian and realized he was watching her with an odd look on his face. She shifted uncomfortably and gestured towards the table. "This one okay?"

"Fine."

"The food smells heavenly. I'm starved." Nicole set out the paper plates and pulled the food cartons out of the paper sack. She had to slap a hand down on her plate to catch it as a breeze whipped past them.

"Let's Wok and Roll," Ian said with a wink as he swung his long legs over the bench and opened a carton.

Nicole shook her head and laughed as she folded back the flaps to her container. She forked the steamed rice out, spread the chicken evenly over it, and topped it with the sauce. Nicole savored the first sweet and tangy bite. "Mmm."

"It's good, isn't it?"

"Mmmmm." She repeated and opened her eyes to look at him. He was eating with chopsticks. "How do you do that?"

"Do what?"

"Eat with those. I'm not coordinated enough."

"It's not hard."

"Says you."

"I do say," Ian confirmed. "Here. Let me show you."

He stood up, came around to her side of the table, and straddled the bench facing her.

"Give me your fingers." He took her hand and wrapped her fingers around one stick.

"Okay." *He's too close. So close I can smell his spicy cologne.*

"Now, you take your other stick and put it between your fingers like so."

His hands were warm. His long tanned fingers sent shockwaves through her. Heat seeped from them, snaked through her hands, and spiraled up throughout her entire body. She knew she wasn't quite hearing what he was saying, but for the life of her she couldn't make herself concentrate on his words.

"Got it?"

Nicole looked up at him, startled. "I … think so."

He sat watching her paltry attempts to pick up her food and cheered her on. She kept dropping the chicken half way to her mouth.

"I'll starve to death at this rate. Like it would hurt me to miss a meal."

"Why do women do that?"

"Do what?" she said glancing at him and moving her fingers back into the contorted position around the chopsticks.

"Put themselves down if they have curves."

"I can't speak for all women everywhere, but I know when I've passed curves and headed to slopes. It's time to scale back."

"You gals don't get it that men like to take slopes and curves. It all gets us to the same place. We just wanna enjoy the drive."

She dropped her chicken in her lap.

"I'm hopeless." She laughed uncomfortably and cleared her throat. *Not to mention nervous. How on earth did we get on this topic anyway?*

Dickens' ferocious barking interrupted the moment.

How I love that dog. She was grateful for the reprieve. After brushing rice off her lap, she took a deep breath. When Ian had gotten up to check on his dog, it created a much-needed distance between them. She leaned over and waved a fly away from Ian's plate.

This whole thing was insane. She stabbed a piece of chicken with one of the chopsticks and ate it. There was no way she could let herself give in to this growing attraction she felt towards him. *And what was that curvy slopes comment of his? Could he be feeling something, too?*

She looked over to where Ian was talking to the dog. The pull of magnetism she felt for him was unsettling. She didn't do casual affairs, no matter how good the man filled out his jeans.

Ian turned and sauntered toward her and she concentrated on her next bite.

"Dickens is pretty proud of himself for treeing a squirrel," he reported, sitting across from her and picking up his chopsticks.

She glanced over to where Dickens lay in watch and smiled. "I take it you like to read the classics?"

"Me? No, sweetheart, I only read criminal reports and gun magazines."

"Oh, I just thought with Dickens' name you enjoyed reading."

"Don't make me into something I'm not."

"Where did you come up with his name then?"

An awkward silence fell between them.

After several minutes, Ian spoke again. "As I explained last night, my father and I have never been close. After my mother died of breast cancer, well, let's just say, we've not gotten any closer."

"Oh, Ian, I'm so sorry."

She'd placed her hand on his arm without thinking.

"Yeah, well, I didn't go around him much after that. A little over a year ago, when Dickens was just a pup, I took him along to my father's house. I guess he got a good laugh."

"What do you mean?"

"Well, my father hunts with his coon dogs. He said he didn't see any sense in having a fancy dog like that." Ian glanced at her and then picked at his food with his chopsticks. "He took one look at him and said 'That's a damn dickens of a dog. What you need, boy, is a good hunting dog.'"

"Boy?"

"Yeah, in the same condescending tone he's always used."

"I'm sorry you and your dad aren't closer."

"It doesn't really matter." Ian shrugged his shoulders and crushed his food container.

"Were you ever close?"

"No. He was stationed overseas my last couple of years in grade school. When he came back after that I was turning into a teenager."

"Those teenage years are hard ones."

"Tell me about it." Ian chuckled "Anyway, he's a fourth-generation decorated Army man. A colonel. He couldn't understand why I didn't want to go off and save the world."

"Just a part of it."

She realized she shouldn't have said it after the words were out. Too late. The muscles along his jaw line bunched as he turned those hard blue eyes on her.

"I didn't see anything in your file about being a psychologist," he gritted out. He crushed his paper plate, stuck it in the sack, stood to his feet, and began clearing away the other empty cartons.

"Sorry. It's just that … sometimes someone on the outside can see things a little clearer, you know, by not being in the middle of all the conflict."

"Am I going to get the bill for this?"

"Ian," she said, stilling a hand on his, "your father lost her, too."

His eyes flickered something she couldn't quite decipher before his face became guarded and he turned his attention to the dog. "Come on, Dickens. Get over here."

He polished off the last of his tea and tossed the cup into the trash.

Nicole decided her tongue had gotten her into enough trouble and added her sack to the trash. A tug at her heart made her wonder at the hurt that must run through him. The loss of his mother. His partner. At odds with his father. It made her count her blessings for two wonderful parents devoted to one another, a sister and her family that she adored even more.

"I'm eager to see what Brian comes up with," she said following him to the car.

"I probably should make some more calls with the information we dug up at the library," Ian said opening the passenger car door to let Dickens in the back. He then stepped aside for her to climb in. He was too close again. Flustered, she dropped her sunglasses.

She started to bend down to pick them up at the same time he leaned over to scoop them off the ground.

A loud pop echoed through the air.

Ian grabbed her arm and jerked her to the ground. His hard body covered hers, pinning her underneath him.

"What's happening?" she whispered as the breath rushed out of her.

"Stay down," he rasped in her ear.

"What was that noise?"

Chapter 15

Ian didn't answer. He shifted his weight. He pulled a gun out from somewhere behind his back.

Realization coiled up her spine. *That pop noise was a gunshot. Someone's found us.* She tried to swallow but the lump wedged in her throat. "What are we going to do?"

"I'm going to roll off of you and open the car door," Ian explained in her ear. "You're going to crawl in onto the floorboard and lock the door. Got it?"

"Okay. Okay." She was trying to fight down the panic threatening to rise up in her throat.

"Ready?"

"Where will you be?" she asked.

"I'm headed off to play FBI."

"Please be careful," she whispered.

"And if I don't come back, drive off." He pressed the keys into her hand. "Now."

The door swung open and she scrambled onto the floorboard. The door slammed behind her. Her heart lodged in her throat. She reached one hand up and locked the door. Her breath came in quick pants as she tried to regain her wits.

Dickens sniffed her face and licked her cheek. He jumped back up in the seat and started barking. She wondered if she should let him out or not to help Ian.

She strained to hear something, anything. The temptation to rise up and sneak a peek ate at her. She shivered, hugged her knees, and wondered what to do next. *Dear God, please let him be okay.*

Moments passed that stretched on into what seemed like an eternity in her mind. Fear gave way to worry. The longer she sat hunched in that cramped position the more worried she became. She couldn't bear the thought of anything happening to Ian. He was out there defending her while she was curled in the fetal position. She had to do something. Worry turned into anger. Someone had tried to kill them. Ian was out there alone. Her fingers curled tightly around the keys until they dug into the palm of her hand. Adrenaline kicked in and she scrambled up into the driver's seat and crammed the key in the ignition. The Mustang roared to life. Dickens jumped from the back to the passenger seat.

"Let's roll, Dickens!"

Looking all around and checking her mirrors for signs of Ian, she peeled out and headed in the direction he had run. She drove across the grass scanning the row of pines ahead for any signs of movement.

Nothing.

She gunned the car forward. Her eyes intent on the trees beyond the park's edge for any movement. She swallowed and stared straight ahead, focused on the dense brush, and pushed her foot down on the accelerator. Her heart beat erratic as she watched for Ian. Dickens jumped into the back seat and barked.

"What? What do you see, boy?"

Dickens barked again and jumped around the back seat. Everything had happened so quickly. She saw Ian emerge from the bushes and jerked to a stop by the trees.

The passenger door flung open and Ian jumped in. "I told you to stay put, dammit."

"Well, tough," Nicole said. "Did you get a look at who shot at us?"

"He ran to his car and headed that way." Ian hooked a thumb to the right to indicate the direction. Nicole cranked the steering wheel right and floored it. Ian barely got the door closed before his body leaned towards her with the whipping of the car.

"Are you sure you're up to doing this, Nicole?" Ian asked as he frantically tried to stab his seat belt into the buckle.

"I'm doing it, aren't I?"

Ian grabbed hold of the dash to steady himself as he leaned into the next curve. Nicole caught her first glimpse of the black SUV. It was kicking chat and dust up ahead. One driver. A man. She increased pressure on the gas pedal. "What do I do now?"

"Over there." Ian motioned as the SUV headed around a grove of trees and made for the main road.

Nicole followed in hot pursuit. Ian rolled his window down and pointed his gun out. She realized she'd have to get a lot closer for Ian to make contact. She raced to lessen the gap between them and the SUV. Beads of perspiration popped out on her forehead. Her knuckles were white in their death grip to control the wheel. The car bumped along the grass until it, too, hit the main road. Even though they were now on smooth pavement, she couldn't will her hands to relax. Worried, she took her eyes off her target long enough to do a frantic glance to make sure there wasn't anyone around to get hurt.

The SUV's tires squealed around the next corner. Nicole's tires made much the same sound as she leaned one way and then was tossed the other trying to keep up.

"Nicole, you're driving like a maniac!"

"He started it," she accused.

Nothing would stop her now. That man had tried to kill her. Ian could've been hurt in the process, too.

When they were closer, Ian raised his gun and aimed for the back right tire of the other vehicle. The bullet skinned off the rim just above the tire. The SUV swerved but continued on its path from the side street to the next major road.

Adrenaline thrummed through Nicole's veins as she leaned closer toward the steering wheel and willed the Mustang to go faster. She was intent on her task but still trying to be aware of the surrounding area for any pedestrians.

"I think he's going to turn left up there," Ian said.

"Gotcha," Nicole said, ready to follow.

"Good girl, you're doing great."

The SUV swung left and bounced over the curb in the process. Nicole cleared the curb, but the Mustang fishtailed at the sharpness of the turn.

She and Ian rocked in their seats. The motion cost them several seconds in the chase.

"Hang on," she told Ian.

"I wouldn't dream of letting go."

She smiled but didn't take the time to laugh. Her eye was on the goal. Nailing the bastard who had the gall to aim a gun at her.

"Watch out," Ian yelled.

The SUV had barreled around another corner. Nicole followed suit. The SUV lurched forward. A red truck merged into the street from a side stop sign and right into their path.

Nicole slammed on the breaks. She squeezed her eyes shut. Both she and Ian jerked forward. Their seat belts snapped them back in place against the seats. The Mustang swung in a semi-circle before it came to an abrupt halt in the middle of the street.

Nicole sucked the air back into her lungs and gasped.

"We're headed the wrong way," she cried, still unsure how they managed to avoid ramming into the red truck.

"We almost had him." Ian smacked the dash with the palm of his hand.

"He's hit the highway by now." Nicole whooshed out the air in her lungs in defeat.

"There'll be too many people around to get hurt," Ian said as he wiped his brow and looked over at her. "Where the hell did you learn to drive that like?"

She shrugged her shoulders. "I just pretended I was playing one of my niece's video games."

Ian's mouth dropped open. She noticed he still hadn't let go of the chicken handle.

This time she took a moment to laugh.

Chapter 16

Peter Roark paced the hallway of the old farmhouse, counting every irritating minute he waited for his cell phone to ring. He needed all the loose ends wrapped up. Today. By this time tomorrow, he would be on an island so far removed from this hellhole it would make everything he'd fought for to this point worth it. He paused to admire himself in the cracked oval mirror hanging on the wall. His eyes had healed up nicely after all the recent Botox injections. He fingered his thinning brown hair to spread it out just so. There was one hair that wouldn't cooperate. He smiled at himself. He'd always had a wild hair, come to think of it. He was looking forward to sampling a few tropical beauties even if he had to pay them for the pleasure. He'd have enough money to keep quite a few on a string from here to his dying days. What a way to go!

Roark sighed and paced to stand in front of the dust covered window. First things first. Right now there were too many henchmen in the mafia pressing in on him for answers. Closure. He needed to be able to tell them the negatives and pictures were in his possession. And that Mulherin and the girl were dead. A closed case.

So far, it had been a win-win. The greasing of both palms had worked out well. The mafia got to keep their men out of jail, and he was getting richer by the case. He wasn't letting some too-good-to-be-true wonder agent fuck it up.

Mulherin was a loose end that needed to be eliminated. Him and that damn girl with the camera. He'd trusted Mulherin to take her out, and the man had double-crossed him. Too bad, too. Mulherin would've made a great double agent. Every man had their price. It looked like Mulherin's was going to be six figures.

"Six feet under, that is." Roark lifted his shoulders and laughed at his own joke.

The cell phone he held in his fist vibrated. It was about damn time.

Roark thumbed the answer button and pressed the phone to his ear and answered gruffly, "Tell me something I wanna hear."

There was a pause.

"Boss, it didn't come off like I'd planned."

"Shit." Roark spun around and pushed his fingers through the front part of his receding hairline. "Just why the hell not?"

"They dodged the bullet by dropping something. It was a freak fluke."

"You're a freak fluke," Roark yelled into the phone. Of all the shitty luck. He closed his eyes and dragged in a deep ragged breath. "Barret, you've a pretty little wife and young daughter ... Bella, isn't it?"

"You leave them out of this, you—"

"No, you look, if you want to keep them both alive, you will see to it this situation is resolved. You'd better have the goods soon or I'll make sure you'll never see your wife and brat again. I'll be in touch." Roark ended the call and rammed the phone into the pocket of his Dockers with resolve. He was damned tired of imbeciles fucking up. It was time to get his hands dirty. He paced over to the window and leaned a hand against the windowsill. "Do I have to do everything myself?"

And his mind began to form a plan.

Chapter 17

Ian let go of the "oh shit" handle above his head. It felt as though his fingers were still curled around the damn thing. They didn't want to relax. He glanced over at Nicole. Her face was white, her body stiff and rigid. "Okay, Nicole, back away from the wheel. Come on. Let go."

She laughed at that, but he could tell she was shaken. He got out and went around and opened her door. "You can let go of the steering wheel now."

"Right." She nodded, but still sat there a moment. She squared her shoulders and took a deep breath. Her fingers relaxed and she flexed them from their white-knuckled grip as she swung her legs towards him to stand.

Her feet hit the pavement and she paused. He tucked his arm under hers and helped her up.

"I'm fine. Really."

"When the adrenaline wears off you're going to shake and probably get hysterical on me," Ian said.

He let go of her arm, but hung close in case her knees buckled.

"Well, I can't vouch for the shaking thing yet, but I can promise you, I will not become hysterical."

"There's my girl," Ian said, easing her around the car. He helped her into the passenger seat. She slid in, her fingers shaky, fumbling as she tried to work the buckle. He did it for her in one swift movement. He shut the door and shook his head as he made his way to the driver's side. Who knew what other surprises lay beneath her surface. She was, indeed, one hell of a woman.

"It's so invasive to think someone had been watching us the whole time we were in the park," Nicole said, and rubbed her hands up and down her arms as they drove on at a more comfortable speed.

"I know," Ian said. He looked over at her to make sure she was doing all right. Her voice sounded so small it tugged at his heart. He leaned across and gave her knee a reassuring squeeze.

"Just think, what would've happened if I hadn't dropped my sunglasses."

Ian raised his hand to cup the back of her neck. He massaged at the base and worked his way up. "Shh. Don't think about it. It won't do any good to go over what ifs. You're safe now."

She merely nodded and looked off at the scenery trailing by. He continued to massage her neck, not wanting to stop touching her. She was alive. It had been a close call. He couldn't have stood it if anything had happened to her. He was there to protect her after all. It was his job. He was just needing to do his job, nothing more. He looked over at her thoughtfully.

She flashed him a spunky look again. "See, I am not even bordering on hysterical, am I?"

He laughed. "No. I wouldn't say that."

"Good."

Ian checked his rearview mirrors again. He admired the way her chin lifted and her shoulders squared in determination. "I didn't get the license plate number because there was mud conveniently splattered on it."

"Yeah, I noticed that, too," Nicole said, and sighed.

"Do you have everything with you that you need?"

"What do you mean?"

"Tell me you have your prescription with you."

"I do. Why?"

"Good, because we're not going back to the hotel. It's too risky," he told her.

"I agree."

They took many turns on their way back down the highway, both keeping an eye out for anyone following. Once Ian was convinced their trail was cold, he cruised along blending in more with the traffic.

"We'd better not chance going to Brian's yet." Ian glanced at her. "We'll get somewhere secure first."

Ian gave her a sideways glance. Her hands were in her lap and she was twisting the ring with a blue square stone she wore on her right hand. Her face white.

"Are you okay?" he asked her.

"Yeah, I just … yeah."

Ian checked the mirrors again. He saw nothing out of the ordinary. In processing what had just happened he realized for a gunman to try something in broad daylight, Roark must be getting desperate. Sure they'd been in a forgotten park but it was still risky. Ian took note of Nicole. Her face was still pinched. She'd been through a lot in the last few days. He couldn't believe how she'd commanded the wheel and taken over like that earlier. She was feisty and fire all mixed into her sweet little package. How many women would've been able to hold up like that? Driven like that? He shook his head and smiled to himself.

What he ought to do is turn her over his knee and spank her for not staying put in the car and staying out of harm's way. What he wanted to do was kiss her. Hard. Instead, he surfed the radio stations hoping to find something good to listen to. Something to create a lighter mood. He paused on a station that advertised playing light rock and eighties music. Deciding a little funk in their tunes might help the mood, he left it on the channel.

The next town over was small, too small to get lost in. Ian opted to drive on. He was trying to work it out in his mind how he and Nicole might have been located. Once he figured that out, his next step would be to figure out just who all was after them. Roark. The Mafia. And maybe someone connected to man number three?

He leaned to the side to feel for his folder with his maps he stashed in the pocket of the door. He handed it to her. "Do you mind getting out the Virginia map? See how close we are from the nearest airport, I'd like you to see how far we are and the exits we need to take."

"Are we going to be taking a plane trip?"

"No. We're going to park the Mustang in the long-term parking. We'll get a rental on a fake ID of mine," he said.

"Aren't you afraid they'll be able to trace you?"

"That's a good question. Not with this card. I have a few tricks in reserve at all times," Ian said, and winked at her.

"Why am I not surprised?" Nicole laughed. He was a man of all trades. She couldn't believe how he had darted off after the gunman like that. Thank God he'd been okay. If anything had happened to him, well, she didn't think she could face it.

Nicole ripped the Velcro flap apart and thumbed through the plastic coated maps and selected the one she needed. She pulled the visor down to block the afternoon sun from blinding her as she ran her index finger down the opened map.

"We get off the highway at exit 152A," Nicole reported, "It looks to be about ten miles right off there."

"Great."

They moved with the flow of traffic and it didn't take them long to make their exit. As soon as they got off the highway they spotted an airport sign leading the way to the terminal.

Planes started appearing across their path overhead. They were so close they sounded like they were going to land on the roof of the car. It was a maze of terminal signs with traffic zigzagging in all directions. Nicole spotted the long-term lot first.

Maneuvering the car to the correct lane, Ian grabbed their claim ticket as the lever went up and pulled through to the parking lot.

"We can catch the tram to the rental car agency over there," Ian said, helping her and Dickens out of the car after they parked.

Once they'd been assigned a black Durango, they headed on to find a hotel.

"We'll be checking in without luggage. And what are we going to wear?"

"You have a point. We'll look for a store and run in and get some things to wear. I feel better about being on a different set of wheels."

With several strip malls to choose from, they turned into the parking lot of Peterson's.

"They'll have both men's and women's departments," Ian said, locking the car. "Here's our plan of attack, we'll undertake your side first and then head to mine. Our targets are shorts and T-shirts. Got it?"

"We need a plan of attack for shopping?" Nicole asked, laughing at him. She had to run two steps to keep up with his one.

"You woman. Me man. Definitely a plan of attack if we're to get out of there before I need another shave."

She shook her head in wonder at the man's logic as they entered the first set of doors looking at the cosmetic aisle ahead. When they opened the second set of doors the vast array of fragrances were sucked their way. It was much too much. Nicole fanned her face and cleared her throat. "Did you start the stopwatch?"

"Funny," he muttered as he snagged her elbow to guide her down the main row. "Ladies first. Your side appears to be this way."

He led her to women's clothing. She had no choice but to follow him. Rolling her eyes and shaking her head, she walked beside him. At least he'd slowed his pace some in the store.

In under forty minutes they both came out with a couple of sacks each with a few changes. Ian carried the handled bags and stashed them in the back of the Durango.

When Nicole climbed into the passenger seat, she checked the clock on the dash.

"Not bad. You were close by eleven minutes."

"Well, we'd have made it, too, if you hadn't stopped to gawk over the shoes."

"I did not gawk."

"Oh, excuse me, drool."

"You're so terrible." She looked over at him as he darted her a reproving look.

"Well, I'm certainly worse for wear after all that shopping, I know that," he said.

"Oh, would you stop your whining." She chuckled as she kicked her sandals off and flexed her toes against the floorboard. She was on to him. He'd been trying to distract her, lighten the mood and try to help her forget they'd been shot at.

For a brief time it had worked, too, and she loved him for it.

Startled at the way that thought rolled across her mind, her fingers curled around the door handle. She stared out her window. A hot flush crept up her neck.

She glanced back in Ian's direction. His eyes were trained on the row of hotels. She wasn't in love with him. Couldn't be. It was just the fact that they were in this together. Both victims. He was trying to help her. And she was grateful.

That was all.

That's all it could be. He wasn't her type any more than she was his.

She wondered what his type was. *Probably some voluptuous blonde. Figures.*

She absently watched the row of hotels passing by in a blur. Did she even know what her type was? Her type was, well, like her ex-boyfriend. She cringed and closed her eyes. *I need a new type.*

"I think we'll try this hotel and see if they have any vacancies."

She sat up and looked around as they pulled into the entrance of the hotel lined with white roses and red cannas. The building sat back from the street and appeared to have all their parking in the rear. A field stretched out at the rear of it, which would make the rooms quieter and offer a place for Dickens to run.

Ian turned the motor off and reached for his door handle. "Stay put this time, okay?"

"Yes, sir."

His eyebrows raised, he looked thoughtful for a moment, and then his eyes narrowed on her. She smiled back at him sweetly and batted her eyes. *Keeping him on his toes is a nice way to pass the time when you're a fugitive on the run.*

Watching him saunter into the hotel lobby, her mind ran back to her wayward thoughts. He had many sides to him. All tough agent one minute, and telling her bedtime stories to help her sleep the next.

She smiled. Even though he was complex, and with many layers, he had such a kind side to him that he didn't try to let out.

Her attention turned to Dickens with his movements in the back-seat. He dashed from side to side pawing at the door and looking out the window.

"Do not even tell me you have to use a tree. If your master comes back and finds us out of this car again, he'll have both our hides."

Dickens' paws rested on the back of her seat as he rolled out his tongue. She chuckled, thinking he looked like he was laughing.

"We've got him pegged don't we, boy?" She scuffed the fur around his neck and ran her finger under his collar. "You are just a treasure, you good dog, you. And you've got a good master, too. Oh, Dickens, I think I'm falling for him. What should I do?"

Dickens barked twice and licked the side of her face.

"Are you telling me to split and run?" she chuckled and kissed the top of his head.

Nicole noticed Ian exiting the doors. He was swaggering his large frame with ease towards their car. She took the liberty of drinking in the sight of him. The sun highlighted his hair and played across his good looks. He really was drop-dead gorgeous in a dangerous-sexy kind of way.

She sighed, knowing just who was in danger. Her heart skipped a beat.

He swung the door open and hopped in, pausing to look at her as he inserted the key in the ignition. "What?"

"Oh … Dickens and I were just having a moment, that's all." She smiled and then cleared her throat. She could feel the heat circling her neck and rising.

His eyes studied her for a moment before he went on. "We're in luck. They've got a room on the second floor in the back. I'll pull around and we can go up the stairs there. They also have a continental breakfast."

Their room held two double beds adorned with navy and tan plaid comforters. There were two complimentary bottles of water and mints sitting on the desk. Dickens sniffed his way across the room and jumped up on one of the beds. He looked at them as if to say, "Well, what are you waiting for?"

She laughed, "It would appear the room has the Dickens seal of approval."

"That's all it hinges on for me," Ian replied dryly.

She moved into the room, set her bags down on the other bed, and kicked her sandals off to wiggle her toes. The day's events were catching up with her. She could almost feel the cloud moving in.

Ian bolted and chained the door. He walked over to the window, looked out on the parking lot, and snapped the blinds closed. "I'm going to call Brian, fill him in on why we have a new phone number and ask him if the pictures are ready."

She decided to put her clothes away in the drawer and freshen up a bit. Luckily, she had her makeup in her purse and she always carried her tortoise-shelled brush. She heard Ian talking to Brian on the phone and recounting the afternoon. She wanted to escape away from hearing the replay of the events. Living it once was enough. She hurried into the bathroom, shut the door, and leaned her back against it and exhaled. She didn't even have to close her eyes to hear the gunfire all over again.

It all had been so close. Too close.

Ian had told her not to dwell on it, but she could still hear the shot ringing through the air again and again. She shuddered. Ian was always telling her to stay focused. With a deep breath she pushed herself away from the door and walked over to the sink. Pulling her purse off her shoulder, she sat it on the marbled vanity and looked around. The bathroom was good sized. Neutral, calming colors. The normal hotel toiletries lay by the sink in a little basket with wash cloths rolled up in it.

She twisted the white knobs at the sink and let the water cascade through her fingers until it felt slightly warm. Unwrapping one of the soaps, she rubbed it between the palms of her hands. It was refreshing to massage the cucumber melon bar in rhythmic circles on her face. After splashing with cool water, she patted her face dry with a wash cloth and wiped her neck.

Her reflection looked a little more relaxed now. She still hadn't gotten used to her new hair color. Her skin had darkened to a golden glow from the self-tanning lotion.

When she was done, she pulled the door open to listen. Once satisfied Ian wasn't still talking on the phone, she stepped out into the bedroom.

Ian had kicked off his shoes and socks and was lying back against the headboard stretched across on the bed. Dickens was belly up getting the rub down of his life.

She went to stand at the end of the bed and Ian broke his stare to look over at her. Curiosity got the better of her so she couldn't stop herself from asking. "What did Brian have to say?"

"To stay alive. The pictures will be ready for us tomorrow morning."

She backed up and sank down in a rounded-back navy chair across from the bed. "This could all be over then."

"Yeah," he said, tucking his hands together behind his head. "Hopefully, the pictures will clearly show who the men are. We know two. Things look good from that aspect."

"But?"

"I can prove Borland and Adams lived beyond their graves," Ian said. "But I can't prove how Roark is involved yet. There's still that link missing. I need more evidence."

"Roark has to be taking payments to stay quiet and orchestrate all of this," she said, rising in a half standing position to lean forward and pull her chair up closer to the bed. She sat back down in the chair and lifted her bare feet up to rest on the end. "Can't you trace that?"

"No. He could have it hidden in any number of ways," Ian said. "People hide money in off- shore accounts all the time."

She nibbled thoughtfully on her bottom lip. "Maybe one of the men in the picture will rat on him."

"It's a possibility, but not a probability," Ian said, pulling his T-shirt out of the waistband of his shorts. "We also have to find them first."

"Yeah, there's that too," she said, trying not to notice the way his shirt rode up a bit on his chest exposing his flat, tanned stomach. *It's a tad close in here.*

Ian raised himself up on one elbow and looked at her with serious eyes. "Nicole, when that time comes, and it will, we'll need you to testify that those pictures are from your trip to Mexico. It'll need to be on record that you took them."

She regarded the wary expression on Ian's face. The idea of testifying seemed scary. She noticed he seemed almost hesitant to approach her about it. He was trying to prepare her for the reality to come. She appreciated the fact that he was being up front and honest with her. "I realize that. And I will."

"You'll also need to be put in protective custody until after the trial."

He watched her closely. She tried to keep her expression neutral. Her stomach bottomed out at the thought of being kept under surveillance. She tried to remain calm. "I see."

"It would be for your own protection," Ian assured her.

"Yes. I'm sure it would be. Well, I don't see any way around it." She agreed as she swung her feet back to the floor. Resting her elbows on her knees, she tucked her chin down and massaged at her temples. *I can do this. I can do this. I have to do it.*

Ian appeared so comfortable lounging across his bed that she looked over at hers. Giving in, she walked over and stretched out on top of it. She lay on her back and stared at the picture on the wall in front of her. It was a serene setting in an English garden. She sighed. Would her life ever calm down and return to normal again? And what of Ian? The thought of something happening to Ian caused her heart to hammer with such force it made her eyes sting.

She rolled over to face him. He was staring up at the ceiling. She tried to swallow the tightness in her throat. It took her a moment to be sure that when she did speak, her voice wouldn't crack and give her inner emotions away. "You've told me what will probably happen to me, but ... you've not said what will happen to you?"

Chapter 18

Ian swallowed while he continued to stare at the ceiling. *What should I tell her? The truth? That I don't have a clue in hell how I'm going to get my ass out of this sling?*

He turned his head in Nicole's direction. Emotions he normally kept in check threatened to break free when he realized the worry etched on her face was for him. It did something funny inside his chest. No one ever worried about him. Nicole's huge chocolate-brown eyes shimmered with tears in their corners. She actually cared about what happened to him. It was a staggering thought.

"If you think I had a plan of attack when shopping, you'd be floored with what I have up my sleeve now," he lied, and winked.

They both shared the laugh and she threw her pillow at him. He caught it in one easy sweep. His voice dipped low and seductive as he bounced his eyebrows up and down. "Does this mean you're coming over to my bed?"

"In your dreams."

"You've already been there, sweetheart," he teased her and then his smile slipped, leaving his voice husky, "Now I'm ready for a little reality."

Her smile died with the teasing and she looked serious again. "Roark is trying to pin a bunch of things on you that you didn't do. You can't let that happen. You'll be careful?"

"Always."

She looked like she was mulling that over, but still wasn't convinced. Sadness played across her face. He decided a subject change was in order. He sat up and raked a hand through his disheveled hair. "What type of movies do you like?"

"Why do you ask?"

"I thought it would be best if we stayed in, ordered a pay-per-view movie and called in a pizza to the room," he told her. "Is it a date?"

"Um … it all depends."

"On what?"

"Pepperoni?"

"Whatever the lady wants."

"Deal. Pepperoni it is. Okay, sure, it's a date."

He smiled, relieved to tread back into shallow waters. Things had turned a little too deep for him back there. It had been too easy flirting. He didn't want to get involved with her. It wouldn't be right. *What the hell do I even have to offer her? Especially if she found out the truth about what happened with Dan.*

He pushed off the bed and strode over to the desk where the TV Guide was sitting. He leafed through it and suggested a few titles. Trying to steer clear of anything with violence in it to remind her of being shot at, he suggested a comedy. "There's a British one listed. I don't know anyone in it, though."

She looked over his shoulder and hair brushed his neck. He tried not to notice.

"Fine with me. I may go ahead and take my shower."

"Hmm," he half grunted, flipping the page to the articles in the guide. He pretended to be absorbed in something he was reading. The last thing he wanted to do was think about her naked in the next room. Silky and wet. His fingers tightened on the pages. This was all going to be over tomorrow, he told himself. He could do it one more night.

When the bathroom door closed with a click, he sank down on the bed and dropped the book in his lap. He shook his head and sighed. She was getting to him. He wiped a hand across his face and took a deep breath.

The sooner they picked up the pictures in the morning and he turned her over to protective custody the better.

Or she was going to need protection from him.

God help me.

He stood and paced the room. Stopping in front of the desk, he opened the hotel reference booklet. After a quick dial down to the front desk, he asked the clerk for the nearest pizza delivery number. He called in the pizza and added a two-liter of Coke to the order.

The shower shut off at the same time he set the phone back in the cradle. He swallowed and turned to stare at the bathroom door. The sound the shower curtain made when the rings slid across the bar caused beads of perspiration to fight their way to his forehead. He swallowed again. Looking around almost frantically, he spotted the TV remote lying on the nightstand. He grabbed it and pointed it at the TV.

By the time the bathroom door handle clicked and Nicole emerged from the steamy room wearing a gray, oversized, cotton sleep shirt, he acted like he was engrossed in the TV. He remembered her buying the shirt, but it sure hadn't looked like that on the hanger. While modest at past her knees, it hinted at luscious curves he was all too aware of her having.

Great. Just great.

She smelled like a gift shop. The kind that sold the scented dried flowers in decorative bags. Her sweet fragrance enveloped him.

I'm a goner.

The room seemed smaller all of a sudden.

"You like game shows?" she asked, sitting down on her bed and uncapping the little bottle she held in her hands.

"Game shows?" he repeated, stalling a moment to stare at the TV, taking in what was on for the first time. Letters were being turned over by a gal with in a flourishing green dress. He blinked. "A … just passing time. I called the order in. The pizza will be here pretty soon."

"Oh, good."

She sat and drew her legs up on the bed. Taking the cap off the hotel bottle of lotion, she lathered the cream onto her hands and rubbed it into her skin. He watched transfixed as her fingers massaged the lotion into her supple skin in circular motions. She took her time patting the bottle on the palm of her hand and then transferring the lotion to her legs. His mouth ran dry. He should look away, do something else. He couldn't think of anything. What he wanted to do was pull her into his arms, comfort her, and tell her everything would be okay. He wanted to kiss her hard. He wanted—

A rap at the door set Dickens off barking at the same time both of them jumped. Ian drew his gun and motioned for Nicole to go back into the bathroom.

Once she was out of sight, he confirmed through the peephole that the young pimply-faced boy on the other side was holding pizza boxes and a two-liter. Not taking any chances, Ian opened the door slowly, keeping his gun hidden from view, but ready.

The kid swapped the food for cash and went on his way. Ian looked up and down the vacant hallway before latching the door behind him.

Nicole came out of the bathroom and resumed her spot on her bed.

He distracted himself by ripping off the box lid to use it for a plate. He tore the pizza in half and divided it between the two sections of the cardboard. After handing one to her, he went to perch on the side of his bed and started eating. His stomach growled. He picked up the remote with the other hand and ordered the movie to the room.

"Lights off or on?" Nicole asked.

"Off is fine with me. You?"

Nicole snapped the light off that sat on the nightstand between them and settled in with her box lid to eat.

The pizza was good even without beer, Ian decided. Nicole poured more soda in both hotel glasses and curled up on her bed while he sprawled out on his. They ate while they watched the movie. The British comedy had a hint of mystery and was just mediocre. He kept feeling distracted thinking about the woman lying on the next bed. She smelled like sweet roses. Good enough to eat. He hadn't ordered dessert to be delivered. He wondered if she tasted as good as she smelled. He was so preoccupied with his thoughts that he lost track of the movie.

"Are you getting into this movie, Nicole?"

After no answer came, he raised up on one elbow to look over at her. He could see her from the glow of the TV that she had fallen asleep with one hand tucked under her cheek and the other curled around Dickens' neck. Her mouth slightly parted and a peaceful look on her beautiful face. And in that moment, he realized he was jealous of his dog.

Damn.

Dickens raised his head and looked over at him with what Ian could've sworn was a smug expression.

He scowled at the dog, pressed the off button for the TV, and lay there quietly watching her sleep. He wanted her. He wouldn't touch her though. She deserved better than the sorry likes of him. Once they had the proof they needed she was as good as going into protective custody until the case went to trial.

Satisfied seeing her relaxed, he quietly unsnapped his jeans and tugged them down his legs. Once they were removed he slid beneath the cool sheet. It felt good to stretch out. She'd found peace and he didn't want to interrupt that. It wasn't easy being shot at. He should know. He yawned and slung an arm over his forehead.

There were still some parts of that night in the warehouse that were fuzzy to him. Everything had happened so fast. He couldn't change things no matter how much he wanted them to be different. He hadn't told the department shrink why he felt so responsible for Dan's death.

He blamed himself.

Ian pressed the palm of his hand to his forehead. *Dammit.*

He curled up on his side with his back to Nicole. Why couldn't he remember? Was it because he'd really shot Dan and blocked it out? Trey had said the lab matched the bullets. He hadn't been able to accept it. He wanted to believe that Roark set him up just like with the bogus file on Brandy.

But, what could he believe?

Would all this second guessing ever end? Would he ever remember? And if he did, could he live with the truth?

Nicole frowned. Her head turned to the side. Something in her subconscious dragged her from her sleep. Was somebody talking to her? She rubbed at her eyes and yawned. Ian must've left the TV on and fallen asleep.

"Get down!"

Her eyes flew open at the sharpness of Ian's voice.

"What?" she whispered, fully awake now with the sound of Ian's command. Her heart pounding against her chest, she clutched at the sheet.

"Don't talk. Move."

She slid off the bed and onto the carpeted floor. Her hands curled around the sheet she'd drug with her. She listened. *What should I do now?*

The glow from the bathroom light didn't offer much help in the way of seeing. The room was too full of shadows she was afraid were going to move. *Where is Ian?* Moments passed until she started to breathe again. She exhaled slowly and snuck air back in her lungs.

What on earth is happening?

While she lay there with her back on the hard floor, Dickens' face appeared over the edge of her bed. He cocked his head and looked down at her. She raised her head up and stared back. *He's not barking.*

It was then she realized Ian was thrashing around on his bed.

"Dan. No. No."

She rolled over on her knees and pulled herself up into a position to see Ian. His head rocked back and forth, and his arms flailed in the air. She lightly touched his arm and called to him. "Ian."

"No."

"Ian, you're dreaming."

He jerked and twisted his head from side to side. "Why, Dan?"

"Ian, it's okay."

"Oh, my God, Dan."

She placed her palm flat against his bare shoulder trying to calm him down.

A hand shot up and grabbed her wrist. With one hard yank, he hauled her against him. He pulled his gun out from under his pillow with the other hand and pointed it at her head.

"Ian! It's Nicole," she shrieked.

He froze. His eyes were wild, the grip on her wrist iron clad. Breath rushed out of his lungs, moving her bangs. He stared at her for a long moment and blinked. "Dammit, woman. What do you think you're doing? I could've shot you."

"You-you were dreaming."

He let go of her arm then. Running his hand through the back of her hair he said, "Don't come up on me like that ever again, okay?"

She chewed at her bottom lip worriedly and nodded. "I'm sorry."

"No. No. I'm the one who's sorry." Ian untangled his hand from her hair, trailed his fingertips down to the small of her back, and swirled a circle pattern against her nightshirt. He kissed the top of her head.

The warmth of his hand scorched a trail where it had run along her back. His breathing still heavy, fanning her cheek. She ran her tongue along her mouth. The urge to turn her head and claim his lips tore at her. Just one kiss. Just to know what it was like. *What would it hurt?*

Her fingers brushed along his heated skin. His chest hair curled between her fingers. She flattened her palms out again and pressed against him to push away. *We shouldn't be doing this.*

The hand on her back tensed and held her to him. She paused and looked down at him with uncertainty. "I ... should get you a cold wash cloth ... or something."

"Why?"

The huskiness in his voice sent shivers through her. She paused and looked away, still trying to avoid his mouth. It was too tempting being this close to him, drinking in the warm male scent of him. *Air. I need air.*

"Oh, I don't know, I heard somewhere that they were a cure all for everything." She laughed, trying to lighten the situation. Afraid he could feel her heart thudding against his chest, she moved away from him.

His arm locked around her waist. "Not everything."

"Oh, well, um, a drink of water maybe?" *Help!*

"That's not what I'm thirsty for."

He made his move. She was suddenly lying beside his bed, the weight of his hip pressing her to the firm mattress. His warm sensual lips claimed hers. Seeking. Searching.

And she was gone. A helpless moan shuddered its way up. Trapped. She was trapped. Buried in the back of her mind was the thought she should put a stop to this. His fingers danced along her spine. His kiss deepened, his tongue explored her mouth and a searing heat spread through to her lower limbs.

Oh, well. Tomorrow is another day, but it's not here yet.

The exploration was exquisite. She gave up all reason.

She wound her arms around his neck and laced her hands through his silky hair. His body tensed. She smiled inwardly at the power she felt over him. She pressed her body into his, loving every moment of it. His breathing hitched.

His mouth hardened on hers. After a few minutes, she moved her head slightly to the right, tracing her tongue along the top of his sexy mouth. His hands spanned her waist and pulled her against him harder.

He was as aroused as she was.

Her hands traveled down his broad shoulders to hard biceps. His mouth trailed from her lips and across her cheek. He nibbled at her ear and rained kisses down to the nape of her neck.

A trail of fire.

He leaned over her, pressing her back against the bed. A delighted *purr* escaped her lips. She didn't want him to stop. Ever.

One knee parted her legs. The pressure divine. His lips worked with practiced finesse. He nipped at her mouth. He groaned and deepened the kiss. His tongue sought hers in caressing motions. A tease. A promise. Her heart lay against his, and they beat in unison. Flames licked through her whole body.

He grabbed a handful of her hair and wove it through his fingers. Breaking the kiss, he moved back. "Tell me you don't want this."

She thought about it a nanosecond. She did. They shouldn't.

His face inches from her own. His body male and hard against hers.

Who was she kidding? She raised up to gaze into his eyes filled with passion and uncertainty, she laid her hand alongside his face.

"I." She kissed a path down his neck.

"Don't." She planted more kisses along his collarbone.

"Want." She took the tip of her tongue and circled his nipple.

"This." She moved lower, paused and looked up, "Do you?"

He growled at her and the next thing she knew she was under him.

"I was counting on you to put on the brakes," he rasped.

She laughed then. "Sorry. No can do. I'm here for the scenic ride."

He chuckled a low throaty laugh that sent chills on a collision course through her system. Rolling over, he dragged her on top of him.

He smacked her playfully on her bottom. She wound her arms around his neck and sealed the deal.

His mouth took savage possession of hers. Her whole body pulsed with pleasure. Their tongues kissed, danced, and stroked one another. His hands kneaded and massaged the muscles along her back and down, down to her waist. She loved the feel of his day's growth under her hand as she ran it along his chin.

His hands closed around her mid-section as he pulled her to him, moving her up and down over his erection.

Sensuous anticipation heated her skin, every cell of her being throbbed, her body cried out for release.

His hand ran under her nightshirt to caress her bare bottom. She hooked a thumb in his underwear and gave it a downward tug. He yanked at her nightshirt and slid it along her body in one upward motion. She lifted to allow room for the wretched barrier to be free. She tucked her head to go through the shirt and he flung off the offending article of clothing. He caught the tip of one breast in his mouth.

She moaned with agonized pleasure.

"You like that, huh?"

"I more than like it."

He went back to sucking on her breast as he grasped her other nipple between his fingers. Sucking. Tugging. Both nipples beaded and throbbed.

She arched her back. His hand fell from her breast to snake around to her back and press her to him. There was no escaping. There was no point in trying to convince herself she wanted to. His mouth kissed a path across her chest and downward. She fell to her side, weak-kneed and wanting.

He leaned over to kiss the flat of her stomach. The hot tip of his tongue circling her navel.

His hand found her soft mound. Her muscles bunched.

"Shhhh. Relax."

"Easy for you to say," she gasped with pleasure.

She ran her hand along his rippled chest, lower, and reached for the male length of him. He stiffened at her touch. His breathing ragged.

"Relax," she mimicked, releasing a husky laugh.

"Witch."

She thought her heart would surely beat itself to death before it was over. The hammering shot adrenaline throughout her entire body.

What a delicious way to go!

His hand closed over hers and eased it away. She broke the kiss, a pouting noise escaping her lips.

"You first." His hot breath fanned into her ear.

His finger slipped inside her velvety moist folds. Her legs stretched out in a rigid stance. The rhythm began. Slow. Deliberate. His long, hard fingers danced in and out of her until she exploded in a sweet agonized frenzy against him.

Her breath labored, she buried her face in his neck a bit, embarrassed at all of her moaning.

His other hand drug through her hair and tugged her head back gently. She loved the way his strong hands caressed her body. His blue eyes pierced through to her soul. His lids heavy with passion, their expression tender.

She melted against him pressing her lips against his.

He returned her kiss with a passion. A hunger. A promise.

She didn't think she could wait much longer.

He moved then, stretching out an arm to the night stand and groped for his wallet. Retrieving a foil packet, he tore it open with his mouth.

Her pulse skipped a beat with anticipation.

He leaned her back and moved to kiss her stomach while he tweaked her right nipple. He then kissed the satiny skin above her thighs. She almost lifted off the bed. He pressed her back against the pillow as he thrust deep inside of her.

"Oh," she moaned.

She begged for release as his thrusts increased. Her fingers dug into his buttocks. His breathing changed. Just when she thought her heart couldn't go any faster, it escalated to try and outrun them.

Right as she crested the edge and gasped, his mouth clamped over hers.

She groaned into him as his arms tightened around her. He bucked harder. She gripped him to her. After a minute, his body went rigid, paused. He drug his mouth from hers and shuddered against her ear and bit down on her lobe.

They collapsed together. Bodies pulsating against one another. Damp. Slick and sated.

They lay there, their breathing slowly returning to the natural state. They dozed; their legs tangled in the sheets, and basked in the warmth and nearness of one another.

She closed her eyes and breathed in his musky scent, wanting to burn everything about this moment into her memory. The sex had been incredible. Intimate. In tune with one another.

She smiled.

"Are you comfortable?" he whispered against her ear, moving back to allow her more room on the bed. He smoothed her hair from her face.

She pressed her hand against his chest to stop him. "I'm great."

To emphasize she ran her toe along his leg and purred.

He gave her bottom a squeeze and said, "Give me a few more minutes and I'll just be trying that out."

She laughed and then sobered. He had a scar above his right hipbone she remembered seeing. She trailed her index finger down his right side where it was.

His hand moved and closed over hers. He brought her fingers up and drew them to his lips to kiss.

"That scar. Is that why you rub your right side sometimes?" she asked, raising up on one elbow to look into his eyes.

"I do it that often?" He seemed surprised.

"Sometimes."

"I guess I'm not aware when I'm doing it."

"Is it a recent wound?"

He sat up then, the sheet dipping low around his waist, and dragged a hand through his hair.

He stared across the room in silence.

Nicole rubbed the palm of her hand across his back. She pulled the sheet up over her breasts and tucked her hair behind her ear. "I'm sorry, I shouldn't have asked. I didn't mean to upset you in any way."

She watched the muscles bunch along his jaw. He reclined against the headboard and inhaled slowly. His eyes closed.

Nicole looked over to where her shirt had landed on the floor and decided to retrieve it. His voice stopped her.

"It was the night Dan died."

She paused and looked over at him. His expression strained. Solemn. She started to say something and decided to stay where she was and be quiet.

They sat there for a few more minutes. The air conditioning kicked on in the room. The sound of someone collecting ice from the machine down the hall and talking could be heard. An elevator dinged.

Nicole wished she could just kiss away the pain etched in Ian's face. "I guess being shot at today triggered the memories for you?"

"It could've been that but not necessarily."

"You mean you've had these nightmares before?"

It was then that he turned his head towards her. His piercing blue gaze flickering pain and sorrow. Her heart turned over.

"Yeah."

Knowing the last thing he would want was pity, she averted her eyes to lean over and kiss his shoulder. Her heart broke thinking about all the pain he'd endured. "If you don't want to talk about it, I won't press, but if you ever do …"

"They're always the same. The nightmares. Dan and I are busting in the door of the warehouse. Gunfire breaks out. Dan moves in."

Ian stopped speaking. His voice had begun to crack. He cleared his throat. She laid her head on his shoulder and ran her hand across his waist to hug him. He ran his fingers up and down her arm absently in a circular motion.

He cleared his throat again. "The next thing I see is Dan lying on the floor. There are two other men dead, and the rest have escaped."

She kissed his chin.

"I make it over to where Dan is laying on the floor. He's … bad. A chest wound and blood … so much blood."

She could feel the tension coil in him. What a thing to have to go through. He was lucky he hadn't been killed, too. Tears welled in her eyes. Her throat was hot. She tried to swallow discretely. She cleared her throat and blinked furiously.

"I knew he was bad off. It didn't look good. Not with so much blood." He went on, his voice strangled. "He said he never meant for things to end this way. And then … he was gone."

She leaned up and cupped his face. "I'm so sorry. So very sorry."

He took her hand and kissed the palm. "Yeah. Me too. It was such a waste of a good human life. And if it hadn't been for me he would be alive."

She sat up fully then. "You don't know that. Ian, listen, you can't blame yourself with this."

He lowered her hand to the bed and looked her in the eye. "Of course I can. Don't you see it? I killed him."

Chapter 19

Nicole sat stunned for a moment trying to process what Ian had just said. She shook her head from side to side. "No. No, you're just blaming yourself. You couldn't have shot your best friend."

"Then why can't I remember what happened more clearly?" he shot out at her, whipped the sheet off, and stood.

She watched him stalk to the bathroom and debated whether to follow him or not. There was more. She could sense it. He was blaming himself for something he couldn't have had any control over.

The urge to go to him won over the thought she should give him some time. Her feet hit the cool floor, she scooped up her sleep shirt, and tugged it over her head as she walked through to the bathroom.

She found him bent over the sink splashing water on his face. She waited for him while she debated what to say. When he finished, she handed him a towel. He wiped his face with it and then hitched it around his waist.

"You can't go on blaming yourself with this, Ian."

He brushed past her and strode out of the bathroom to pace around the room. "You just don't understand."

She stood in the doorframe to the bathroom. "So, help me to. Explain it."

He stopped at the window and moved the curtain to look out. With his back to her, she could see the muscles knotting along his shoulders. The curtain fell into place as he rested the flat of his palm against the wall, the other hand on his hip.

"I have some blackouts during the dream. The same as I have in real life when I try to remember what really went down that night."

The quietness of his voice while he said it sent a waterfall of icy chills down her spine. She swallowed. "Our minds protect us from things we can't quite process sometimes. What you went through, Dan's death, it was a traumatic thing to happen."

"Yeah, that's one way of looking at it," he snorted.

She didn't quite follow what he meant. Frowning, she asked, "And another?"

He dropped his hand from the wall and turned to look at her. The torment in his face contorted his features. "Maybe I did shoot him."

"No. I don't believe that." She went to him then and wrapped her arms around him, wanting desperately to convince him he was wrong.

"Then why can't I remember it?" He buried his face in her hair and spoke against her ear. She pulled back to frame his face in her hands. "Ian, even if it is true, if, then it was just an accident."

"And that is supposed to help me feel better?" His hands closed over hers. "That is supposed to make up for his wife Leslie and his three sons not having him?"

Her heart ached for the pain she heard in his voice. Raw pain. The kind that could eat a man from the inside out. "Do you think it would be any different for Dan if the tables were turned?"

"Yes. I do."

"How do you figure that?"

"I don't have any family."

"You have your father."

He stepped back and waved his hand through the air. "A man who hates me and I don't care to ever see again."

"You can't mean that."

"Oh, but I do. The day I go back for more from him is the day Hell forms icicles."

She didn't know how to help him. He was like a wounded animal trying to retreat. She didn't want to let him go through this alone. "I know you're hurting. Let me help."

"I don't see how," he told her. "It's hard to feel anything anymore."

A step toward him brought her close enough to smooth her hands across his shoulders and wind them around his neck. His muscles rippled under her touch. She leaned in and pressed her breasts against his bare chest.

His hands traveled down to her waist and gripped together.

"Do you feel this?" she whispered against his lips.

Her mouth closed over his, hard. She moved against him, feeling him, promising him whatever he wanted, he could take.

The warmth of his mouth melted hers and she deepened the kiss. His hands traveled down to cup her bottom and pull her against his hardening body.

Delighting in the feel of his body reacting to hers, she reluctantly tore her lips from his. "Or this?"

She trailed kisses over his jaw line and down his neck. At the same time, she hooked her index finger in his towel and gave a playful tug. The towel fell to the floor in a thud.

"What I want to feel is every inch of you. Know every secret. Create some more of our own. I want to feel myself inside of you," he answered, and backed her up against the wall.

The movement was so sudden, she gasped. He covered her mouth with his. After a minute, he yanked the nightshirt up over her head and threw it somewhere behind him. He swung her into his arms and carried her over to the bed. She clung to him as he lowered her onto the mattress, and came down on top of her.

The look in his eyes, dark with desire, fanned the flame inside of her. She pulled his head down to kiss him hard on his sensuous mouth at the same time she lifted her legs to wrap around his waist. He returned her kiss with a fevered pitch.

Heat flared deep in her pelvis. When he reached for her, he began massaging her tender core. She moaned. His kissing intensified as he thrust himself deep inside of her. She tugged at his hair and arched into him.

"I feel," he breathed into her ear before biting it.

"I feel it, too," she moaned. "And if feels so good."

And they rode the waves of passion together in perfect union. Each basking in this time they had created for one another.

Nicole lay there, her breasts rising and falling as she tried to catch up with her heartbeat, loving the feel of him inside of her.

After a few minutes, his weight shifted to lie beside her. He curved an arm possessively around and spooned into her. A sigh escaped her lips as she rested her cheek on his arm.

They were sharing one bed. She looked over to see Dickens sprawled out on the other bed. He looked up at her, his ears picking up, and rolled out his tongue. He then rested his chin back down on his paw.

A slow happy smile spread across her lips as another sigh escaped.

Ian felt a warmth before he rose to the surface. Warmth and curves. He almost drifted back to sleep his body was so relaxed. He lay still for several minutes basking in the moment. It was as if he opened his eyes it would break the spell and the dream would fade.

The dream was tickling his nose.

He raised a hand and brushed Nicole's silky hair away from his face. Memories from the night before replayed behind his eyes. He was in deep trouble and he knew it. How should he play this one out, he wondered.

The sex had been bad. Bad news. Nothing like he'd expected. Nothing like he had ever experienced before. And it scared the hell out of him.

Always before, he had been able to remain detached. He thought of the women he had dated before. They knew the game, the score, and how it ended. A clean break. He never played with women that wanted to win for keeps.

Yeah, last night had been bad, all right. Nicole had been different. It hadn't been just sex. It had been emotional sex. Something he didn't think he was capable of having. Last night had more than proved him wrong.

His body hummed from the intimacy of the night before.

And he felt more alive than he ever had.

Being with her was like a drug. He'd been satisfied, but now wanted more. She made him feel whole. A part of something bigger than himself.

Not wanting the moment to end just yet, he lay there on his back with Nicole's soft cheek resting on his chest. He kissed the top of her head.

How in the hell am I going to be able to act nonchalant after a night like that?

With the realization of the type of impact it could have on his life, both eyes sprang open.

Remorse settled over him. She wasn't for him. He'd never do her justice. She deserved Sir Noble, not some idiot who ruined the relationships he had. The thought of someone else touching her welled up feelings he didn't even know he was capable of having.

He didn't feel like he could breathe.

There would be a full investigation into Dan's death. It would get ugly before it was all over with, said and done. Even if he had accidentally shot Dan, Roark would make sure he was framed for it and went down. It would even the score. He'd lose either way. And he wasn't taking Nicole down the tubes with him. He cared for her too much.

He had to protect Nicole from that at all costs. She'd already been through enough, he didn't want to put her through any more.

He eased his arm out from under her. She moaned a bit and shifted in the bed. The expression on her face was content. She deserved to be happy. She deserved someone else. He had to do this for her. She'd thank her lucky stars later she hadn't stayed involved with the likes of him. Better to make a clean break now.

He wiped a hand down his face and swallowed. They needed those pictures from Brian, and then he needed to hand Nicole over to those who would protect her, and she could testify.

Careful not to wake her, he eased from the bed to go and take a shower.

Nicole moaned. Her head was keeping tempo with her pulse. She wasn't even fully awake and yet she knew. She was ill. The muscles along her spine were wrapped tighter than a loaf of braided French bread. The last knot was at the base of her neck, throbbing and vibrating her brain.

A migraine.

Up on her side, she slowly moved her foot back. She was alone in the bed. Just as well. Any movement and she might throw up. She put a hand to her head. Here after the most incredible night of her life she was held captive by her chronic enemy.

It sounded like Ian was banging around in the bathroom. Every noise more pronounced with her head pounding. The door snapped open. She cracked her eyes open. The light hurt.

"Good morning."

She attempted a smile and winced.

"What's wrong?" he asked with concern laced in his voice.

He came over to stand beside the bed and looked down at her worriedly.

"My head is vibrating."

"A migraine?"

"Yes," she whispered. She was miserable. So much for the morning after. Not very romantic.

"Have you taken your medicine?"

"No, not yet."

She heard him move about the room, the zip to her purse, and the rummaging for the bottle. Still unable to open her eyes, she was happy to lie there and let him do it. His footsteps retreated to the bathroom where he ran the water.

"Here," he said, and pressed the pill into her hand.

She raised it to her mouth and rose up half way on her elbow to sip the water he offered. The top in her head spun to the side. She sank back onto her pillow and stifled a moan.

Ian's warm hand rubbed reassuringly along her arm. "How long does it take for one of those things to work?"

"A good couple of hours to really take the edge off. Then I'll just be tired," she said, trying to get still again and concentrate on breathing.

"I see."

She did risk a peek then. There was something in his tone that warranted her looking. "What?"

"Not a problem. I'll just call Brian and let him know that we're not coming."

She moved a hand out to stop him but missed. "Don't do that. Just go, I'll be fine. The sooner this is resolved the sooner we can work on getting you cleared."

"I can't leave you here."

"I'll be fine. I'll be better alone. Quiet. I need to sleep."

"I don't like it."

"It'll be okay. We weren't followed. I'm obviously down for the count and won't go anywhere."

Dickens leaped off his bed, trotted over to the chair, and scooped up his leash between his teeth to bring it over to lay it at Ian's feet.

"Well, it would appear Dickens needs to pee on nature," Ian whispered to her with a chuckle.

"You better help him out then," she said, smiling weakly.

"We'll discuss this when I get back."

The chink of the leash and the closing of the door behind them triggered a sigh to escape from her. It was quiet again. She always preferred to be completely alone during one of her spells. She readily gave her blessing for the world to go on without her until she could join it later.

Ian must have pulled the curtains. The room was in darkness once again. *What a time for something like this to happen. Last night was incredible. No, Ian was incredible. His hands traveled every inch of my body.* More than that, he had touched her heart. The moments shared before they'd been intimate had been priceless as well. Sharing such buried pain, giving so much over of himself had made her want him all the more.

"I'm going to help you clear your name, Ian," she vowed in a whisper. *As soon as I can sit up.*

She lay there several minutes trying to breathe as deep as she could and allow the medicine to work.

There was a soft tap at the door and next the card inserted in the slot.

"Dickens, no," Ian called out.

It was too late. Her eyes sprang open just as Dickens bounded up on the bed. She flung a hand up out of reaction as Ian grabbed the dog's collar. The jarring of the bed made her wince.

"Down boy. Nicole's sick."

Ian hauled Dickens off the bed and commanded him to sit.

Nicole cringed at the loudness of Ian's sharp order to Dickens. She tried to pretend she didn't feel like throwing up.

"I'm sorry," Ian said.

"It's okay."

"Maybe I should run over there and pick up the pictures really quick."

"Do. I really relax better when I know I'm alone and can just sleep."

Dickens stood up, propped his paws on the arm of the chair, and snorted.

"I said to sit your hairy butt in the chair and I meant it."

The dog snorted again but sat down. He gave a whine and wagged his tail.

"And when we get home you're going back to obedience school for a refresher course."

Dickens leaned on his left foot and pawed the air with his other. He then rested his paw on his nose and hid behind it.

"Look, he's sorry," she whispered with a weak smile.

"Sorry looking."

"Ian."

"Well, a two-year-old kid would take commands better."

"Shows you what you know, hot shot, two-year-olds do not mind well at all."

She watched Ian pace the room and go over to the window. He pulled the drape back slightly and peered out.

"All clear?"

"What?" He looked back at her. "Oh, yeah."

"Ian, why don't you go? Please."

Dickens barked.

She put her fingers to her temple and turned her head to the side and groaned.

"Dickens," Ian scolded.

"See? If I could just get some quiet and allow the pills to work, I'll be better. What else are you going to do? Sit here and watch me sleep."

"Maybe I should go. I wouldn't be long. I'd feel better if Dickens stayed with you but since you're ..."

"Right. No. I'll be fine."

She watched indecisiveness play across his face. He was sweet to worry, but she just didn't think she could take all the commotion.

"You don't answer the door to anyone, got it?"

"I won't even leave the bed."

"I don't like it," he said coming toward the bed. He leaned over and brushed his lips gently against her forehead. "I'm going to write Brian's number by the phone."

"Okay."

He placed the note pad by the phone with Brian's number, grabbed the DO NOT DISTURB sign, and eased the door shut behind him. She heard him try the door to make sure it had caught and locked.

Peace, blissful peace at last. Nothing to worry about but sleep. She would be just fine alone.

Chapter 20

Roark jabbed the end of his cigarette in the old flower pot he'd found in a window sill of the abandoned farm house. He blew the last of the smoke out the side of his mouth and squinted thoughtfully. The wicker on the old ladder-backed chair creaked as he leaned against it and smiled to himself. He was satisfied with his plan. He'd given Basset his orders. The man should be bright enough to follow them. He knew what to do. Failure wasn't an option. If the man valued his wife and brat at all, he'd see to it the job was done right, or else.

Roark drew air through his nostrils and tilted his head back as he weighed the thought that he'd never killed a child before. Would it bother him?

He shrugged his shoulders. *Not really.*

He scraped his chair against the narrow boards on the floor, raised his arms in the air, and stretched while he contemplated his next move. Timing was going to be everything. He looked around the old gate-leg table. He'd have Miss Hewett's sweet little ass tied to one of these chairs by the end of the evening. Mulherin would play the part of the ever-noble agent and come to her rescue. He laughed to himself. "How touching."

Roark slapped his hands together and a resounding *clap* rang through the air. Soon Mulherin would be right where he wanted him, as would the girl, and the pictures. He'd be able to call Grisso tomorrow and tell him the job had been completed. The coast would be clear and the money would be added to his hidden accounts.

The mafia would get what they wanted and he would be free. He made a mental note to purchase several pairs of diamond earrings to spread about to all the women he would line up to love and leave. He'd retire early on the island, soak up the sun and dip his wick in every girl he could find. Not a bad way to live out your life.

Yes, things are really looking up.

There were just a few minor details that he needed to tend to first before his final plan. This was going to be the wrap up to conclude it all.

He reached in eager anticipation for the wires of the explosive device.

Chapter 21

Ian hurried to the Durango and motioned for the dog to jump in. He drove around the parking lot surveying the area. Nothing set off his instincts.

"I don't like leaving her, Dickens." *I don't like it one damned bit.*

He gunned the vehicle out of the parking lot and shot down the street that led to the freeway. Brian's shop was no more than twenty minutes away, give or take a few. He'd go in, grab the pictures, and head back. The quiet and chance to rest would do Nicole good.

The scenery whirred past him in a blur as his mind turned things over. They would need the pictures as evidence, and Nicole would need to testify. He and Trey would see to it that she would be safely placed in protective custody and have around-the-clock protection until the case went to trial. With this being such a big case, the courts would take forever to slap it to the jury. Nicole might have to miss some time teaching in the fall. That wouldn't make her happy, but she'd be alive.

He needed to figure out how to prove Roark's involvement. And quick. Frustration settled over him. He pounded the steering wheel with the palm of his hand. Damn! He and Dan had been so close to nailing the bastard. So close.

Words his father used to say suddenly came to the forefront of his mind, as clear as if the man were in the next seat. "Boy, when you feel you've taken a wrong turn in life, go back to where you last stood."

His eyes narrowed as he glanced over at the passenger seat, half expecting to see his father in the flesh. It was just as empty as his relationship with the old coot. He turned his gaze back to the road.

Just thinking about the old man set Ian's jaw on edge. Nicole didn't understand. There was no way she could. She liked her father. But a good father-son relationship just wasn't in the cards for him.

Go back to where you last stood.

He tapped the steering wheel with his thumb. His mind raced back to the week before the warehouse raid. The week when he and Dan had the file on Cordoza. It held evidence that would take the man down. Roark was the last to have the file. The buck had stopped there. He and Dan both felt that Roark had destroyed the file, but they couldn't prove it. Roark was probably paid quite a hefty sum to aid the drug lords. *Where could he have stashed the money away?*

The traffic clipped along at a pretty good pace. A minivan cut him off and then slowed down. He growled, his fingers curling tighter around the steering wheel. His eyes flew to the rearview mirror as he crammed his foot on the brake. "Come on. Come on."

He hadn't liked the pale, dark shadows under Nicole's eyes. A part of him felt responsible for some of it. He'd not really let her sleep most of the night. After all she'd been through in the last week, she had to be exhausted. He'd had a few headaches before but had no knowledge of migraines. Just sympathy to those who were unfortunate to suffer from them.

As he neared the exit, he signaled and pulled over into the next lane. He was close to his exit. "We are in and out of there, Dickens. We need to get back to Nicole."

Dickens barked and looked back out the passenger window.

Ian wheeled into the first available parking space he found and threw the SUV into park. It sure wasn't as easy as parking the Mustang. When Ian stepped onto the sidewalk leading to Brian's shop, his gait slowed as he approached the storefront. A CLOSED sign hung face out on the door. He turned his wrist out to confirm it was almost ten-thirty. He frowned. *Brian knew I was coming.*

He walked ahead, went to the door, and pulled slightly on the handle so as not to move the cowbell hanging on the hinge of the door. It wasn't locked. Instinct kicked him in the gut. Easing the door open, he covered the bell with his hand, and slipped inside with Dickens. The shop was empty. His eyes ran to a mug sitting by the register. A donut with one bite out of it rested on a napkin.

He pulled his gun out of his waistband and took a careful and deliberate step forward. With a quick motion for Dickens to heel and stay by the front door, Ian treaded carefully across the store.

His eyes locked on the curtain beyond the counter. *The passageway must lead to the back and to storage, no doubt.* Adrenaline pulsed through him.

Making his way around the counter, he strained to hear any noise coming from the back of the shop.

Nothing.

He pushed his way through the curtain and cupped his hand that held the gun. He panned the hallway from side to side, aiming for anything that moved.

The shadowed hallway was still. He quietly made his way down the passage. His footsteps calculated, he zeroed in on a door at the end, ready for the moving target. His heart rate escalated another notch as he padded over the carpet.

He placed his hand on the knob and started to turn it in one slow motion. The door suddenly yanked open and was swung open wide. He jerked his hand back to cradle the gun in his other hand.

"Ian," Brian's voice stormed.

A nanosecond more would've sealed the fate of one of them.

Ian blew out a breath in relief, thankful for not having to know which one. Brian stood in front of him, his gun pointed at Ian's heart.

"Shit," Brian said, lowering his weapon to his side. "That was too close."

Ian had to agree on that one. He wiped his brow with the back of his hand and expelled a breath. "Well, that was fun. What shall we do for the encore?"

"How about a game of show and tell?"

Ian frowned. "What's up?"

Brian stepped aside to allow him entry and waved him into the room. Ian walked into a storage area stacked with boxes all around the room.

Brian pointed to the left, just behind the door. Ian's gaze followed the direction. A dark haired man lay crumpled against the wall in the corner, a bullet hole between his eyebrows, a blank expression frozen on his face. He wore black jeans, a dark T-shirt, and black tennis shoes.

"A friend of yours you could introduce me to?" Brian asked from behind him.

Ian raised an eyebrow and studied the man's face for a long moment. He had angular features and short brown hair. Ian guessed he was somewhere in his mid-forties. He was sure he'd never seen him before.

"No ID?"

"None."

"What went down here, Brian?"

"I came in earlier than usual to work on some layouts. I got set up and came back here for some more supplies. He was waiting there behind the door to welcome me."

"Nice."

"Yeah, tell me about it."

Ian tucked his gun back in his waistband. "I don't know him, he could be an agent. My guess is one of Roark's men, no doubt."

"I'm sure of it."

The adamant tone in Brian's voice made Ian turn and eye the other man. "How so?"

"Because he smelled bad before I killed him."

Ian regarded those words carefully. Brian hadn't gotten to be the top in his field by chance. If it went down like Brian thought it had, it was another agent gone bad, and an even deader end.

"You got Nicole out in the front of the store or in your car?"

"Neither. She's still in bed back at the hotel."

"Oh? Do tell." Brain raised a brow and grinned.

Ian ignored the bait. "She has a migraine. End of story."

"Hmm."

"What is this, hmm?" Ian asked, irritated.

Brian clapped a hand on his shoulder. "Don't be afraid to reach out and grab that one. She's a keeper."

"Sure," he shrugged, trying to look bored with the subject. "For someone else."

"Oh? Why not you?"

"Look, Cupid, put your arrows away," he said, pointing to the dead man. "Don't you think you have better things to do with your time?"

"Oh, but I'd much rather harass your ass."

"Yeah, well, some other time. I came to see a man about some photos."

Brian shrugged his shoulders but let the subject go about Nicole. Ian was glad, too, because he still desperately needed to try to sort out his feelings. The best thing would be for him to detach himself and focus on sorting out this case. Brian led the way back up the hall and into a side room while Ian recanted in detail what had happened to him and Nicole in the park. He motioned to Dickens to come to his side.

"You were both lucky to be alive," Brian answered. He went over to twirl the dial on the wall safe. A click sounded, and then he twisted the handle. He produced a manila envelope and spread the glossy photos out. "With it being in broad daylight, I'd lay odds it was a sniper."

"What makes you say that?"

Brian's face hardened. A distant look took over his expression. A darkness shadowed his eyes. "When you kill a lot, it gives you a rush to do it in the daytime. More of a challenge. You need something to keep you going, to keep you killing."

Ian regarded his friend with sadness. A moment passed. He knew that feeling of having to kill or be killed. Even when you were on the winning side, fighting for justice, it still didn't make it any better. "Brian, you did a lot of good for your country over there."

Brian's eyes wandered back to his, a ghost of a smile spread across his lips. "Thanks for the reminder."

"None of it's easy."

"No. Far from it."

The two men nodded in agreement.

"Ian, these pictures are the real deal. I detected no tampering to them."

"Excellent," Ian said, going with the flow of Brian trying to change the subject. Ian spread the varied glossies across the counter and ran his fingers over them. The largest blow-up showed the faces of all three men clearly. He held up one to study, paying close attention to Mystery Man number three.

"The pictures have authentic dates and times stamped on the backs of them from the camera." Brian said. "Another thing I tested for is to see if the pictures had been altered to where someone might have spliced an old picture in or a picture taken at a different time and altered into the mix."

"And?"

"They're the real deal."

"Good. I wanted the works. A lot hinges on these photos."

"Yeah, you're good to go. I didn't see signs of any altering whatsoever," Brian said.

Ian stared at the larger photo. He was satisfied that the man he and Nicole thought they found a match for in the library clippings was the same guy, Kevin Adams.

"What is it, Ian?"

He pointed at the second man in the photo. "Guess who this man is."

Brian took the picture from his hands and scrutinized it. "Don't believe I know him."

"Meet dead man number two. Kevin Adams," he said.

Brian stared at the photo for a moment and handed it back to him. "I recognize the name. That's who was under Mafia man Nick Grisso."

"Yes."

Ian looked up and caught the expression on Brian's face. "What?"

"I had a run in with Grisso about eight years back. I knifed one of his head snipers before he took down Senator Bronson."

Ian appraised his friend closely. "Grisso's men are the best."

A slow smile spread over Brian's face and he cocked an eyebrow. "There's always somebody better."

"Nice," Ian laughed.

"So, do you know who this third guy is yet?"

Ian shook his head. "No. I don't know him but that doesn't mean I won't find out."

"Let me see if I'm following this correctly. You have the FBI after you, the Mafia, and who does man three represent? And, is he dead or alive?"

"Good questions," Ian said thoughtfully. He rested his hands on the edge of the counter and rolled his neck from side to side. "My guess is, it's probably a bodyguard."

"When's the reunion?"

"Adams and Borland are more than likely staying put in Mexico."

"You know … I've not been to Mexico in close to ten years, maybe more," Brian said, rubbing his chin thoughtfully. He turned and pulled out a couple of bank bags and snapped the wall safe shut.

"Is that right?"

"Yeah," he said going over the cash register and collecting the money from the till. "I think it's about time I got a little parasailing in, don't you?"

Ian smiled. "Maybe get in touch with some old contacts. Cash in a few favors."

"Now you're talking."

"What about Mr. Scarecrow in the back?"

"Hey, did you hear about the mugging in the back alley this morning?" Brian said and winked. "I just happened out there to take the trash and found this guy keeled over with a bullet hole in his forehead."

"No," Ian matched his tone to Brian's.

"Yes. It's the darnedest thing, and no witness, either."

"Pity. And the gun used just happens to be unregistered."

Brian pulled his cell phone out of his back pocket and tossed it over to him. "You take my cell phone so we can stay in contact. I've got another one at home I'll grab."

"Thanks, man." Ian palmed the phone as he caught it in mid-air. "I need to get back to Nicole."

"Understandable. And Ian, don't forget what I said about claiming a little piece of the pie for yourself. I never regretted the precious time I had to love my wife before she had to leave."

Ian merely nodded, unable to think of anything else to say. He wanted to be sensitive to Brian's feelings. His wife had been a beautiful and caring woman. Brian meant well. He just didn't understand the situation. Things were different for him.

"I'm outta here," Ian told him and pocketed the cell phone. He shuffled the pictures back into the manila folder. "I can't thank you enough for these, Brian."

"Don't mention it." Brian walked him to the door. "I'll fly out after I take care of a few things around here and take Cindy to her aunt's house. I'll be in touch."

Ian shook his friend's hand. "Be careful."

"Always. And Ian," Brian said, "be a little reckless with your feelings once in a while."

With that parting shot, Brian chuckled and shut the door in his face.

Be a little reckless with my feelings? Hell, I already did that last night and I don't think I'll ever be the same again. He could still taste her. Even now, he couldn't wait to get back to the hotel and catch another glimpse of her. He was going to have to reel in his feelings or trip over them. *Stay focused, pal.*

He walked past the row of shops on the way to his car with Dickens trotting along at his side. When his attention wandered to the florist's shop, his step slowed. A sign advertising "Friday's Fresh Flowers Today" caught his attention.

Ten minutes later, he laid the half a dozen red roses and baby's stuff, whatever the sales woman had gone on about, on the seat next to him.

Dickens sniffed his way over the seat, his nose leaning toward the flowers. Ian brushed the dog away with his elbow. "Get back. They're not for you. And if you tell anyone about this, you've seen your last bone, understand?"

The dog snorted.

Ian sighed. He'd never bought flowers for a woman before. It was official now. He was in deep.

Nicole frowned and moved her head to the side. Something smelled foul. Her brain throbbed all the way down to the base of her neck. She twitched her nose and her eyes blinked open. The strong bitter smell that had an awakened her grew stronger. She placed her hand over her mouth and coughed. She looked around the room bewildered. The pungent odor robbed her of her breath. She coughed again.

A noise above her to the right caught her attention. A spraying sound. It was then that she noticed a dark mist floating out of the air vent over her bed. She could feel the moisture from the vapor falling on her skin. She coughed harder.

Horrified, she slung the sheet back and tried to sit up. Her body weak, she teetered. She reached back to grab a pillow. Holding it to her nose, she struggled to get her feet out of the tangle of the sheets, and tried to stand. She swayed.

I've got to get out of here!

Her eyes on the door, she took another step and then another. She pressed a hand to her stomach, trying to fight the nausea building in her stomach. Knees threatening to give way, she forced herself to keep moving. Her eyes watered with the burning behind them. She took a few more steps. The room began to spin, the pillow falling to the floor.

Air. I've got to have air.

She pressed her nose into the crook of her arm, coughing, she tried to hurry for the chain on the door. Her eyes blinked furiously with tears as she reached for the door handle. Her vision blurred.

She had to get out.

I can't breathe.

She groped for the handle. Disoriented, she tugged the door open. A figure stood in front of her. She wiped her eyes and blinked furiously.

A tall dark-headed man in a personnel uniform stood beside a covered laundry cart.

"I … help … me," she pleaded, coughing and rasping in the clean air from the hallway.

The man looked up and down the hall. His dark eyes returned to hers.

Fear poured down her spine and instinct rose. She gripped the door with all the strength she had left and tried to slam it shut.

The man rammed the cart into the door and pushed it back, knocking her to the floor.

"No! Please …" she sputtered, her body wracked with coughing.

He swiveled on his heel, shut the door behind him, and ripped the security chain across the slot.

He turned back to the laundry cart, reached in and fished out an air mask and tank.

She tried to scoot away from him. If she could make it to the bathroom, she could lock the door.

His dark features started to blur.

She rolled up on her knees and tried to crawl to the bathroom. Fingers grabbed her hair and yanked her around.

She let out a cry, which ended up in a coughing spell. Pain registered across the back of her skull.

Dazed and coughing, she looked up at him. The man had an air mask over his face now.

She tried to scream again and only coughed harder.

Out of the corner of her eye, she spotted her shoes. She reached out to grab one of them to use to hit him with. His black rubber-soled shoe stomped her arm. She let out a howl of pain and curled away grabbing her hurt wrist with the other hand. Tears welled in her eyes.

"Help! Somebody help me … please," she managed to croak out over the burning in her throat.

Weak, she rested her forehead onto the floor. He kicked her over face up and checked his watch. Air gasped through her lungs. The mixture of pain seared through her stomach combined with the sharp intake of contaminated air created a numbness.

"Please ... no ..." The rest was lost.

Chapter 22

Ian felt like an idiot carrying the roses through the lobby. An older woman passed him on her way to the parking lot pulling out her keys and stopped to eye him with interest. He pretended not to notice her smile and curious glance, opting to look down at Dickens and murmur something instead.

He hoped Nicole's medicine had kicked in and she was feeling better by now. The elevator door dinged, he stepped inside and jabbed the button to their floor. They really needed to travel as soon as she could, now that they had the pictures for proof. He was excited to share what he'd found with her. Taking out his wallet from his back pocket, he fished for the card to open their hotel room door.

Nicole was probably sleeping.

While shuffling down the hall he wrapped Dickens' leash tighter around his hand. He could just see the dog bounding up in the middle of Nicole's bed. The key entry blinked green and he eased the handle down to push the door open quietly. He paused, and feeling a little sheepish, he tucked the roses behind his back. With any luck, she was still resting and he could lay them on the nightstand beside her. No sense in a big production.

The room was dim with the drapes pulled. His eyes took a moment to adjust. The bed lay empty. Sheets were strewn about and a pillow had been thrown on the floor. He frowned and glanced around the room.

"Nicole?"

No answer.

Eyes trained on the bathroom, he headed to the door to knock. It flew open with the force of his knuckles and he rushed inside. "Nicole!"

The room was empty.

He stormed back into the room to hear Dickens' growl. The dog was crouched down and inspecting the floor.

It was then that he noticed a faint bitter smell. The window had been opened. Ian ran to look out. The view of the parking lot offered nothing. He turned and scanned the room. Dickens whimpered and sniffed around the floor still tracking the scent of something. Heart hammering, Ian dropped the roses and ran to the door. He wrenched it open and dashed to the stairs. Taking two at a time, he opened the side door to the lobby and hurried over to the desk.

A dark haired, young Hispanic man glanced up from his paperwork and nodded. "Good morning, sir."

"Did the lady in room two-seventeen call down?"

The desk clerk moved down in front of a computer and pounded out something on the keyboard. He scanned the screen. "No, sir. No calls have come through from your room."

Panic kept Ian from speaking. He turned and tore back up the stairs. He almost barreled over a couple strolling in the hallway in his effort to get to his room. Dodging to the right, he reached for his card to the door. He jammed it in the lock. It flashed red.

"Come on. Come on."

He tried it again. Red. He slid it in and back out dramatically. Green. Smacking the door handle, he rushed into the hotel room. Going over to the bed, he ripped the rest of the covers off of the mattress looking for some sort of clue.

Nothing.

He dropped to the floor to look under the bed for something, anything. The frame was boxed in. He jumped to his feet to go over and inspect the door. A scan showed no signs of forced entry.

He paced the room, running his hand down the base of his neck. *The closet.*

Yanking the doors open, he didn't find clothes hung on the bar. He quickly moved to the drawers. They'd just checked in with a few sets of clothes each. With a hard tug on the last drawer, it dropped out and fell to the floor with a thud. Nicole's new shorts were folded up neatly with her T-shirt underneath them. He grabbed the T-shirt and squeezed the material between his fingers.

Wherever she was, she hadn't changed to go out in search of food or anything. Not in her oversized T-shirt. He rested his forehead on the shirt in his hand. *Had she known whoever was at the door? Why in the hell did she open it?*

They've got her. But who? Roark? The Mafia?

He backed up, sank down on the bed, and stared straight ahead. His gaze fell to the roses lying trampled on the floor where he'd stepped on them in his frantic search of the room for clues.

She was gone. And not of her own free will either.

His chest rose and fell with short quick breaths that did nothing to ease the uncomfortable feeling within.

On autopilot, he pulled out the cell that Brian had given him, glanced down, and punched number two. "Answer. Come on."

He only had Brian's cell phone number, not his home number. He needed back up. The phone dialed but no one picked up. The answering service clicked on. "Brian. They've got her. Call me."

"Damn." He jammed the phone back in his hip pocket. *Surely Brian can't be on a plane yet.*

Dickens sat down at his feet, whined, and pawed at his leg. He hugged the dog's neck. "We'll find her, boy. We have to."

He contemplated his next move.

Nicole could hear herself moaning, but her eyes were too heavy to open. Her head felt even heavier. Her chin was practically resting on her chest and her neck and shoulders hurt all the way down her spine.

The fog in her brain was starting to lift. The memories flooded back. She twisted around.

"No. No …"

She moaned some more as she tried to fight the haze in her head. It was then that she realized her hands were tied behind her. Each movement caused the ropes to cut into her wrists. Her eyes fluttered open as she jerked her head up. The pain in her shoulders ached more than they had with her head bent over in the cramped position. She let her head fall back and tried to stretch her neck. Her muscles knotted. Her neck protested the movement and she groaned. She was tied to a chair. Her ankles were crisscrossed and bound together by rope. A sense of fear and self-preservation started to war with one another in her chest. Her mouth went dry.

There was an old brown and black oval, braided rug at her feet. It looked like rats had been chewing on it.

She swallowed as best she could and tried to remain calm.

Clearing her throat, she tried again to struggle against the ropes. The stinging in her neck and shoulders shifted and shot pain further down her back.

Directly across from her sat an old torn couch with faded stripes. Rotted doilies clung to the arms. Beyond the couch, a cobblestone fireplace with a charred mesh screen in front filled the wall. The dark wooden mantle had broken shards of blue glass scattered across one side from what was probably once a vase. The blackened wall to the left of it showed signs of smoke damage. Discolored fuzzy wallpaper hung in shreds. Cobwebs covered two dirty windows that allowed very little light into the room. A busted staircase with a worn brown carpet runner trailed up the stairs. She spied an oval doorway leading to another part of the main level.

Voices rumbled from the next room beyond the oval doorway. Possibly a kitchen. She strained to hear what they were saying. A man with a smoker's voice was speaking. His tone rose in anger, but she could only make out a few jumbled words. Then it sounded like someone hit something or pounded their fist on a table. A scraping of chair legs followed.

Someone's coming.

Footsteps approached closer and a tall man with thinning hair appeared in the oval doorway. He looked right at her with dark eyes that were much like a wolf's. She shivered and tried to look away. It was as if she couldn't tear her eyes from his. They were unemotional. Void of life. She swallowed. His angular face gave nothing away either. His thin lips curved into a secretive smile that made her blood run cold.

Her stomach clenched.

"Well, look who is wakie."

She glared at him then, hating the sound of his voice that dripped with sarcasm.

"Such fire when you've not a hand free to fan it." His laughed a deep throaty laugh. The kind that was hollow. Dead.

She lifted her chin. The ropes cut into her wrists as she twisted her hands.

"We should call lover boy and let him know you're awake." He winked at her.

Another man, shorter with a bald head, appeared in the doorway. He held a cell phone in his hand and in the smoker's voice said, "Roark, they want to know if you're ready for them to move the truck?"

Nicole closed her eyes as her heart sunk.

Ian splashed his face with cold water and patted it dry. He stood at the sink, praying Nicole was all right as he waited for the call he knew would come. What was taking Roark so long? Surely he wouldn't kill Nicole until he got what he wanted? She was the trump card right now. The perfect carrot to dangle in order to get Ian to turn over the pictures and himself. He had to have time to get to her before—

The hotel phone beside the bed shrilled through his thoughts.

He knew who it would be before he picked up the phone.

He snatched it up. "Hello."

"Missing something?" the coarse voice rasped out, followed by a sickening laugh.

"What have you done with her?"

"Nothing … yet, although, as pretty as she is, I have a few ideas I favor. Want to hear them?"

Ian's grip tightened on the receiver. "If you harm her, Roark, I swear I'll kill you, slowly."

"Aw. Would I do that?"

"You bastard."

"Tsk. Tsk. Is that anyway to speak to your superior."

"Superior, my ass," Ian gritted out.

"No matter. It would appear that I have something you want, and you have something I want."

"Get to the point, Roark."

"I want those damn pictures and all the negatives. You don't know how much trouble and money you've cost me."

"I feel so bad."

"Not like you will if I don't get what I want," Roark warned.

"Let me speak to Nicole."

"As you wish. Oh, honey ..."

A shuffling noise crackled through the line and then, "Ian?"

His heart flat lined at the sound of her voice. "Are you okay?"

"Yes. Ian, forget about me and do whatever you have to do to nail this guy," Nicole pleaded.

"Nicole, I want you to listen to me—"

"Okay, golden boy. Time's up. She's alive. For now. Alert anyone and you're both dead. Her first. I'll be in touch."

The click on the line echoed through Ian's head.

He slammed the receiver back in the cradle. "Dammit!"

When he came face to face with Roark, he was going to kill him with his bare hands.

Nicole gasped as Roark ripped the cell phone away from her ear. He smacked her across the cheek with the back of his other hand. "You whore. All of you women are whores. You're only good for one thing."

Her head snapped to the side. A roaring echoed through her head. Tears gushed from both corners of her eyes. The room drained of color.

Fire spread along the side of her right check and trailed down her neck. She caught her breath and tried to steel herself against the pain. He stood in front of her, clenching and unclenching his fists. Slowly, color returned to her vision but the ringing stayed.

He snatched his hand through her hair and whipped her face back around to look at him. His eyes almost glowing in their fury. "If you ever try something like that again, I'll blow your brains out through your eye socket."

Nicole sobbed and tried to bite back the next wave of tears that threatened to overcome her. She let out a breath and sobbed again. She sunk her top teeth into her bottom lip and tried to concentrate on breathing. Her cheek was bruising, she could feel the blood pooling under her skin.

"Next time I allow you to speak, you'd better do as I say. Got it?"

Nicole nodded numbly and fought the wave of nausea that welled up in her throat.

Roark started to pace the room. His hands were clasped behind his back; he radiated evil with his contorted features.

She watched him with wary eyes. He paced like an angry lion on the prowl for prey.

She caught her breath and chewed on her bottom lip. Just the sound of Ian's voice had made her hungry for his touch. She'd give anything if she could sink into his strong arms again. *Help him to find the answers he needs to put Roark behind bars.*

Roark paused, pulled his cell phone out of his pocket and held down a number.

She wondered how many others there were besides the smoker and Roark. Maybe it was just the two of them. She had to figure a way to try and escape.

"Are you in place?" Roark inquired in a boss-like tone. Listening a minute and glancing her way, he said, "Very good. Make sure you can see the road clearly. No more screw ups."

He snapped the call off, turned on her, and bared his white teeth.

Chapter 23

Ian stood up abruptly from the desk where he'd been staring at the phone, willing it to ring, for the last half hour. Roark had him right where he wanted him. A game of dangling a carrot in front of a starved rabbit. Ian paced the room.

Once.

Twice.

He should be out there finding her. Instead he had to wait for instructions from a maniac. He strode back over to the desk and plucked up the manila folder, the damning evidence that was sending all of them on a downward spiral. Pinching up the clasp, he reached in and whipped out one of the photos. He held it up toward the light from the window.

Evidence that had ruined so many lives.

He frowned.

Stunned for a moment, his fingers tightened on the photo. The only sound in the room was his heart beating in his ears. He hurried over and slapped the picture against the window. His eyes zeroing in on unknown man number three. Something was very familiar about the man that he hadn't noticed before. The thick bushy hair was wrong, the mustache wrong, the funky clothes were all wrong. It wasn't the way the guy looked, but the way he stood. Right foot to the side, hand out in a gesture, and the posture was right.

Could I be so lucky?

Why hadn't he seen it before? He'd wrongly assumed it was someone he hadn't seen before and passed off too easily that it was a bodyguard.

This was it. The proof he'd been looking for. He narrowed his eyes. Even past the disguise, there was no denying the similarity.

Roark.

In that moment Ian knew what he had to do. He swallowed. Resolve settled over him like an acid rain. He shook his head. His eyes closed as his chest rose and fell while he tried to pump oxygen back into his lungs again. There was no way he wanted to go through with what he was thinking. Having a leg lobbed off would be easier. But his mind replayed Nicole's words, "Ian, forget about me and do whatever you have to do to nail this guy."

The hand that held the photo dropped to his side. The picture slapped against his leg. He stared out the window and tried to swallow the lump rising in his throat. He exhaled and his shoulders slumped in resolve. A lot of people's lives had already been destroyed by these three men. *How many more will suffer if they aren't stopped?*

None.

It looked like Nicole was going to get her wish after all.

Nicole's pulse ricocheted as Roark walked toward her, his lecherous eyes trained on her mouth. He curled his index finger under her chin. She jerked her head away.

"My aren't we a prim one now? It's a shame we don't have more time for me to work that out of you. It's even more of a shame that I'm going to have to kill you."

Nicole refused to show reaction, to give in, and let him have the upper hand he so badly wanted to have. Instead, she stared at the braided rug beneath her feet.

Roark turned away and began pacing again.

She fought against the rope. Her fingers working deftly digging the side of her sapphire ring into the coarse fibers, trying to weaken more layers of it. She had frayed a tiny fraction. She focused on trying not to show any movement with her shoulders, leaving it all to her wrist action.

The thought of never seeing Ian again, of not telling him how she felt about him was hard to take. She had to think of a way out of this.

Nicole sawed back and forth at the ropes harder with her ring. Roark turned to look at her. She froze. Careful to keep her eyes averted, she concentrated on displaying a worried look on her face.

Roark stopped his pacing and came to stand in front of her. "How does it feel to kill someone?"

Startled by his question, she looked at him then, despite her resolve not to. Her brows knitted together in confusion.

"Oh, yes. You see, many lives have been lost since you snapped that damned picture," he said, walking over to stand at the window. With one finger, he swept back an old dingy lace curtain and looked out. He stood for a moment assessing the area.

Keeping her eyes on his back, she sawed the ring across the rope a couple of more times. His eyes returned to her, a smirk played across his lips. He dropped his hand, the curtain falling back into place. "And now, Ian is next."

She shook her head and tried to swallow. The air wasn't getting through to her. Her lungs burned and her face throbbed all the more.

"Yes, because of you, he will die," Roark said. "Too bad, really, he's excellent at what he does. He'd rather die for the side he's on, though. He could've been rich."

"You won't get away with this in the end," Nicole told him, as another stroke of her ring rubbed over the rope.

His lips curled into a thin line. "I already have. By this time tomorrow I'll be in another country with two big-busted blondes that just wanna have fun."

"How will you live knowing the authorities could catch up with you at any moment? You'll always be worried, always hiding."

His eyes narrowed on her for a moment and then he threw back his head and laughed. "Are you trying to prick my conscience?"

Nicole stared him down and opted not to answer him.

"Won't work, baby. News flash, I don't have one," he replied, throwing up his hands.

She tried to think of something else to say that would stall for more time.

"You see, doll face, that is where all the money comes in. There are some things it can buy, and I will have more than enough," he said, leaning over to twirl a section of her hair between his fingers. His rank coffee breath fanned in her face.

Repulsed, she turned her head away.

His cell phone went off again. He stared at her with hungry eyes until the third ring. He clicked the call on and listened to the caller.

"Very good." He straightened and backed away. "Is there anyone else in the house besides the woman?"

Nicole watched Roark's face intently trying to figure out what was going on. He was listening, obviously pleased with what the caller had to say. She could almost hear his mind ticking away ready with orders.

"Make sure you tail him, give him time to get away, and then grab the girl," Roark ordered. "I don't care if you kill the woman or bring her, but I must have the child as an insurance policy to make sure Helms does exactly what I want."

Nicole gasped. *Brian's daughter, Cindy. No.*

Roark hung up and turned his eyes on her with a pleased look on his face. "It would appear you're about to have company soon."

"No," Nicole cried, horrified at his words.

"Rumor has it that Helms has dropped off his little darling at the babysitter's house and has a flight out to Mexico of all places. Funny the timing on that, wouldn't you say?"

Nicole just looked at him, her spirits sinking even farther. He really didn't have a conscience.

"Well, no matter, he'll stop in his tracks once he hears I have his stupid kid."

Nicole's stomach churned at the thought of that poor little girl with pigtails she saw in the picture enduring the impending nightmare. Tears burned her eyes.

He laughed, almost to himself as he checked the windows again.

She started to work harder with her ring. Her wrist she was working with was rubbed raw now. She prayed Roark would be needed in the other room for some reason. She'd have to get her hands undone and then her feet. "Do you think I could have something to eat?"

Chapter 24

Ian absently picked up the coffee pot to pour, and frowned. Empty. Had he really drank the whole pot of horrible coffee? He must've lost track while he'd paced the room. It had been almost three hours. Waiting. Roark hadn't called back yet. The bastard was enjoying making him sweat.

His cell vibrated in his back pocket. He snatched it out, checked the screen. *Thank God.* He answered. "Roark has Nicole."

"Shit. When?" Brian asked.

"She was gone from the hotel room when I got back," Ian explained, pacing the room and rubbing at his temple with the other hand. "Where are you?"

"I delivered Cindy to her aunt's house, and I'm about ten minutes from the airport. I'm turning around. What do you need?"

"You. Here. A block from the hotel. Parked and ready to follow out."

"I'm over an hour away from where you are."

"Step on it," Ian ordered. "Roark hasn't called back yet, maybe we've got some time."

"I'm on my way."

"One more thing, I just figured out who the third man is in the photo."

"Elvis?"

"Concerning this case, better than that," Ian said. "Peter Roark."

"That's your last piece of the puzzle."

"I'm ready to put the lid on it."

"Watch your back."

"More importantly, I'm going to watch Nicole's. She's my priority." Ian clicked the phone off and slipped it back in his pocket.

He had ransacked the room for hidden cameras or listening devices and had found none. Walking by the window, he swept the drape aside and looked out again. Nothing had really changed since he'd looked five minutes ago.

He let his forehead fall against the glass and exhaled. Now he knew what a caged animal felt like. Any longer and he was going to lose his mind. He turned away from the window and stared at the bed. Memories of the night before with Nicole in his arms came flooding back.

The sweet way she'd given herself to him. The way she'd comforted him, heated his blood, and made him feel again.

As if in a trance, he walked over to the bed and picked up the pillow from her side. He held it to his chest and inhaled. Wild flowers. He breathed in deep. His fingers dug into the pillow. He had to find a way to get her back. To get her safely out of the sick snares of Roark's world.

Alive.

He tried to swallow over the thick lump in his throat. He'd never gotten a chance to tell her what he felt for her. What she meant to him. He hoped he still had that chance.

A knock sounded at the door.

His fingers released their tautness on the pillow. He took a deep breath and steadied his resolve. This was the moment he'd been dreading. He would rather have had a different option, anything but this one, but it was his only avenue of help. Placing the pillow back on the bed against his, he squared his shoulders.

He had no other choice but to get the door.

Drawing his gun as a precaution, he quietly stalked over to the peephole and peered through. Satisfied the right person had arrived, he shoved the gun in the holster. He set his jaw, ripped the chain across the door, and opened it.

"Pizza," the man with eyes to match his own replied. He stood there with a pizza-warmer bag propped in one hand and rested on his wide shoulder. His manner gave nothing away. If they'd been playing poker, he'd have won.

His father hadn't changed much in the last year. The dark color of his hair hadn't faded, nor had the stern expression on his face.

"Thanks," Ian said, whipping out his wallet and placing a dollar in his father's hand.

Dickens pressed between the two men, sniffed the older one's shoes and legs before snorting.

The deliveryman palmed the money and ripped apart the Velcro to pull out the pizza box. He handed it to Ian, his eyes narrowed, and assessing.

"Got it. Thanks," Ian said.

"Thank you for your order," the man announced before leaning over to pay attention to the dog. He held Dickens by the neck and rubbed his fur. He looked like he was checking the dog's eyes for healthiness much like a vet would. "Fancy dog you got there."

And with that retort, he nodded and turned away to walk down the hall.

That just figures. His father wouldn't pass up a chance to establish their places. Him forever in the role of the colonel and Ian the *boy.*

Ian scowled and motioned for Dickens to move back from the door. The dog complied. Ian kicked the door shut behind him and hurried over to place the pizza box on the desk. He turned back hurriedly and slid the chain across the door. He lifted the lid and inspected the contents. Phone tracing equipment and other tracking devices he'd asked for were all there.

If he could get a trace on where Roark was and get to him there might be a chance to get Nicole out. He set to work on hooking the tracer to the phone.

After several minutes of arranging, things were in place. He sat down on the bed and stared at the phone, willing it to ring.

He set the transmitter up and spoke into it, "Have I made connection?"

His father's voice crackled back, "Yes. Transmitter in place?"

"Yes."

"Very good."

Ian sat connected to his father by wires. The gap between them was just too wide to make any changes. He'd spent years trying to figure his father out and never could. The man was an elusive mirage.

Come on. Dammit. Ring!

"Now that you've got some time on your hands, mind telling me what kind of trouble you got yourself into, boy?"

And there it was. That one word summed up their whole relationship. The boy that would never be a man in the colonel's eyes no matter how hard he tried.

"A witness I had under protection was kidnapped this morning. She's in a lot of danger."

"She?"

"Yeah."

"This woman, she isn't just a client is she?"

Ian paused a moment, his hands stilled on the cord to the head piece. He shrugged. "What else?"

"You're lying," his father's voice accused in a matter of fact tone. "I wonder, to me, or to yourself."

"What the hell is that supposed to mean?"

"Your voice is shaking. I can hear the fear. You care about this woman."

Ian considered saying no, but then that would only be a lie. He did care, too much, and he couldn't deny it. How could this man know him so well when he'd been looking the other way his whole life?

"Let's just stick to the business at hand," he told his father between clenched teeth, drumming his fingers on the desk.

The awkward silence stretched between them. Both sat listening to it, a reflection of their past with one another.

His father broke the barrier first, "Would your mother have approved of her?"

Ian pulled in a deep breath and closed his eyes. He rubbed the back of his thumb across his forehead. "I don't want to talk about Mom, but … yeah, she would've liked her."

"That's all I needed to hear then."

Why now? Why in the middle of all this going on does my father pick this moment to try and do a little father-son bonding time?

He pinched the bridge of his nose and massaged in upward motions. Rolling his neck from side to side, he tried to pop his neck. Release evaded him. He pushed his feet against the carpet and scooted the chair back from the desk. He stood and stretched his arms out and headed over to the coffee pot. A fresh pot of coffee was in order. While he longed for something stronger, coffee would have to do. He needed to keep his wits about him.

A few minutes later, the phone rang. He barely got the coffee pot under the drip before he headed over to snatch up the receiver.

"Hello."

"Tsk. Tsk. Eager, Mulherin?" Roark laughed. "I don't even think it rang."

"What do you want?" Ian asked, knowing full well it was the pictures, but hoped to keep him talking.

"Don't get your boxers in a bunch."

"Let me speak to Nicole."

"Your lover boy misses your sweet nothings. Call to him." Roark's voice sounded away from the phone.

Ian pressed the receiver against his ear and strained to hear her.

"I'm okay." Her voice sounded distant, like she was across the room.

At least she was alive.

For now.

Thank God!

He tried to think of a ploy to keep Roark on the line while the transmitter tried to pick up a location.

"Roark, I swear, if you hurt her—"

"What? You'll put me in time out?"

A click sounded and then the dial tone screamed in his ears.

"Shit." Ian threw the receiver on the bed, retrieved it and smacked it on the cradle twice before getting it hung up.

The phone rang again.

He dove for the phone. "Dammit, Roark—"

Roark's voice barked out orders of a meeting place. Ian pulled the plug on the listening device just before the directions were announced. He'd disconnected his father. The last thing he needed was his father playing Army hero and jumping in the mix.

"And Ian, come alone, or she's dead."

The call ended. Ian grabbed up the photos and raced Dickens to the car. He wheeled out of the parking lot while putting on his seat belt. He checked his mirrors. No sign of his father detected. He punched in Brian's speed-dial number as he scanned the area. Nothing seemed out of the ordinary. Still, he didn't want to risk anything. He wanted to make sure he left his dad in his dust.

"Ian?"

"Yeah. Where are you at?"

"I'm on the road headed your way. I'm roughly about twenty minutes away."

"Good. Here are the directions." Ian related the route Roark had given him. "Do you know anything about the area?"

"Hmm … farm roads … cow pastures … corn fields … an old barn or two, I'm sure … gravel roads," Brian said. "Mostly desolate. A good place for them to be waiting for you."

"That's just great."

"I've made a few calls. Called in some favors. I've got connections lined up, Ian," Brian told him. "I have someone ready for a signal who can be in the air. I also have two cars headed our way as back up. Now that we know the locale we can place them."

Ian flipped his turn signal and slid into the changing lane. His fingers tightened on the phone, his knuckles draining of color. "We have to be careful, Brian … he'll … kill her if—"

"We won't let that happen. My men are good, and that's all I'm at liberty to say. Just know they're some of the best."

"Helluva thing, here I'm an agent and I can't even contact anyone because I don't know who is on the take and who isn't," Ian breathed into the phone.

"We're going to flush them out, pal."

"There'll be no room for error, Brian."

"Give me a few minutes to make the calls and I'll get back with you."

"Thanks, Brian."

Their connection ended. Ian leaned forward and pushed the cell phone into his back pocket. He watched the road signs for his turn off. After checking all the mirrors, he was certain he was still on his own. His dad wouldn't be pleased with him, but what else was new.

He'd made haul-ins for years, there was the adrenaline rush beforehand. He was used it, sometimes even thrived on it. Not this time. This time it was personal.

His jaw bunched. The muscles in his neck protested. His foot pushed down on the accelerator. The pit in the bottom of his stomach got heavier. Everything rode on how this thing would go down. There couldn't be any room for error. He had to work out a plan of action. He noted the changing terrain. The road was swapping out houses for more trees. Signs of civilization stretched fewer and farther between. There was a metal utility building with yard ornaments for sale scattered about on the left behind a rusted chain-link fence. He started seeing firework tents raised just outside the city limits.

His cell phone went off, breaking his train of thought.

He retrieved it from his back pocket and verified the caller in the screen. "Yeah."

"I've got operatives headed our way. They'll be a few minutes getting into place. One of the men said he knew that area pretty well, so there's a trump card for us."

"Tell them to hold back. We can't have a chopper detected."

"Don't worry. He's going to be stationed ten minutes back from the main area in question."

"Okay. Good. What else?"

"After checking, there's a north road beyond where you're to meet. I have someone headed there to set up a road block."

"Brian, I can't thank you enough."

"You've already done it, man. Remember the Mancoza case?"

"Yeah, we go a long way back," Ian said, remembering the man he'd brought down after he'd killed Brian's brother.

"Yeah, we do."

"Brian, these placements know to stay outta sight until they're signaled?"

"Affirmative."

"Keep about fifteen minutes behind me."

"Ian, I don't think you should—"

"I didn't ask you what you thought. He'll kill her if he sees you."

"All right. All right. Your call."

"Thanks, man."

Ian clicked off and set the phone beside him. He had to concentrate on a plan. The traffic thinned with the now two-lane highway. He checked his mirrors. After close to two miles, the hardtop gave way to a gravel road. His Durango came in handy as the road crunched beneath his tires. He slowed to keep the haze of dust at a minimum so he'd have optimal vision. He watched the road signs until the farm road he needed to turn on came up on the right. A black furry mutt ran out to the road to race him down it, barking all the way. Dickens growled at attention in the back seat.

The gravel road became a dirt road as he progressed down the way. Dust kicked up on both sides. The farm road was narrow and overgrown. Old oak trees loomed overhead.

The sun was backing off from the day and setting on the surrounding cow pastures. Up ahead he could make out a black car parked to the side, angled in a corn field.

This was it.

His cell phone rang. Brian's name filled up the screen.

Ian kept the phone on the seat, but put it on speaker. He leaned his elbow on the door and covered his mouth with the back of his hand so as not to be detected talking. "Yeah?"

"Ian, what's your location?"

"I've just turned off the main road and I'm on the dirt farm road now."

"Drive a bit slower, pull over, look a bit lost. That'll give us time to catch up. We hit a traffic jam a few minutes ago which slowed us way down. I'd like to be a little closer."

"No can do. I'm in sight."

"Shit."

"Ditto."

"I'm alerting back up."

"Showtime."

After the click, Ian hung up. His eyes never left the road or the black target in front of him. He traveled along the road at a steady pace. Breath held and heart pounding, he made his way closer and closer to the car. As he approached, his mind raced back over both plans of action, trying to narrow it to one. It had to work. He needed to get Nicole out of there safely.

If it was the last thing he did.

Chapter 25

Ian drew closer to the black car, near enough now that he could make out it was a sedan. He slowed. The windows were tinted too dark to tell how many passengers there might be inside. He guessed Roark sat among them. He reached for his cell phone and thumbed in the license plate numbers and typed "BLK SEDAN." If something happened to him the record would be a clue.

The passenger door swung open and a tall red-headed man with wavy gel-fingered hair emerged. Too much gel, Ian noted as he tossed the cell phone back under the driver's seat. Pretty Boy stood watching him through mirrored sunglasses, held up a hand and signaled him to stop the Durango.

Ian slowed to a halt as two more men threw open the opposing doors of the sedan. They got out and came to stand at the tail of the car and drew their guns. Pretty Boy raised a gun eye level to Ian and mouthed, "Lower the window."

Ian made sure his movements were slow and concise so the dual bulldogs with the guns didn't get excited.

"Now get out nice and slow. Hands up," Pretty Boy ordered.

Ian moved the door farther open and started to swing his legs out.

"Hands up," Pretty Boy said and motioned for the other two to check the car. "Slow movements. Don't try anything heroic."

Ian raised his hands into the air in one even motion.

Dickens growled and tried to peek around Ian.

"He's got that damn dog with him," one of the men said.

"We're supposed to bring the dog back if he showed up," the other said.

"You're kidding right?"

"Hell if I know," the other man argued back. "I just take the orders."

"Call him off," Pretty Boy called out.

"Dickens. Stand down. Stay."

Dickens whined and sat on the seat, watching them.

"Step around to the hood, Mulherin, and put your hands on it," one of the men said and followed him watching every move Ian made.

Ian did as he was told and spread his hands flat on the warm hood. He was on high alert for any signs of Brian or his men.

"Now, legs apart."

Lead man patted him down gruffly, pausing to retrieve Ian's gun, the knife inside his sock, and pulled his wallet.

After the other two did a thorough search of his vehicle, they handed their leader the things they'd confiscated from his car. The manila envelope of pictures and his cell phone.

Ian was puzzled as to why the one man said they had orders to take the dog back. He was careful not to make any eye contact with Dickens. The German Shepherd watched him for signs of orders to attack. While the thought appealed to him, he needed a face-off with Roark and he needed to know where Nicole was.

"Now get back in your car and curl your fingers around the steering wheel and hold them there," Pretty Boy told him.

Ian found that an odd request, but he got back in his car and shut the door, and did what he was asked. He had assumed he'd be put in their car and taken away. There was still no sign of Roark.

Just what are they up to?

He scanned the grove of trees beyond, but detected nothing of Brian or his men. He wondered how close they were.

Out of the corner of his eye he saw a moving van backing out of a thicket of trees. It came to a rolling stop in front of him, leaving about 100 feet of room. The driver flung his door open and leaped down. Ian didn't recognize the blond man. He seemed to be the youngest of the lot. The guy came around to raise the door of the van. Jumping up in the side rear rail, he pulled out car ramps and put them into place on the ground. He then straightened and motioned for Ian to drive up the ramps and into the back of the van.

Ian could literally feel his heart sink along with his hopes.

"Do it," the lead man commanded, waving the gun.

Ian left his car window down purposely, drove up the ramps, and into the back of the truck.

He turned the car off at the same time the door behind him lowered, blocking out what was left of the daylight.

"Damn." He pounded the palm of his hands on the steering wheel and then gripped it tight.

So much for plan A.

The moving van started to roll forward. Ian swayed with the unevenness of the road. His mind went into overdrive.

Brian wouldn't have a chance in hell of finding him now.

Dickens moved beside him and sniffed his neck.

"Somehow we need to figure a way out of this," Ian told him, putting a hand around the dog and rubbing his neck back and forth absently.

Dickens whimpered and then snorted.

"I was afraid you were going to say that. I was counting on you to come up with the way out."

Ian prayed that Brian or one of his men had seen everything go down. He tried to gauge the time spent in the dark for the approximate distance they'd traveled. They bumped down the dirt road a good twenty minutes and veered to the right before coming to a stop.

He heard the motor shut off and then voices. Two car doors slammed somewhere outside. The back gate raised, flooding light into his prison.

Ian motioned for Dickens to get onto the floorboard. "Lie down. Stay."

Dickens obeyed.

Ian hoped to create a diversion and maybe they'd forget about Dickens. The dog was his only trump card at the moment.

"Come out with your hands in the air," a new voice called to him in a New Yorker's accent.

Ian opened his car door and stood, squinting against the light. For some reason this man's voice was familiar but not his long thin face. Ian couldn't place him. He was younger, maybe in his late twenties, and had a New Yorker look to him.

"Go round to the front of the truck," the man said, waving his piece at him. "And if you try anything funny, I get to blow your head off."

Ian hopped to the ground and turned to his left to see a small run-down old farmhouse. Once white paint had faded and peeled off the spindles. Flecks now lay on the rickety porch. A green vine curled around the rails and sprawled over the rusted gutter and onto the roof.

"Go ahead and head over, they're expecting you."

Ian walked toward the house, his hands in the air, his shoes snapping twigs as he stepped. His foot tested the first step to see if it would hold his weight. The creak wasn't reassuring, but neither was the gun jabbed into his back. He made it up the three steps and onto the porch without breaking the wood beneath him. With his hand cupped around the rusty, oval handle on the screen door, he glanced up and caught the reflection in the dusty glass of another shorter figure alongside Mr. New York. That made two men outside. He opened the screen door, the oxidized spring groaning in protest. It took force to push open the warped front door in to enter. He burst through it into the front room of the farmhouse and stood.

His heart slammed against his chest and stopped. His breath hitched. *Nicole!*

She looked up from the ladder-back chair she was tied to. Her beautiful face was stained with tears and bore a purple bruise on her right cheek. Her lips were swollen.

He clenched his fists into the palm of his hands.

"We've been expecting you." Roark stood up from his position on the old torn brown couch.

Ian's full attention was on Nicole. He forced himself not to make any sudden movements and rush to her even though he wanted to so badly. Just to hold her in his arms, tell her she was going to be safe. Instead his eyes searched hers. "Are you okay?"

He made an attempt to step closer to her. A gun cocked behind him, stopping him in his tracks. He raised his hands back up into the air slowly.

Counting Roark, that made a fourth man.

Nicole nodded, but looked past him, over his right shoulder. She was trying to tell him something. The gunman behind him moved around to stand to his left side. Ian swung a glance over to take in the fourth man and assess his size.

His mouth went dry and heat flushed from his neck down to burn the pit of his stomach. "Trey."

"Hello, partner," Trey returned, his voice smooth. An arrogant smile played across his lips.

"I don't believe it," Ian said, his head shaking, his heart accelerating to a fevered pitch.

The look on Trey's face made him sick. His partner. A man he had trusted with his life. A man that now had a gun pointed at his heart. How could he have been so wrong about him?

"What's there not to believe? Hm? That I don't want to continue making pennies for a shit job?" Trey laughed, keeping the gun level to Ian's heart. "Well, guess what, I don't."

"Don't do this," Ian pleaded with him, shaking his head.

The smile dropped from Trey's face. "Too late. I already have."

"He's right, Ian. He's in too thick now," Roark gloated.

Ian turned a hard glare on Roark. "You'll never make it out of this alive."

Roark merely sent him a scathing look and motioned to Trey in an impatient gesture. "Tie him up."

Ian watched the man he thought he knew as his trusted partner pull another chair across from Nicole.

"You make one wrong move," Roark said, cocking his pistol and raising it to press against Nicole's temple, "and it'll be her last."

Ian gritted his teeth and tried to breathe. The betrayal he felt was unbearable. He stared at Trey trying to let it all sink in.

Trey grabbed him by the shoulder. He ushered him across the room and slammed him down into the chair. With Ian's back to the fireplace, he quickly assessed the room. Not much to go on. A braided rug at their feet, no fireplace tools, and an oval opening to another room beyond them. Behind where Roark stood was a broken staircase leading to the upstairs. He wondered if there were any more men around. He hoped to have an opportunity to ask Nicole. He looked at her now and tried to give her a reassuring nod. She looked at him with sad eyes, glanced to Trey, and back at him. He nodded in agreement. Betrayal was a bitter word to swallow.

A rope dropped down over his face, paused at his neck and then fell around his chest with a sharp snap. He grimaced and caught his breath. He was pinned to the ladder-backed chair. Trey wound the rope around his chest and tightened each loop with every trip.

"Some pal you are," Ian bit out through clenched teeth in disgust.

The rope pulled tighter. Then, suddenly, Ian felt the end of the rope being pressed into the palm of his hand and his fingers closed over it tight.

Trey came around and leaned down into his face. "Don't mention it, *pal.*"

Their eyes locked.

Trey winked.

Ian kept his harsh expression frozen on his face, careful not to give away the soaring elation he felt on the inside. *Yes!*

Trey straightened and turned to head over to stand beside Roark. He then turned back and stared at Ian. His expression gave nothing away.

Ian kept the scowl on his face as he looked at both men. How he managed it was a mystery to him. His hope restored in both his partner and the situation, he kept his eyes trained on Roark.

"So, my informants tell me that Brian Helms is your sole crony in this," Roark said casually, as if he was making chit chat over a luncheon. "That will keep this little matter tidy."

Ian gave him a blank look. Let Roark go on. If he could keep the man talking, maybe Brian and his team would have a chance to find them.

He was willing to bet Trey had a back-up system in place as well. At least he hoped to hell he did.

"Well, just so you know, I'm ahead of the game on that, too," Roark said. "A plan is already into effect. I've ordered Helm's little girl to be picked up. Our alternative plan, is if he makes it onto the plane, it's rigged to take a nose dive."

A gasp escaped from Nicole's lips.

Ian's jaw clenched. "More innocent lives, Roark?"

"Ah, well, they've all done something to deserve it at some point," Roark said, laughing at his own joke. "And if—"

"There are no ifs about it. You'll be caught," Ian said.

"Looks like I already have. After you, your bitch, and Helms are gone, I'm home free."

Ian slowly began to unwind the rope.

He was careful to sit stationary and move only his fingers. The process was slow, but the promise was sweet. He was going to wrap his hands around Roark's neck and enjoy choking every ounce of air out of him until he drew his last breath.

He chanced a glance over to Nicole. She sat stiff, rigid, and eyes wide. Her eyes lifted to his. Her face battered and bruised. She was beautiful to him. He managed to work off another loop. He curled it around his index fingers so the excess rope wouldn't drop to the floor. His muscles tensing with the anticipation of overthrowing Roark. He wanted his head on a platter with an apple shoved up his nose.

"Roark, you're working with Mirano's men. Just how long do you think it'll be before the Mafia figures out that your purpose for them is over?"

"Nice try," Roark sneered. "I've got them right where I want them. I've saved their asses so many times they owe me and my next three generations. I'm rich."

"You're delusional. They all suffer from short-term memory. You know that as well as I do. They're not about to let you walk free and roam the earth, even somewhere foreign, with what you know."

Roark regarded him a moment and then turned on his heels and strode back over to the window. "Enough. Valuable time has already been wasted. Trey, pick those pictures up Ross brought in and check and see if the negatives are there."

Roark busied himself pulling back the tattered curtain and checking the front yard again. Trey went over to the beat up coffee table where the other man had tossed the pictures down they'd found in Ian's front seat. Trey glanced over at the back of Roark's head before setting his gun down on the coffee table. His eyes deliberately held Ian's. The meaning was clear.

Ian nodded slightly and looked to see if Nicole caught it. She had. She glanced from the gun to Roark and back to Ian quickly. Relief was dawning in her eyes.

Roark turned to look at Trey. "Are the negatives there?"

Trey held the strips up and smiled. "Affirmative."

"Good to know," Roark said, "If you'd just put them back in ..."

Trey obliged and folded the flap down on the manila envelope.

Roark lifted his gun. Aimed. And fired.

"No!" Ian realized what was going on a nanosecond before the shot rang out.

The warning came too late.

Trey's body jerked. A look of surprise sprang to his face. The envelope slipped from his fingers and dropped to the floor. Trey's hand went to his right temple. Blood seeped through his fingers. He crumpled forward and pitched face down onto the floor.

Nicole's scream brought two men running in the front door with their guns drawn.

Ian looked up from Trey's motionless form to see the gleam in Roark's eyes, a sickening smirk on his face.

"Men, I've got things under control here," Roark addressed the two at the door. "Why don't you guys drive back up to the front road and keep an eye out there, hmm?"

The men looked at the body on the floor and at one another before they retreated. The screen door closed behind them with a smack. Ian watched Trey's body to detect any signs of movement.

Roark laughed. "You recommend it then?"

Ian glared at him. His mind whirled from the situation at hand. Trey shot at that close range wouldn't be good. It was probable he wasn't faking lying there. Roark had just sent the other two away. Ian could see the men out the window loading up the truck and getting ready to pull off.

The odds were soon going to be one on one.

He unwound another loop.

Roark went to stand by Trey's body. He kicked him over with his foot. The right side of Trey's head dripped with blood, the edge of the carpet saturated. His eyes remained closed, his face deathly white.

Ian had to react quickly. He wanted to keep Roark talking so he wouldn't notice Trey's gun on the table. He needed to keep the conversation going to distract him. As soon as the truck roared off, he'd make his move. "You really think you can get away with this?"

"Looks like I already have," Roark rose, his eyes looking directly at him. He twirled the cylinder of his gun. "And I've bullets with both your names on them to ensure it's so."

He walked over to Nicole and rubbed the end of the barrel along her cheek. "Pity, and so pretty, too."

"Leave her alone, Roark," Ian warned, his blood to the boiling point.

"Oh, like you're in any position to make me," Roark said, shrugging his shoulders. "It's just you and me here. I sent the others away, remember? Who are you going to have help you now, Ian?"

Ian stared at him.

"Dan's not here to bail you out this time."

Ian's hands stilled on the rope. "What are you talking about?"

"That's right, smart guy. You've not figured that one out yet, I see. Don't you see it? Dan was in on the whole thing."

Chapter 26

Ian blinked. His mind stalled, unable to process the words spilling out of Roark's foul mouth. Dan. It wasn't possible. This was just another one of Roark's twisted jokes. He and Dan had been more than partners. They'd been friends for many years. He was there for the birth of all three of Dan's sons. Ian found himself shaking his head. It simply wasn't true. "No. This is just another one of your lies, Roark."

"Is it really? You think I'm lying, huh? You just can't admit you were sold out for a price. And by your best friend."

"I'm not falling for your shit."

"You were there that night. Don't you remember?"

Ian's mind flashed back to the night in the warehouse. This time he remembered how it began. Dan had insisted he go in first. Ian followed up. Dan raised his gun and ducked behind the first group of boxes. Immediately after coming in behind Dan he'd felt a gun shoved into his back. He remembered thinking at the time how quick that had gone down. But Dan had made it in safely. There was a lot of yelling, a gun shot fired followed by more shooting. Dan was standing there in front of him. Safe.

Always before, the memory went to him storming into the warehouse and then cut to him holding Dan after he'd been shot. Only now Ian saw what happened in between. The gun was in his back. Dan turns and for the first time, Ian can see his face and how odd his partner's expression appeared to him. A look of horror and whatever else played across his partner's face. Remorse? Yes … that was it. Remorse.

The bitter moment of realization on Dan's part prompted him to act. Ian remembered it all and heard Dan's words clearly this time. "Leave him alone. I was told Ian would be safe."

The gun in his back pressed into him harder and its owner said,

"Well, let me show you how things are *really* going to be."

Ian tried to swallow the pain that welled up in his throat.

Dan dove between him and the gunman.

Ian's eyes shut as he heard the gun go off again. He recalled the look of pain that flashed across Dan's face. He caught Dan as he was going down. He lowered him to the floor and held him while he died. Dan's last words echoed through Ian's mind. "I never meant for it to be this way."

His partner and best friend had betrayed him.

Ian's heart broke for his own loss, but his mind quickly ran to Dan's widow and three young sons. All victims.

He sucked in a deep breath and opened his eyes to see Nicole watching him. Compassion apparent in her eyes. Tears trailing down her cheeks. She'd been right all along. He hadn't killed Dan. She'd believed in him.

The pain in his chest constricted his breathing.

Roark came to stand in front of him, his back to the stairs. "First Dan dies. Now Trey's dead. Both betrayed you. So, who are you going to call on this time to save you, Ian? Your Guardian Angel?"

Ian stared him in the eye. He held him there to try and keep Roark from looking over his shoulder. Ian kept his own eyes from looking to the right, and his expression blank so as to not give anything away.

"If my Guardian Angel were here, I'd yell … *attack!*"

The puzzled look on Roark's face was wiped off as Dickens leaped off the stairs behind him and knocked him to the floor. Roark hit the ground with a thud. The gun clattered on the wood and skittered across the floor to land just under the coffee table.

Ian uncoiled the last of the rope. He threw it off and jumped to his feet. The chair fell backwards and he dove on top of Roark.

Roark lifted himself off the floor with his arms and bucked Ian off his back. He tried to stand.

Ian clasped his hand around Roark's ankle and tugged. Roark fell to the side, slamming into the end table. The old dish on the table fell to the floor and shattered.

Ian grabbed Roark by the shoulders and hooked his head in the crook of his arm with one hand. He banged Roark's head against the floor. Once. Twice.

Roark reached a hand up behind him, jabbed at Ian's face, and tried to flip him.

Both men rolled around on the floor exchanging punches.

Roark socked the right side of Ian's face. Ian gritted against the pain and pinned Roark's arms to the floor. Roark head butted Ian and staggered to his feet.

Dickens snapped at Roark's leg and sunk his teeth into the man's ankle.

Roark howled out in agony and shook his leg. "You damn dog."

Nicole stood up, her hands now free, but feet still tied to the chair. She swung her hips to the right, chair and all, and banged it into Roark, knocking him to the floor.

Out of one corner of his eye Ian caught sight of a figure darting out of the kitchen. He poised his hands, ready to throw a punch.

It was his father.

Without taking the time to figure that one out, Ian grabbed Roark's arm to roll him over, facedown. "Who are *you* going to call, Roark, to save your worthless hide? You sent your thugs packing."

"I'll—"

Ian smacked the man's face on the floor again. He tried to tie the man's arm behind him. Roark bucked Ian hard until he was able to throw him off. Roark rolled across the floor and jumped up.

Ian shook his head to clear it. Roark was coming at him again. Ian stole a quick glance over to see his dad cutting Nicole loose from the chair.

He reared back and threw a punch across Roark's jaw line. Ian jerked his wrist back and slung his hand to try and ease the sting. His knuckles burned. The pain was well worth it to see blood spurt from the side of Roark's head.

"Things are just getting good," Ian taunted.

Ian ducked as Roark swung at him. He came up swinging again.

Aware that his father had his arm around Nicole and was hurrying her out the front, his mind ran to the gun Trey had left on the coffee table.

Ian went for the revolver. Roark hurled a shoe at Ian's hand. They both lunged for the gun at the same time. Ian fell to the side.

Roark grunted and grabbed the gun. Ian's hand encircled Roark's wrist, his fingers biting into the older man's flesh. Dickens' teeth sunk into Roark's butt. The man yowled with pain. The gun, pointed at the ceiling, went off. Plaster crumbled to the floor. Ian blinked and sputtered as his eyes felt the particles floating in the air. Ian advanced before Roark had time to aim. Roark slammed the gun against the side of Ian's head. Pain shot across his forehead. The room blurred. He kicked Roark in the stomach. Roark clutched his abdomen and doubled over. Ian dragged a ragged breath into his lungs. The room was still spinning and everything was gray to black. He leaned against the chair for strength and tried to breathe again.

Roark crawled through the doorway onto the kitchen floor. Ian jerked his head up, determined. He tried to focus. His head roared like thunder, his temple throbbed.

He leaned over, pushed up, and swayed to his feet. He followed down the hallway staggering from side to side catching himself against the wall for support with his hands.

The hall opened into a room full of kitchen cabinets partially hidden behind an array of cardboard boxes. It was impossible to see Roark. Where was he?

A movement to Ian's left got his attention. He could see the side of Roark's head but couldn't make out what he was fumbling with. Seeing Ian, Roark moved, darting to the nearest stack of boxes.

Ian hit the floor behind an old trundle cabinet as bullets rained over his head.

Roark turned and fled, the back screen door sounded with a creaking slap.

Ian bolted after him.

He made it out the door in time to see Roark running across the yard. Ian closed in on him. Roark turned halfway and tried to aim the gun. The movement slowed him down.

Ian caught up to him, clapped a hand on his shoulder, and forced him around to face him.

"This is for Nicole." He pelted a blow across Roark's face, his knuckles ramming into his nose. Blood gushed in every direction. Roark returned the punch. Ian's lip busted open as he stumbled to the side.

Roark staggered and ran.

Dickens shot past the both of them and circled in front of Roark.

Roark aimed the gun at Dickens.

Ian jumped on top of him, pinning him to the ground. He held the gun to Roark's temple.

"And this … is for Dan … and Trey," he gritted out, his chest heaving from all the fighting.

He cocked the pistol.

For a long minute, he hovered there. His heart pulsated in his ears. He wrestled with the urge to settle a score and the need to do what was right. He rather enjoyed the fear in Roark's eyes.

"Your blood isn't worth it." He moved his hand an inch to the right and fired the gun into the ground.

The whirring of sirens and the screech of police cars racing to a stop broke through the night.

Ian backed off and stood. Chest cramping and lungs burning, he wiped his mouth with the back of his hand. He kept his gun trained on Roark's battered body until the first officer approached with his gun drawn. Ian watched as two officers ran up on the scene and hauled Roark up to a standing position and cuffed him.

Ian then turned to the newcomers. "I'm Agent Mulherin. A plane leaving the airport later this evening, destination Mexico. It was to have a Brian Helms on it. Peter Roark ordered a bomb to stop it."

"I'm on it," an officer called as he whipped out his phone and ran ahead to his squad car.

"Is there an ambulance on its way?" Ian called.

"Yes, sir," another officer replied. "One has already been dispatched."

"We've an agent down in the house from the result of a head wound."

Ian cut a glance to Nicole. His father had been holding her back. She broke away and ran to him. They both turned to head toward the house.

They cut across the yard running for the front door. After they'd only made it a few feet, a fierce boom shook the ground hard. The next thing Ian knew, he was lying flat on his back on the ground with Nicole a few feet from him. A loud explosion popped in his ears like a million fire-crackers set off at once. A blinding flash went off and then mushroomed through the air. Its fire lit the night's sky, obliterating the stars. From somewhere behind, he heard cries of confusion as people scattered like picnic ants.

He tried to catch his breath into his chest as realization sunk in. The sky rained debris from the house. His eyes stung. The first air he drug back into his lungs burned with heat.

"No," he cried as he pushed himself up to a sitting position. He inhaled again and coughed as he stood. "Nicole, are you all right?"

"I'm o-okay."

Satisfied with her answer and seeing she was getting up on her own, he covered his nose and mouth with his arm. "Stay here, Nicole."

He headed for the other side of the house from where the flames were leaping to try and gain access that way.

"Ian, no, come back. It's too dangerous!"

Nicole's words reached him but he wasn't stopping. He was going to pull Trey out, or else. One buddy didn't leave another to die.

Greedy flames engulfed the old farmhouse and trailed a line of fire over to a large elm tree to the right of the porch. The fire blazed through the vine adorning the roof. Ian swallowed as he tried not to think the worst. His mind ran back to the scene where he'd run into the kitchen and had seen Roark back behind a cabinet. At the time he hadn't known what the man was doing. He'd guessed he was reloading a gun. Roark must have had a bomb on location.

Hands fell on his shoulder and pulled him around. He came face to face with his father, breathing hard, face flushed. "I can't let you do this, son."

The two men stood eye to eye glaring at one another.

"You can't stop me." Ian's chest heaved with limited oxygen. He tried to throw his father's hands off of him. "Get out of my way."

"Ian, you can't go in there," his father pleaded. "Nicole's right, it's too dangerous."

Ian dodged his dad. "The hell I can't."

"Ian, please." Nicole's voice cut through to him as she dashed up.

He shook his head when he turned and saw her tear-streaked face. "I have to try."

"Ian … the house is bad. It's almost gone. There could easily be more explosions," she sobbed.

Ian turned to look at the house as the front porch crumpled inward and fell to the ground, the roof completely engulfed in flames now.

"I'm sorry. I'm so sorry, Ian."

He felt her hand on his arm. Her soothing words were trying to penetrate the part of his brain that was fighting the truth.

Trey didn't deserve to die.

Ian couldn't hear any more. There was no way he could accept the fact that Trey was dead. He turned to run to a side window of the house. Maybe he could break it and slip in. Ambulance sirens grew louder. Time was wasting.

"I have to try, dammit." Ian began to move across the yard, his destination his only focus.

He barely took a few of steps before another explosion, smaller this time, shattered through the night. Ian turned to wrap his arms around Nicole and shield her from the fall out.

Nicole flung her arms around him and held tight.

His heart plummeted as he was forced to let go of hope. It was over. He had failed his partner. He buried his face in Nicole's soft hair and took a deep breath.

Ian pulled away from Nicole and grabbed her arms. "Are you okay?" He cupped the side of her face gently where she was bruised. She was so beautiful.

She merely nodded and hugged his waist.

They stood there together, helpless against the fire, watching the blaze engulf the remainder of the house.

The sadness that washed over him was almost too overwhelming. Trey had died saving him and Nicole. All the emotion of the night with Dan, and now Trey, pressed in on him. Two men. Two very good friends. Two lives wasted. He hugged Nicole tighter and kissed the top of her head.

"I'm sorry, son, about your partner."

Ian glanced over his shoulder as his father walked up behind them. He nodded at his dad and swallowed. "He was trying to save us ..."

"He kept trying to get word out to the right people that Peter Roark had ordered the plane down," Nicole offered, wiping the back of her hand across her eyes.

"He was a good man," Ian said, his eyes stinging from the fire and something more.

"I knew you couldn't have killed Dan," Nicole said quietly.

Ian hung his head. "No, he killed himself. His family doesn't need to know. It will kill Leslie. She needs to go on believing he died in honor. She has three young boys to raise alone. I can't stand the thought of them finding out."

Nicole nodded and then turned to the older man. "I want to thank you for helping me get out of there."

"You're very welcome," the colonel said.

"Nicole, this is my father, Colonel Aiden Mulherin."

Nicole's startled glance ran between the two men. Ian watched as his father's grim expression softened.

"I'm just glad you're safe. My son was going out of his mind with worry."

"There's something I don't have pieced together yet. How were you able to get a location on me?" Ian asked his father.

"When I leaned down to pet your dog, I put a track on his collar."

Stunned, Ian was both impressed and grateful. "Thank you."

His dad smiled and nodded.

For a moment, something passed between them.

Ian's attention turned back to the fire as a crackle popped and part of the porch caved in. He stared at the blaze as the grief he felt caught in his chest. "Trey wasn't on the take. He didn't really tie me up."

"I know," Nicole's calming voice spoke to him. She placed her hand on his chest near his heart. "He stopped Roark from hitting me again. He even ordered the men to bring Dickens to the house if he was with you."

Ian grabbed her wrist. He didn't hear any more. Realization sliced through his mind. Alarms went off in his head.

"Dickens!" He cupped his hands to his mouth and shouted, turning all around to survey the perimeter of the yard.

"Oh, Ian, no," Nicole cried. "Dickens."

All three of them began calling for the dog.

Chapter 27

Ian and his dad spread out and alerted everyone in the area the German Shepherd was missing. Ian inserted two fingers into his mouth and whistled as hard and loud as he could. The blazing roar of the fire competed with his calls. He put his hands to his mouth and yelled, "Dickens!"

No answer came.

"Dickens!" Ian shouted again. He could hear the echoes of others calling the dog's name. The woods behind the house were still close enough that the German Shepherd should be able to hear him and come, but thought he'd check it out anyway. *Where the hell could the dog have gone?*

His dad parted through the throng of onlookers and asked, "Any luck?"

"No. I'm going to take this side. Dad you take that whole area. I may head back into the woods a bit."

They fanned out, calling for the dog.

Ian whistled again. He tried to recall the last time he'd even seen Dickens. He remembered the dog biting at Roark's heels, and then he seemed to just disappear. That meant the dog was out of the house before the bomb went off, unless ….

He and his father had circled the entire yard. Ian heard Nicole calling for Dickens. The dog should've responded by now. He saw his father heading in his direction. The colonel wiped his brow with one hand and breathed by holding his shirt tail up to his face. The smoke was swirling thick through the night's air.

"I'm sorry, but there's just no sign of your dog."

Ian nodded at his father. Resolve burned its way through to his brain. Dickens adored Trey. The dog would've gone back into the house to get to him.

The emotion of the evening's events came to rest its weight on Ian's shoulders. A tightness expanded across his chest. So much loss. His eyes wandered back to the fire and his eyes fell shut. He placed his hands on his hips and bent over to try and take in a deep breath. When he straightened, he saw the officers put Roark into the back of a squad car and slam the door.

"May you rot in the eyes of your inmates," Ian muttered under his breath. When the fellow prisoners found out Peter Roark was FBI, they'd make his life hell. Ian relaxed a fraction at that thought. *Justice comes in many forms. Irony even serves its purpose.*

"Agent Mulherin?" a policeman said, breaking into his thoughts.

Ian, on autopilot, nodded as he watched the house burn as if the blaze had him hypnotized.

"We have a total of four men we've rounded up and cuffed. Is there anyone else that you know of that we need to be on the lookout for here?"

"Not that I'm aware of."

"We also were able to stop the plane from taking off."

"Very good. Did you—" Ian stopped speaking. A dog's faint bark sounded from the woods behind the house. Elation lifted Ian's heart. He cupped his mouth and yelled, "Dickens."

More barking broke out, only closer this time. Through the haze of smoke Dickens bounded out of the thicket of trees.

"Here, boy. Come on, Dickens." Ian slapped his knees and crouched down. Nicole came running over to stand by him.

A few gasps followed as people gathered around Ian. He motioned again for the dog to come to him.

Dickens didn't advance toward them but stopped to bark and paw at the ground. He then turned and dashed back into the woods.

Ian raised his hands to cup his mouth and command the dog to come back, but stopped halfway. Hope rushed adrenaline to his heart. His hands dropped to his sides. *Could it be?*

"Trey."

Ian broke into a run across the yard. His legs could barely carry him fast enough. Others followed suit behind him. Ian met Dickens on the dog's third trip out. "Show me, boy. Show me."

Ian strained to see through the darkness as he crunched over the brush, trampling the growth beneath his shoes. He held his arm up to shield his face from the lower branches of the trees smacking him. He could make out Dickens turning circles up ahead as he barked. The dog announced his prize.

He heard his father call out behind him and ask if an ambulance could be pulled down to the edge of the woods and shine their headlights into the area.

Somebody came up on the right of Ian's shoulder and scanned the ground with a flashlight. Dickens was straight ahead of him and still barking. The moon cast shadows enough that Ian could peer through the brush and make out the outline of a body lying on its side. He swallowed and prayed it wasn't too late for Trey.

"Good boy. Good boy." Ian fell to his knees on the ground beside his partner's body. He reached out to touch his shoulder. "Trey?"

Careful not to move Trey's injured body, Ian eased his hand down his partner's arm until he came in contact with his wrist to check for a pulse.

Trey moaned and rolled onto his back.

He's alive.

"Trey, I'm here. It's going to be okay, pal."

Someone behind Ian yelled, "That dog's in here with a body."

"We need a stretcher brought in here now," Ian called over his shoulder. His partner's pulse barely throbbed beneath his touch. He prayed they'd have enough time to get him to the hospital. The officer knelt beside Ian and scanned the flashlight over Trey, mixing with the moonlight seeping through the leaves of the trees. It was still hard to assess the extent of the injuries.

"We'll get the paramedics," another police officer called out and took off running.

"Trey? Can you hear me? Help is on the way," Ian breathed, releasing some of the tension. Worry had him coiled pretty tight.

Trey coughed, sputtered, and then tried to raise his head. "Dickens …
drug me … away … he …"

"It's okay. Don't talk. Save your energy. We've got you now. The paramedics are coming with the stretcher. Just hang on, pal. You're going
to be fine." Ian cradled Trey's head, he wanted Trey to move as little as
possible.

Trey's face was covered in soot and blood trickled from his right temple. Ian picked a leaf from Trey's matted hair. Ian could tell that the side
of Trey's face was burnt and the dark shadow mixed with angry flesh
trailed down past the collar of his neck. The stench of burnt flesh filled
his nostrils. Ian swallowed. He turned his face upward and refused to
show the emotion that made his eyes sting.

Trey's body jerked and his eyes fluttered open. "Nicole?"

"She's fine. Nicole's just fine. Thanks to you."

Trey's hand dropped back onto his chest and his body relaxed a bit as
he tried to swallow. "Guess you owe me … a steak … dinner."

Ian couldn't help but laugh. It was so like Trey. He took comfort in the
fact his buddy still had his sense of humor working for him. "You're on."

"I … just … hope …" Trey coughed and winced with pain, "I'm
around to eat it."

"Easy. Quit trying to sit up." Ian sobered. Trey had been given another
chance in life. Ian couldn't lose him now. "You will be. Just concentrate
on all the women you haven't kissed yet."

"Well … there is … that." Trey's voice trailed off as he passed out.

Ian glanced up through trees to the sky and thanked God for a new
hope.

The headlights from the police cars flooded the woods. He looked
back down at Trey. He couldn't tell how much of the face was burnt and
how much was soot. Ian tried to calm himself. At least Trey was breathing. He was alive. They'd worry about the rest tomorrow.

Leaves crunched and footsteps pounded closer as two paramedics barreled through the brush and lowered the stretcher on the ground beside

Trey. Ian squeezed his hand, stood, and backed away so the two men could do their job. One checked his pulse while the other one slipped an oxygen mask over his head. They prepped him for the stretcher ride.

Ian watched all the commotion feeling helpless.

Nicole caught up to him, took hold of his arm, and breathing hard asked, "Is he—"

"Alive. He's alive." He turned to wrap his arms around her.

"Oh, thank God."

They hugged one another close as the paramedics loaded Trey carefully onto the stretcher. The two men worked their way back through the brush, an officer leading the way with his flashlight, and carted him across the lawn.

"Man," one of the policemen said pointing at the German Shepherd, "that sure is one helluva dog."

"Yeah. Yeah, he is." Ian leaned down and hugged Dickens' neck, stroked his fur, and then looked up and met his father's eyes. "He's a damn dickens of a dog."

Nicole laughed as she wiped tears from her eyes.

A slow smile spread across the colonel's face. "That he is, son. He's the best hunting dog around."

Ian stood up then and studied his father for a long moment. There were things he saw for the first time. He held out his hand.

His father looked down at his outstretched hand for a second, blinked, and then accepted it in his own. One pump of a shake and they were both thumping one another on the back and exchanging hugs.

"Thanks, Dad." Ian cleared his throat.

Something passed between the two men that hadn't been there before.

The ambulance turned on its siren announcing its departure.

Ian cleared his throat again and turned to take Nicole by the elbow. "We'd better follow them to the hospital."

The three of them trudged across the yard back to where his dad's SUV was parked.

The farmhouse had caved in the middle in a heap of flames. The fire department was hosing down the scene and outlying areas to keep the flames confined.

"Agent Mulherin?" a policeman called after him.

Ian turned to see a police officer coming up to them holding a phone in his hand. "Yes?"

"You have a phone call on this cell we found on one of Roark's men." The officer handed Ian Brian's cell phone. "Hello?"

"Well, thank God you're still alive for me to ball you out. I was worried I wouldn't get the chance." Brian's voice crackled through the airwaves. "You changed the game on me in midstream and didn't bother to tell me. So, did our side win?"

Ian snorted. "Yes, Mr. Cavalry."

"Hey, you failed to mention we were playing hide and seek instead of cops and robbers."

"Roark had me drive into the back of a truck and carted me off somewhere."

"So, that's it. When we came down the road it had been newly graded. That's how we missed you."

"Figures. He thought of everything except he forgot that good always prevails over evil."

"I'm just glad you still have your hide, even as sorry looking as it is."

"Yeah. Me too. Is Cindy Lou Who all right?" Ian asked worriedly. Nicole's hand tightened on his arm.

"She's fine. My sister kick-chopped two men trying to break into her house."

Ian nodded and smiled at Nicole. A look of relief washed over her face as she hugged him to her.

"Some sister," Ian laughed. He made a mental note he'd have to meet her in the future.

"I taught her everything she knows."

"Riiight."

"So how did you get your ass rescued? Come on, tell the truth. Nicole save the day?"

"Funny. I'll buy you a beer and explain it all soon."

"Make it a pitcher and you've got a deal."

Ian's tone turned serious. "Roark shot Trey."

"Shit. Man, I'm sorry. How bad is he?"

Ian climbed into the back seat of his dad's car with Nicole and wearily pulled the door shut. "Bad. We're in route now to the hospital. Roark had a bomb in place. There was an explosion and … well, Trey may be burnt pretty badly, too. We don't know all the details yet."

"Rough break. I hate to hear that. I've always liked him. I know how Trey is. He's quite the ladies' man. He won't do well with it if it's bad," Brian said. "Is there anything I can do?"

His dad drove fast to try and catch up with the ambulance. The siren was still on. "The pictures burned up in the fire."

"Ah, that would be set number one of two. I told you I was good at what I do. They don't call me a professional photographer for nothin'."

"Love ya, man."

"They all say that, Ian. Come up with something new."

Ian laughed then. He covered his mouth and coughed. The smoke in his lungs still burned. "Are you still headed to Mexico?"

"Well, I'd still like to be a part of the action. My contacts are in place and have already got leads on the whereabouts of dead man number one."

"Excellent," Ian replied. "I won't be reporting in any time soon to my superiors. With all this going down about Roark, things will be in an uproar at headquarters before I'm briefed. You'll have a day or two lead on it."

"Works for me. I'll keep you posted and do what I can until you've had time to debrief all those higher up than you in the nosebleed section of the FBI."

Ian smiled. "You're all heart, man."

He flipped the phone shut with the side of his face as he and Brian ended the call. He tightened his arm around Nicole. The night had been almost too much to take in. She was in his arms. Safe. He held her close.

Dickens was sitting up front riding shot gun with his father.

Ian flexed his knuckles on his right hand. They hurt like no other, but he sure had a lot to be thankful for. He peered ahead at the light on in the ambulance. They had to be working on Trey now. He wondered what they were doing. He felt powerless to do anything. His eyes closed and he breathed up a prayer that Trey would make it. He just had to.

Chapter 28

The hospital waiting room was packed. People sat curled up in chairs reading while others crashed, trying to sleep through their worry. Staring at four walls while your loved one was being treated wasn't easy. Ian and his dad took turns pacing the floor and drinking old coffee the consistency of tar. Ian didn't know who looked worse all covered in soot between he and his dad.

Nicole was still back in the examining room. Ian had been checked over first and dismissed. Cuts, multiple bruises, and a split lip were all he suffered, nothing compared to Trey's injuries. They had whisked him to the burn unit and then on to surgery.

His partner had been on the operating table for almost three hours now. No one had come out in that time to offer them an update. When Ian checked at the desk, all they told him was that surgery was still in progress and someone would let them know soon. Their definition of soon clearly wasn't the same as his.

They had dropped Dickens off at an emergency animal clinic where he had checked out fine. When they last saw him, the staff had him undergoing the poodle treatment. He would come out smelling better.

"I wonder what's taking them so long with Nicole?" he asked his dad seated next to him.

"She'll be fine, son. The hospital staff is swamped with emergencies tonight."

"I hope that's all it is." Ian didn't want to think about the possibility of anything worse. He stood up to stretch. One look at the coffee pot made him grimace. He wadded his empty paper cup up in his fist, tossed it into the trashcan across the room and sat down. Bone tired, his mind still hadn't computed what all he'd found out about Dan.

"I ... Dad, I wanted to thank you for all you did ... you know, tonight," Ian said, glancing over at his father.

"I was glad I could help. I've not really been the best father to you. The father that you should have had. Needed." His dad blew out his cheeks and stood.

"It's okay." Ian realized he himself was a workaholic. And that Nicole had been right. He and his dad had a lot in common. A lot more than he'd ever thought possible. He'd never seen it before tonight.

"No. No it isn't okay. I was away so much of your childhood. I'd come home from wherever I'd been stationed and only knew one way to run things," the colonel told him as he placed his hands into his pockets and jingled his change in a nervous gesture. "I must have seemed hard on you. I saved a lot of lives, but lost my family in the process."

His father looked at him with such a strained expression. Vulnerable. Ian had never seen this side of his father before. He cleared his throat to try and loosen the tightness setting in. "Look … Dad … what do you say we just try and start from today forward and not look back? Deal?"

The look on his father's face relaxed into a smile and he nodded. "Deal."

"About Nicole, when she comes in, why don't you take her back to the hotel and she can rest better?" his dad offered. "I'll stay here and call you when they come out with news about your friend. He'll be in recovery for a good while."

"Thanks, but …" Ian paused trying to get his emotions in check. "Trey didn't look too good. He'd lost a lot of blood. His face … well, you'd have to know Trey."

"I saw him through the window back at the farmhouse. Pretty boy."

Ian chuckled then and shook his head. His dad didn't know the half of it. "Quite the ladies' man. I'm afraid … if he … lives … he'll wish he hadn't." Ian ran both hands through his hair and sighed. "I want to be here for him."

"Understandable. I'll take Nicole back to the hotel and sit with her if that will help."

"Thanks, Dad." Ian meant it, too. His dad had been his saving grace.

Who knew things would turn out like this? Too bad his mother hadn't lived to see it. "I'll offer that to Nicole. She needs rest. I somehow doubt she'll go, though. She has quite the mind of her own."

His dad chuckled and his eyes twinkled. "So I noticed. Good for you."

Yeah, good for him. She was good for him. He nodded and returned the smile. *What was taking them so long with Nicole?*

He stood up and paced another loop around the waiting room.

"Ian, have you told Nicole how you feel about her?"

He stopped pacing and dropped back into the chair beside his dad. "She knows I care for her."

"And the translation to that would be that you've not really told her in words."

It was Ian's turn to whoosh air out his cheeks as he leaned forward and put his elbows on his knees. He clasped his hands together and nodded. "Something like that."

"You can't leave something like that too long. Women need to hear those things."

The door opened. Nicole walked in, eyes roving over the room, and when she saw him the apprehension on her face subsided. She wore a bandage on her forehead and a smaller one on her cheek. She smiled up weakly at him, her face pale. "How are you?"

"I'm fine. What about you?"

"I'll live long enough to make you pay for scaring me half to death."

Ian caught her hand, drew her fingers to his lips and kissed them. He wrapped his arms around her. He was determined nothing bad would ever happen to her again. Not on his watch.

"Any word on Trey?" she asked against his chest.

"No. No, not yet." He sighed.

"I'm sorry about Dan." Nicole pulled back to look at him and slipped her hand into his.

He squeezed her fingers. "Me too. I just can't understand it."

"Roark was trying to get rid of you that night in the warehouse."

"Yeah, Roark was trying to frame me. Dan was ..."

She put her fingers over his lips. "Trying to do the right thing in the end."

Ian rested his forehead against hers. She was right. Dan had been a good man, but had let greed get in the way. In the end, their friendship still stood strong. He'd made up his mind to dwell on the good memories, of the good Dan.

All three of them sat down in the line of chairs to wait out the surgery together. Nicole threw off the idea of going back to the hotel to rest. Ian felt selfish because he knew she was tired, but he was glad to have her alongside him when the doctor came out.

The door to the waiting room opened and a slim beauty with raven-colored hair floated in, a worried look on her face. She scanned the room eagerly, her green eyes coming to rest on him.

He swallowed and stood. He wasn't sure he was ready for this. Leslie, Dan's widow advanced toward him.

"Ian. Brian called me. I heard the call-in on the scanner. I had to come. Are you all right?"

He took the hand she offered and smiled. "I'm fine."

"And Trey Bollinger? What of him? The report said he'd been shot. Is he—"

"He's in surgery. We're waiting."

"Oh, I hope it's good news." Leslie glanced at the other soot-covered people sitting with him.

"Leslie, this is Nicole Hewett and my father, Aiden Mulherin."

The colonel stood and shook her hand. Nicole smiled and stood as well.

"Mr. Mulherin. Nicole." Leslie nodded.

"And this is Dan's …" Ian paused, he couldn't bring himself to say "wife" or "widow".

"Ian, it's all right," Leslie said, and then turned her attention back to the others. "Dan was my husband."

Compassion immediately filled Nicole's face, and she grabbed Leslie and hugged her tight. "I'm so sorry for your loss."

The two women held one another for a moment, and then Leslie straightened. "Thank you. Thank you so much."

"I've heard so many wonderful things about Dan," Nicole said.

Leslie pulled a tissue out of her jacket pocket and dabbed at her eyes. "Thank you."

Ian put up an arm around Leslie's shoulders. "He died trying to save my life. He was a good man, Leslie. I want you to be proud of him. The boys need to know what a wonderful man their father was."

Leslie smiled at the same time tears flowed down her face. She mouthed *thank you*, and Nicole hugged her again.

At that moment, a man dressed in green scrubs walked into the waiting room. It was the surgeon who had spoken to them before they'd taken Trey back to surgery.

Ian's dad squeezed his shoulder. The surgeon walked up to them and nodded.

"Mr. Bollinger made it through surgery. We were able to remove the bullet. He's a lucky man. Another inch to the left and we wouldn't be having this conversation."

Ian nodded. "Yes."

"He's lost a lot of blood and he's pretty weak. The next twenty-four to forty-eight hours will determine a lot. If there are no other complications he'll be in the clear. He's young and healthy."

"Thank you," Ian shook his hand, relief soaring through his system.

The surgeon hesitated and looked over his glasses. "The burns were pretty significant. The right side of his face is in bandages. There's a question of possible hearing loss in that ear. Only time will tell how well he'll heal and what amount of scaring there will be."

Nicole lifted a hand to her mouth and shook her head silently.

Ian had realized that much. He took a deep breath. Trey was in for a long haul. No matter. Ian was prepared to be right behind him kicking his butt all the way. "Thank you, doctor."

"He's headed to recovery now and will be there awhile. They'll call you back when he's set up."

"Thank you."

The doctor nodded and left.

The three of them looked at one another. The first of it was over. Ian could tell his adrenaline was ebbing. He knew he was wrung out. The thought of sleeping for a week sounded pretty damn good. He couldn't wait to get a shower.

"Do you think Trey will be ... all right with things?" Nicole asked quietly, clearing her throat.

"I'll see to it that he has no choice but to be," Ian told her, and claimed her hand in his. He was going to help Trey over this hurdle no matter how long it took. He knew with certainty, if things were flipped Trey would be there for him.

After a half hour a large nurse with bleach-blonde tresses and black roots poked her head in the door. "Mr. Mulherin?"

Ian rose to his feet. "Yes?"

She paused, smiled, and said, "Mr. Bollinger appears to be coming around now. I can only allow one person in to see him at a time, though."

Nicole gripped his hand in reassurance and nodded. He followed the nurse back to the recovery room. The smell of antiseptic overrode the stench of smoke on his body. He took a deep breath and braced himself for what he was going to see beyond the curtain ahead.

The nurse slid back the curtain. "I'm afraid you can only stay five minutes. Mr. Bollinger will need his rest."

"Yes, of course, thank you."

Ian walked further into the room toward the bed. Trey lay on the hospital bed tucked under a sheet as white as his face. His face was swollen and his eyes were closed and puffy.

Ian swallowed and squared his shoulders.

The right side of Trey's face was covered in gauze and bandages from his jawbone to his hairline. His brows were knitted together in pain.

Ian forced himself to take another deep breath and relax his hands at his side. He moved over to the bed and pulled up a chair. The chair creaked with his weight as he sat down. He had to be strong for Trey. He cleared his throat. "Trey?"

His friend showed no reaction.

He placed his hand over Trey's arm. "I'm here for you. Whatever you need. I'm going to be beside you every step of the way and enjoy kicking your ass while I am."

Trey frowned, and his lips moved slightly.

"Don't try and talk," Ian reassured him. "I'm sure they have you pretty medicated. You rest."

Ian tried to swallow the emotion that was welling up in his throat.

"I … want to thank you for everything you did for me, for Nicole. You saved our lives, man," Ian said, his voice cracking despite his resolve. "I don't have the words to tell you how much that means to me."

The machine continued its beeping. Trey's chest rose and fell with the oxygen mask over his nose. Ian could see gauze patched on Trey's neck leading down past where the hospital gown fell.

"I'm going to stick by your side on this one. You can count on it."

"Mr. Mulherin, I'll need to ask you to leave now so Mr. Bollinger can get the rest he needs."

Ian nodded and patted Trey's good arm gently. It was hard to leave him there all hooked to tubes and fighting for his life. He wished there were more he could do or say. "They're kicking me out now so you can get your rest. I'll be close by. I'll see you later."

Ian took in one last look and then stumbled out and back down the hospital corridor. He was overwrought with emotion and fatigue. He pushed open the double doors and turned into the waiting room. Nicole was standing in the opening, her hands clasped together looking worried. The care and concern on her face was just what he needed. He wrapped his arms around her.

"Hey," Nicole said, hugging him back. "How was he?"

"Out of it. He's hooked up to a lot of equipment and hoses," Ian said. "I told him I'd be there for him the whole way. I just hope he heard me, knew I was there, you know?"

"I know. I'm sure he did. It's a proven fact that patients can often hear you even under the most serious conditions."

"Thank you for that." He traveled his hand down her arm to take her hand in his and squeeze it.

"How are you dealing with things now that you know about Dan?"

Chapter 29

Nicole stretched her seatbelt out and repositioned in the passenger seat of the Durango. For some reason the belt was cutting into her. Exhausted, every fiber of her being protested when she moved. The taut muscles across her shoulders ached the worst. She couldn't wait for them to reach the hotel. Ian drove most of the way in silence. She knew his mind remained back at the hospital with Trey. She herself had a hard time trying to let it all sink in from the last twenty-four hours. It was a lot to process. He had just shook his head when she had asked him about Dan. He clearly wasn't ready to talk about it. The sad look in his eyes had tugged at her heart.

"I hope they can make Trey comfortable enough," Ian said finally.

"I do, too," Nicole told him. "Try not to worry."

"I wish I could've stayed with him, but they won't let anyone stay back there in ICU." Ian slid the vehicle over into the next lane. "I left my cell phone number at the desk with the instructions to call if there were any changes."

"That's all you can do. You need to get some rest."

"I'm exhausted enough to sleep a week, if I could shut my mind off."

"I know what you mean," Nicole agreed. She kept hearing the explosion repeated over and over in her ears. If she closed her eyes, she saw an instant replay of Ian and Roark fighting over the gun. She shuddered. The outcome could have gone either way.

"I called the hotel and asked them to move our things to a different room," Ian said.

"Thank you. I think that would be easier to take than going back to the room where—" Her voice broke. She blinked furiously to hold back the tears. She didn't want to fall apart. The worst was over. Roark was behind bars. She was free. Ian was okay, and Trey would be all right. And if she wasn't mistaken, the relationship between Ian and his father seemed to have improved. The previous stiffness wasn't there. Ian reached over and covered her hand with his. The warmth of it comforted her. His fingers laced through hers while he continued to drive.

She was so tired, she didn't think she had the strength to walk up to their room once they got there. She was worried about Ian, too. Quiet and withdrawn, he acted like he was on auto pilot. She glanced over at him as he drove. He looked tired and worry rimmed his forehead. He had to be processing the night's events. It must be hard to realize your partner you thought you knew so well had betrayed you. Her heart went out to him. She wished she could do more for him to ease the pain.

As if sensing her worry, he absently squeezed her hand again while keeping his eyes trained on the road ahead. "Are you okay?"

"I'm tired. You?" She put her hand on top of his and curled her fingers around it.

"Same."

Neither spoke the remainder of the time until they pulled into their hotel to park. They walked through to the lobby to pick up their new room key. Nicole was glad to find it was on the second floor this time. She wondered if she had enough strength left in her to take a hot shower. She knew she'd sleep better if she did.

Ian inserted the key in the slot and held the door open for her. She offered a weak smile as she stumbled over the threshold and passed through. Their room was the same as the other one only everything was on the left of the room instead of to the right.

"Do you want to take a shower first?" Ian offered.

"Yeah. Thanks." She nodded and went to the dresser to search which one held her clothes. After finding them, she headed for the shower. It would be heavenly to scrub Roark's filthy touch off of her.

She flipped on the switch and grimaced as she caught her reflection in the mirror. Her right cheek was swollen and bruised. She shut her eyes against the images of the evening that haunted her.

Ian fidgeted with the drapes and scanned out over the parking lot. It had been one hell of a night. He leaned his forehead against the coolness of the window directly above the air conditioner. His fist squeezed the satiny material in his hand. He couldn't even begin to process all the information about Dan. Not yet. No, he was going to focus on Trey right now. The image of his partner lying there completely helpless and fighting for his life almost choked him.

He dropped the drape and straightened. Life needed to be lived to the fullest because you never knew when you could lose it. What was it Brian had said? "Be a little reckless with your feelings."

Wandering around the room restlessly, he put his hands on his hips. His father even said tonight that women needed to hear words. He was nervous. Words. The thought of telling Nicole how he felt, sharing his heart with her, unnerved him.

He ambled over to the bedside table and plucked up the TV remote. Aiming at the TV, he paused.

He heard the shower turn on.

He swallowed.

She was naked.

The remote clattered beside the phone. He rested on the knuckles of both fists and rolled his neck from side to side. He wondered what she'd do if he slipped in behind her and offered to lather down her body.

Be a little reckless with your feelings.

He stood and squared his shoulders. A slow smile played across his lips. There wasn't any reason why he couldn't just show how he felt while he was trying to think of a few words as well.

He reached for his belt and unbuckled it.

Nicole stood under the shower head and let the warm water rush over her body and down the drain. She wished she could wash away the horrible images from the evening as easily. She tapped the opening of the bottle of hotel shampoo against the palm of her hand. Working the creamy citrus suds through her hair, her thoughts returned to Ian.

Her mind held the image of his well-muscled body looming over hers. How small her hands had seemed against his firm chest. The way his chest hair curled under her fingers, a trail of it leading down his flat abdomen before spreading out.

Her mouth went dry.

Should she tell him how she felt about him? Maybe it was too soon. Maybe he didn't feel the same about her. *No. The timing is all off. Too much going on. Maybe after this all blows over, I'll see where we stand then.*

A whoosh of cool air spiraled around her when the curtain whipped back. Her mouth fell open in surprise as she turned to see Ian standing there. Naked. Her eyes roved hungrily over his body. *Okay, maybe he does feel the same way about me. At least his body does, at any rate.*

He raised an inquiring eyebrow at her. She smiled. It was all he needed evidently, as he stepped in behind her. He lifted his hands and worked his way through the suds in her hair. His fingertips massaged rhythmic motions into her scalp. The rest of her body seemed to melt away. A blissful sigh escaped her lips. He rained kisses along the nape of her neck and paused to take his time at her throat. Goose bumps trickled down her spine, even against the warmth of the water.

He rinsed her hair and then reached around her and grabbed the little bottle of cream rinse. Flipping the cap open he squirted some into the palm of his hand. She turned to face him then. Their eyes locked. He smiled that lazy smile of his that turned her insides upside down.

I love him. I really love him.

The words lingered on the tip of her tongue. He leaned down and pressed his mouth against hers.

Hot. Ready.

She wrapped her arms around his waist and pulled him to her. The male length of him felt delicious, just like in her dream. She returned his kiss with all the emotion her heart held.

He was the first to ease back. He pushed his fingers into her hair and worked the conditioner through each strand.

She was on fire. *Forget the hair.*

"You're beautiful," he said huskily against her ear.

"You make me feel that way," she whispered back.

"You make me feel alive. Like life is worth living."

She looked up at him, her heart soaring, and decided it was now or never. Droplets of water clung to his hair. Her hands framed his face, his eyes the darkest blue of the ocean after a storm. "I love you."

His hands glided to rest on her arms. His fingers increased their pressure and he swallowed. "I was going to say that first."

"Oh?" she said, and grinned. "Sorry. Ahem. Go ahead."

"How about I just show you?"

She jabbed a playful finger into his chest. "No way, buddy. You're not getting off that easy, Agent Ian Mulherin."

"Okay, we'll compromise," he said, running his fingertips up over her collar bone, down the middle of her breasts and coming to rest his hands on her waist.

"How are you figuring that one?"

"I'll say the words," he smiled wickedly, "and you show me."

She was had. She bit back a smile and tossed him her best reproving teacher look. It didn't stop him a bit. He wasn't buying it.

"Do I need to turn you over my knee?" he threatened her.

"Hm. Sounds kinky," she laughed.

He caught her chin in his hand. She looked up at him, his blue eyes earnestly searching hers. He pulled her to him and kissed her with such passion her knees almost buckled. His arms snaked around her waist for support.

"I love you." He kissed her cheek. His lips glided to her right ear, and nipped at it.

She couldn't believe how this awful day had turned around. Only hours earlier she had been fearful she'd never see Ian again, never be able to tell him what she felt for him.

"I love you passionately." He cupped her breasts, his lips returning to hers.

He finished the kiss and rested his forehead against hers. "I love you madly."

He reached for the soap to run it over her shoulders and down her neck. "I love you more than I ever thought it possible to love another human being. You're so good for me."

Her heart spilled over as she kissed him back with all the love she felt for him. "Let's get back to that love me passionately statement."

"Now you're talking." He chuckled that throaty chuckle that she loved.

He reached around her and shut off the water. He pulled back the curtain and snagged a towel from the bar. She followed him out of the shower and stood patiently while he took his sweet time drying every inch of her. She returned the favor, stopping for a few kisses along the trail. While she was on her knees toweling off his legs, he put a hand on her shoulder and squeezed it to stop her. "Don't even think it, or I'll never make it."

"Who says you have to?"

He drew her out of the bathroom and led her across the room to sit on the bed and pull her down on top of him. He smoothed back her damp hair and framed her face with his hands. "I was so worried something was going to happen to you."

The tortured look in his eyes said it all. She placed a finger across his lips. She didn't want to remember the feelings she'd experienced back at the farm house when she thought she might never see him again. "Shh. I'm right here. I'm not going anywhere."

"Damn right you're not!" he growled, his hands sliding down her side to span her waist. "I'm going to drag you back to my cabin, woman, and handcuff you to my bed again."

"Promise?" she laughed and kissed his chest, loving the way his rough hands felt on her skin. "I'd love that."

"You'll have to marry me first, though."

The smile on her face slipped as her lips formed into an O shape. She hadn't expected that. Not that she minded.

"Oh, Ian." Her arms wound around his neck, her lips found his.

They kissed for several minutes enjoying one another. Ian was the first to break the kiss. "Hey, you've not said the word."

"Hm?' She nuzzled her cheek against his neck. "What? Oh. I haven't?"

"No. I know you're a major distraction, but I would've remembered."

"Well, then, I'll say the words," she said with a coy smile, "and you can show me what you mean."

"Deal."

"Yes, I'll marry you."

He kept up his end of the bargain and showed her, much to her delight.

The next morning, Ian held Nicole's hand as they stepped off the hospital elevator. In his other hand he carried a brief case. They headed down the hall toward Trey's room as a nurse was coming out with a chart in her hands. She shook her head and laughed. "Are you headed in to see Mr. Bollinger?"

"Yes, we are." Nicole nodded.

"Was he as big a mess before his accident?"

"Worse," Ian told her and laughed.

"Heaven help us all." She threw up her hands, shook her head again, and wandered off with a smile.

Ian pushed the door open for Nicole to go first. Trey sat cranked up in a slanted position in the bed.

"Word in the hall has it that you're harassing the nurses," Ian said.

Trey smiled wearily out of one side of his mouth and winked. "Ah, I do what I can. Don't you know it."

Ian drew a chair over for Nicole and opted to stand at the foot of the bed.

Trey certainly had a good deal more color in his face this morning. His shadowed eyes showed that he was in quite a bit of pain. The right side of his face and neck were still shrouded in gauze and bandages. Ian was relieved to see Trey awake and more alert.

"So, hey, how long are you going to be on vacation?" Ian teased him.

"Up yours, Mulherin."

Ian laughed. The old Trey was in there, just covered up under bandages for now. "You sound cranky."

"You got the goods?" Trey asked him, pointing to the briefcase Ian had brought in.

"Yeah." Ian set the briefcase on the bed and snapped the latches back. He pulled out a box of nutrition bars.

"Thanks. I'll name my first born after you."

"You're going to get my ass kicked out of here."

"You surely deserve it for something you've not been caught doing," Trey said as he took the bar. "So, Nicole, wanna go out with me?"

Nicole laughed at his lightheartedness. "I'm sorry, Trey, but I don't think it will work for us."

Ian walked over to where Nicole sat, leaned over, and took her hand in his. "Get your own girl. Nicole's already taken."

The left side of Trey's mouth turned up in a half smile. "You're smarter than I gave you credit for, Ian."

"Gee, thanks."

"All right, you two." Nicole pretended to scold them both.

"He started it," Trey defended, tucking his sheet around him better with the hand that had wires taped to it, and carefully brought a nutrition bar to his mouth. "And with me on my sick bed."

When the laughter subsided, Ian cleared his throat. "When you're outta here, we want you to be the best man at our wedding."

Trey stilled. "I'd like that. Thanks. Marriage will look good on the two of you."

"You and I ... we've been through a lot together," Ian told him, trying to keep emotion out of his voice. It wasn't easy.

"Yeah. I'm sorry about Dan."

Ian nodded. It took him a moment to answer. Nicole squeezed his hand and smiled up at him in encouragement. He cleared his throat. "Me too. I would've never believed it."

"Yeah. I know."

"But, he came through at the end. I guess … he just got sucked into the vortex of things. The almighty dollar," Ian said, resigned. "Roark has a lot to answer for and I'm going to make sure he does. They've got enough on him to see him serve ten life sentences in prison."

A tap sounded on the door behind them.

"Come in," Trey called from the bed as he handed over his nutrition bar for Nicole to take from him.

A petite blonde with a heart-shaped face stepped in holding a chart and thermometer. She looked from one party to the other. "Oh, I'm so sorry. I didn't realize you had company, Mr. Bollinger. I can come back and check on you later."

"Ah … wait, nurse. Please. The company was just leaving. Weren't you, guys?"

Ian allowed a blank look to form on his face. "Huh? Us?"

Trey crooked his finger, motioning for him to come closer. Ian stepped around Nicole and leaned in. Trey grabbed him by the shirt collar with his good hand and tugged him down within whispering range. "This is my dream, now step out of it."

Ian straightened and laughed. "Yes, well, we were just leaving. Come along, Nicole."

The blonde looked confused, but smiled sweetly. "Well, if you're sure."

"Oh, I'm sure. We don't want to stand in the way of our buddy here getting the best help available." Ian chuckled as he motioned for Nicole to follow him. Trey, ever the ladies' man, lived on.

"We'll check on you again, Trey." Nicole patted his leg and turned to follow Ian to the door.

They both heard Trey say in a pitiful voice, "I'm sorry, I'm so weak, I don't think I'll be of much help to you."

Ian and Nicole entered their hotel room with Dickens in tow. They had picked the dog up after being freshly groomed and fluffed up.

Ian looked at his police-trained dog and laughed. "Dickens, you sure do smell sweet and that ribbon on your head … well."

Dickens sat down and barked.

"That's telling him, Dickens," Nicole applauded the dog. "Come here and I'll take it off of you."

Dickens stood up, walked over to Nicole, and stuck his nose in her hand. She unclipped the bow and tossed it on the dresser. "There. All better."

Ian strolled over and took her soft hands in his. "I'm so damned thankful to have you."

She smiled up at him and his world tilted.

"I'm the one who's thankful."

He pulled her into his arms and held her close. Her hands traveled up his back. He was truly overwhelmed with the feelings of love he had for her. Never had he experienced anything like it. He kissed her gently at first, then deeper. His arms tightened around her.

"Tomorrow's a new day, and I'm so lucky to have you in all my tomorrows after that," he breathed against her ear.

Nicole shivered in his arms. He held her against him.

She looked up into his dark blue eyes, all the love in her heart shinning in them, "Did I hear you say you wanted to get lucky?"

He scooped her up into his arms and strode over to lower her onto the mattress.

"Oh, yeah, baby." He laughed as his lips hovered close to hers. "I love you."

Look for the next book in the Capture Series,
May 2013.

Read Brian's story in

Capture A Memory

About the Author

Sherry Foley has always had a wild imagination which she has used to craft inspired pieces of fiction that often border on the disturbing. While her creative mind races forward, she keeps her feet planted in Missouri with her husband and three teenage children.

Follow Sherry:
SherryFoley.com
Twitter: twitter.com/Sherry_Foley
Facebook: facebook.com/pages/
Sherry-Foley-Author/253958441304150

CPSIA information can be obtained at www.ICGtesting.com
Printed in the USA
BVOW041155181112

305859BV00003B/1/P